ACCLAIM FOR LOST SHIFT

"Lost Shift is an absolute delight of a shifter book. With page-turning action, high stakes, a budding romance, and an ending that is pure perfection, Skelly has penned a gem!"

—CASEY L. BOND, bestselling author of *Where Oceans Burn*

"Fur has never been so fun! AJ Skelly's *Lost Shift* is a perfect addition to her swoon-worthy Wolves of Rock Falls series."

—CAREY CORP, *NY Times* and *USA Today* bestselling author of The Halo Chronicles and The DOON Series

"Lost Shift is a swoon-worthy escape into adventure and romance. Skelly weaves an addicting love story with equal parts friendship and steamy-sweet kisses. She deftly portrays real-life characters, found family, and tops it off with the test of true love. This is a story you won't be able to put down!"

—E. A. HENDRYX, author of *Suspended in the Stars*

"AJ Skelly delivers in yet another thought-provoking and romantic novel. As the start up in a new spin-off series, *Lost Shift* offers many swoon-worthy scenes that will leave you wanting more. With new characters to love and new twists to enjoy, Skelly has created the foundation for a fantastic new series."

—V. ROMAS BURTON, award-winning author of the Heartmaker and Legacy series

"With her usual (and awesome) page-turning pacing and swoon, AJ Skelly's *Lost Shift* had that perfect mix of paranormal romance plus a story focusing on the value of found family. It's those relatable characters that ground what many of us have affectionatly termed Skelly's "wolf books" in reality. Once again, I read it way too fast, and as always, I turned the last page and immediately asked when the next book would come out! And while this story can be read without reading *The Wolves of Rock Falls* series, I promise you that you'll be slavering for more wolf books at the end of *Lost Shift* in the best way."

—BRITTANY EDEN, author of the Heartbooks series

"With new characters and evolving pack dynamics, AJ Skelly takes the reader on an exciting cross-country adventure in *Lost Shift*, as Katie and Donovan try to untangle her family's mysterious past. Along the way, the lifelong friends discover feelings they never saw coming—but the stakes have never been higher and Skelly keeps you guessing until the very end how it will all work out."

—AMBER KIRKPATRICK, author of *Until the Rising* and *Unleashed*

"With characters you cheer for from page one, to stakes that have you on the edge of your seat, Skelly weaves a story of friendship, love, hope, and healing for two people who desperately need it. It will leave you breathless with both wonder and excitement!"

LOST SHIFT

— ANNA AUGUSTINE, author of the Taletha Love Stories series

LOST SHIFT

Also By AJ Skelly

The Wolves of Rock Falls
First Shift
Rogue Shift
Sworn Shift
Dark Shift (novella)
Pack Shift

Magik Prep Academy
Making Magik (Making Magik anthology)
Of Flame & Frost

LOST SHIFT

The Wolves of Arcadia Bay

Quill & Flame
PUBLISHING HOUSE

AJ Skelly

Quill & Flame
PUBLISHING HOUSE

For those who have loved and lost.

Chapter 1

Donovan

My chest was tight. Tight like when my mom died. Too tight. Like I couldn't breathe because the walls were caving in on me. Only, there were no literal walls. Just the darkness, the forest, the trees, the stars shining softly above the dark canopy as I leaned my head against the cool glass of the truck window. Just metaphorical walls and my gloom threatening to crush me.

I hadn't realized how hard leaving Rock Falls without Sarah would be. I wasn't sorry I'd given her up—she was in love with Cade, and he was in love with her. But I think a tiny part of me had been falling for her, too. And coming home from the Lacessere empty-handed, without her Alpha genes to mix with mine, left me feeling hollow. Somehow less. Like I wasn't enough.

"Hey, snap out of it, Donovan," Angus, my older cousin, said as he mock punched my shoulder. "What's going on in that head of yours? You've been quiet the whole way back. And it's been a *long* drive from Delaware back home to Oregon."

I grimaced ruefully. "Sorry, Angus. Just thinking."

"Yeah. I bet." Angus snorted and rubbed his neck. The faintest markings of bruises where Cade had his incisors against his throat during the last challenge still lingered. "Are you sorry you gave her up?" He wasn't condemning my choice, but I could hear his curiosity.

"No." I sighed. "If I'd forced her hand and we'd become mates, it would have just festered between us." I shook my head. "She couldn't love me."

"She respects you. That wasn't enough?"

I sighed and my breath fogged up the window. "No. Not when you love someone like she loves Cade." It had been written on every inch of her once I won the Lacessere—the challenge for her hand. Her look of horror, tinged even with revulsion, when I won the right to Claim her, marry her, be her mate and join our would-be Alpha bloodlines, was burned into my brain. My skin crawled thinking about it.

I'd given her up. I had no claim on her now—never would again. I didn't regret what I'd done, but my confidence had taken a serious hit. For the first time in a long time, I felt unsure of myself.

Who was I?

"Donovan! Angus! You're back. I wasn't sure I should expect you before tomorrow," Dad, Alpha of the extensive Hazelton werewolf pack, called from the doorway, the porch light glinting off his silvering hair.

"Hey, Dad," I said as I dragged myself from the truck, unfolding my stiff joints.

Dad met us at the bottom of the steps and gave me a quick hug. "Welcome home, son." He cupped my jaw in his weathered hand, giving my cheek a fatherly pat. "I've had a Gathering organized for tomorrow night to welcome you home properly with the whole pack." He smiled at me, though there was a touch of sadness in his expression. Some emotion I couldn't identify slithered through my gut, curdling like shame, but leaving a hollowness behind.

"Thanks," I croaked.

Dad squeezed my shoulder. "Angus, we'll see you tomorrow then?"

"Sure thing, Uncle Hal. I'm going to get myself home to Emma." I could see the sparks in my cousin's eyes from where I stood by the house. A thread of jealousy wormed into the uncomfortable mass in my belly. Angus and Emma had Claimed each other last spring. They'd been nearly intolerable in their ardor for each other since then. Sarah flashed across my brain. Wolf raised his head wearily inside me.

"See you, Angus," I said, waving tiredly and shoving the thoughts from my head. I had no energy for anything more than falling into bed.

My dad, as Alpha, had planned an epic party to welcome me back home—I think he'd planned on welcoming his future daughter-in-law along with me, but that hadn't worked out. I needed to marry someone with Alpha or Beta genes to keep the pack bloodlines strong. Girls with Alpha or Beta genes were few and far between. Giving Sarah up would be seen as a colossal loss to some. I sighed. My mom had been the cousin of a Beta. I wished she were still alive to offer some advice in the girl department. I shook off the sadness that came with thoughts of my mom. Werewolves married and mated young. There wasn't an expiration date on when I had to find the girl to carry my genes into the next generation, but at nineteen, I was expected to find that girl in the not-too-distant future.

I was not in the mood for a Gathering. But now that I'd been home all of twelve hours, I was expected to get back out and mingle with my pack.

"Donovan! It's dusk! Are you coming down?" Dad called up the stairs. I sighed again, glancing out my window into the forested twilight beyond the panes.

"Yeah." I swallowed, collecting my courage, trying to ignore the ache in my chest, and headed down the stairs.

By the time I got to the Gathering, the bonfire was lit and everyone in the pack had heard the heroically spun tale of how I'd given up Sarah and her Alpha bloodline so she could be with the wolf she loved.

"That took a lot of guts, Donovan, giving up the girl like that," a friendly older pack member said as he clapped me on the back.

"I'm not sure I would have," another said with a smile and a swig of his soda. My insides crawled.

"I think he did the right thing. It's rare enough for Alphas and Betas to find love early if they aren't true mates. Donovan will always be the hero of that story," a woman called from the shadows.

I smiled politely at it all, responding when I had to, but retreating into myself as the night lengthened and shadows darkened the clearing. Once darkness fell completely, and I was less likely to be missed, I melted into the fringe, letting those around the bonfire tell jokes and stories. I felt like an outsider in my own pack. I'd never felt this way before. It rocked me to my core, leaching concern and trepidation into my normally-healthy confidence.

Watching alone from the shadows calmed my heart, but still left my insides bruised and unsure.

"Van." The soft-spoken word had me wheeling around. I hadn't heard Katie's quiet footfalls over the newly sprouted covering on the forest floor. My heart plummeted, hoping I could escape detection here in the trees, but as she came close, her eyes shined at me in a way that made my stomach dip.

"Hey, Katie," I said, my voice hushed. She came over to me, just inside the borders of my personal space, the moonlight filtering down weakly on her red-black hair only to be swallowed up in large red-brown eyes.

"I hear you made quite the sacrifice back in Rock Falls," she said lightly, her voice betraying nothing. My insides churned. Though her voice gave nothing away, her eyes did. She drank me in, mystery and desire swirling together in the deep pools of her dark cinnamon gaze.

Life sparked inside the dead void of my chest. Feeling returned to my limbs. The pressure in my chest eased enough I drew a full breath as I watched her. Looking at her, I felt *something*. I knew she'd be willing. She'd been half in love with me since the night we found her, bleeding and alone, her pack slaughtered by feral wolves so many years ago. She'd looked at me then with something akin to hero-worship, but as we'd grown older, it had morphed into something infinitely more dangerous.

She was beautiful. Beautiful and alluring. I'd never felt anything beyond friendship for Katie...but looking at her, longing for *something* welled up inside my chest. Any sense I had fled. I took a step closer. Her eyes widened. Her heartbeat picked up, echoing faintly in my ears. My own sped up to match. For just a second, Sarah's pale face, her celery green eyes and light blonde hair superseded Katie's darker looks. I blinked. We were inches from each other. Her fiery-sweet scent of allspice and maple invaded my senses and my blood pumped quicker. My gaze tracked to her mouth. Her lips parted as she inhaled quickly.

Willing the lump in my chest to beat again, to rid myself of the doubt that clung to me closer than my fur, I lowered my face to hers, my lips covering hers as my hands slid around her waist, drawing her flush against me. Wolf jerked inside me.

A shocked, guttural noise sounded in her chest. For one charged second, she stood stock-still against me, but as my lips moved slowly against hers, she melted into my chest, her mouth responding in a way that made my knees weak. Her hands dragged up my biceps to twine around my neck. For long moments, we kissed. The darkness inside me abated as her body pressed against me, as my hands followed the curve of her waist to the small of her back, up to her shoulders, pulling her closer.

I kissed her harder, craving the spark she ignited inside me, the way kissing her made me feel. She groaned softly against my mouth, her hands twisting into the hair at the base of my neck as she went up on tip toes, her chest pressing against mine. The hair on my arms stood on end. Her muffled noise carried so much longing, so much want, that it snapped me out of my trance. My lips froze against hers, my hands stilling where they gripped her sides.

Wait.

Why was I kissing Katie?

Was I kissing Katie? I was thinking about Sarah.

Was...was I *using* her?

Wolf and I recoiled at the realization that it was exactly what I was doing.

Using her unwittingly for my own selfish pleasure without a single thought of what I was doing to her. My stomach heaved as I tore my lips from hers, crashing a step back into the underbrush. My heart pounded as I panted, desperately trying to drag air into my frozen lungs. In horror, I watched numbly as she blinked once. Twice. Then her eyes filled with tears, and she fled.

I was the worst kind of dog alive.

I sat despondently on the porch early the next morning. The Gathering had gone late into the night, but I'd made my glamourless exit moments after Katie had. Guilt tied my insides up in knots. The sun was half-way up over the far horizon and morning birds were calling to each other as spring awoke beneath the chilly remnants of winter still clinging to the landscape.

The thump of footsteps was all the warning I got before Angus rounded the far side of the wrap-around porch.

"Did you kiss Katie?" Angus asked incredulously, anger tinging his words as he swung around the pillar on the porch to face me where I sat moodily on the steps.

"I did," I admitted tightly. Shame flooded me but I resisted the urge to wilt under it.

"You know she's in love with you," Angus accused.

I pursed my lips, refusing to comment as the weight of my mistake pushed down on me.

"Well? What are you planning to do?" Angus's brows knit together, his bicep flexing where his arm still gripped around the pillar.

"I don't know," I said honestly.

"You don't know?" Angus parroted. "Donovan, this is *serious.*"

"Well, crap, Angus, I didn't already know that," I snapped as guilt, irritation, and irrational anger flared beneath my skin.

Angus seethed in silence for a minute, his fingers flexing against the pillar hard enough one of his knuckles cracked. Part of me wished he'd just haul my sorry tail out to the yard and fight me with teeth, claws, and fur. That would at least get rid of some of this tense aggression and confusion building inside me. I was ready to explode. Wolf paced inside, malcontent, and testy, too.

"You need to talk to her," Angus finally said quietly. The fight drained from me, and I risked a glance up at my cousin.

"And what would I say?" I asked, desperation coloring my words.

Angus gusted an angry sigh through his teeth and plopped down on the step next to me, his light brown hair waving slightly in the chill breeze.

"Look. Katie is practically my sister. She's lived with my family since we found her bleeding out on that mountain pass five years ago. I'm incredibly protective of her. I want to skin you alive for messing with her. But you're also more brother to me than cousin. Which is weird when I say both those things out loud in this context." His nose wrinkled. "You've never loved Katie the way she's loved you. What changed?" Angus turned the full force of his hazel eyes on me, and I resisted the urge to wither under their stare. What *had* changed?

The ache sharpened in my chest. Angus sat in silence, waiting for me to get my thoughts in order. Shame welled up the back of my throat.

"I made a stupid, impulsive decision that I've regretted every second since," I muttered.

Angus raised his eyebrows. "That's it?" he deadpanned.

I shook my head angrily. "I don't know why I kissed her, Angus. I just...felt dead inside. Katie made me feel something. It was wrong." I swallowed back the remorse that flooded my mouth.

Angus whistled through his teeth. "Yeah. Not a good enough reason." We were quiet for another minute. "You wanted Sarah, didn't you?"

Angus's words scraped across my skin, leaving me raw and exposed.

"I've always known I'd likely make a political match for the betterment of the pack. That's part of my job as the Beta. I have to marry strong to carry the Alpha gene for the next generation. I made peace with that a long time ago." I paused. "But I didn't expect to actually *want* the person I was obligated to pair with."

"Then why give her up?" Angus asked, his voice gentling and losing some of its earlier venom. "You won the right to Claim Sarah fair and square. She was yours."

"I told you. She'd never love me the way she loves Cade." Bitterness and loss rumbled through me and set Wolf pacing again. "And that would be a nasty root that would wedge itself between us. We'd have never been completely happy with each other. I might have grown to love her, but she'd never love me like she loves Cade." I shook my head. It was painful, saying these things out loud, and I'd already said a version of them to Angus once. Wolf whined.

Angus squeezed my shoulder with his hand. "I'm sorry you're smarting over Sarah. But that still doesn't excuse what you did to Katie. You have to make things right with her."

"I know." I flicked a stray piece of dead grass that had blown up on the porch.

"Just tell her you acted like a Sasquatch's backside and beg her forgiveness," Angus said with a hopeful tone in his voice.

I burned him with a glare.

He shrugged. "That's what Emma prefers."

"Yeah. Not sure Katie has the same tastes as your wife."

"You're right. I think you might be more like the wrong end of a dog than a Sasquatch butt."

I shoved him off the porch step.

CHAPTER 2

KATIE

The mountain air was brisk, fresh, and clean. Though it cooled my face, it did little to cool the turmoil boiling inside me.

Van kissed me. It had been the best moment of my life as his lips pressed against mine, moved over mine, his hands slid around my waist, ran up my back, held me tight. The best moment of my life until I realized he wasn't kissing *me*.

And that about ripped my heart straight out of my chest. In that moment, I think I hated him as much as I loved him. Either way, it was a considerable amount.

Now I was just frustrated as all get out. I wanted to hit him, wanted to cry, wanted it to be real. Not that it mattered. It couldn't be. I could never be with Van. My secrets were too dark. And to have any real chance with Van, I'd have to reveal them.

And then one or both of us would die.

So instead, I took another lungful of crisp early March air, tugged my hoodie sleeves down over my chilled fingers, and continued hiking up the rocky trail towards one of my favorite spots. It wasn't far from the collection of Hazelton pack houses—essentially the wolf village—and its protection, but it was far enough away that I felt sufficiently able to be alone with my thoughts without interruption.

Reaching the pinnacle of the rocky outcropping, I sat down on an overhanging rock, letting my legs dangle over the nothingness as the wind whistled through the trees at my back.

Midmorning light streamed across the land spread out below me in varying shades of lingering winter brown and early spring green. As it always did, it calmed the rage inside me. I let my mind empty as well as it could for a few moments before my thoughts circled back to the same thing I'd been obsessing over for months.

I'd be eighteen next week.

I worried my bottom lip as I lifted one knee and wrapped my arms around it. As I propped my chin on my knee, fear sunk its talons into my midsection.

"You don't know what will happen," I whispered out loud to myself. It was true. I didn't know what would happen once I reached eighteen. Maybe nothing. Maybe something.

"I hope if it's something, it doesn't have deadly consequences," I said to the lichen growing over the surface of the boulder beneath me. I shoved the worry away, but the next thought that popped into my brain wasn't any more helpful.

The memory of Donovan's lips surfaced, bringing with it a confusing mix of tingles, anger, and hurt. How long had I dreamed of his kiss? How many times had I wished it could be true? I growled, irritated all over again. Idiot lip-locking mongrel.

Wolf stirred within me, suddenly pricking her ears forward. An unnatural swish of foliage had me on high alert. My muscles tensed as my belly clenched. A soft waft of earthy clay and hazelnut brushed over my face.

Donovan.

I bit the inside of my cheek and forced the tears away as emotion choked the back of my throat. I would not cry in front of him. Not over this. I'd already cried my heart out in private. But I *would* give him a dose of the anger coursing through me. Wolf peeled her lips back from her teeth inside me.

Moments later the soft tread of his footfalls sounded dully against the gray rock where I sat. He hesitated, and I refused to turn around and face him as the wind whipped a piece of my dark auburn hair across my lips. Lips he'd treacherously kissed.

With pained slowness, he crossed the space between us and sat a few feet away.

We sat in utter silence for several long minutes. Wolf paced. My heart pounded painfully against my breastbone. I ached. Ached with anger, and because I loved the stupid boy next to me. I loved him with a wild abandon that I couldn't turn off no matter how hard I tried. And that's why what he did had wounded me so deeply.

CHAPTER 3

DONOVAN

I was in such a pile of crap. Katie was more than mad. She was steaming. But worse than her anger, I knew her well enough to see behind her veil of wrath to the hurt that lurked there. Wolf gnashed at me, my own idiocy being the cause for her pain.

I swallowed thickly. The breeze blew and birds chirped. A tang of spring lit the air, though it was still cold. None of the peace of this place matched the unrest inside me.

"Katie," I finally rasped when I could stand the silence no more.

She said nothing. Didn't turn, didn't acknowledge me more than the slight indention in her cheek which let me know she was chewing the inside of it. A fresh wave of guilt hit me.

"Katie, I'm sorry," I whispered, my voice cracking on the last word anyway. I *was* sorry. So sorry I'd wounded her. Sorry I'd been so unbelievably selfish, and she was paying the price for my actions.

"You hurt me, Van. You shouldn't have kissed me, and you know it." Fire lit in her eyes as she finally looked at me. Her words cut me deeper than if her claws had opened a gash across my chest. I bowed my head, guilt consuming me, forcing me to drop my gaze. Wolf whined.

"I know, Katie. And I'm sorry. So sorry. I never meant to hurt you. I never wanted that." I shrugged, not wanting the next words to come out of my mouth, but knowing I needed Katie to understand what was going on inside me. "I…I've not been myself since I came back from Rock Falls. What happened there—it kind of made me lose my footing. I got back and I've been floundering, doubting myself, my abilities. And then there you were, looking at me with those big eyes, and I felt *something*." I tapped my chest as my eyes lifted to find hers. Tingles of awareness danced along my solar plexus, my lungs tightening. "And then I kissed you." I swallowed on a suddenly dry mouth. I rushed on, "I was wrong to kiss you like that. But I won't. I won't kiss you again." As the words left my mouth, I had the horrifying feeling that I'd said something wrong—made things even worse. "I'm a Sasquatch butt," I blurted.

Katie snorted. "What did you just say?"

Wolf rolled his eyes in mortification as my cheeks heated in a particularly unmanly fashion. I cleared my throat, squirming at my lack of eloquence and silently cursing Angus. "I…I was wrong," I said instead.

"No, I'm pretty sure you just said you're a Sasquatch butt," she quipped. Some of the hurt lingering in her eyes began to dissipate, replaced by the barest hint of humor.

"I might have," I grudgingly admitted.

"Yeah, Van, you are a Sasquatch butt," she agreed with the tiniest tilt of the corner of her mouth. She gazed back to the sun-dappled hills rolling down from where we sat.

"I mean it, Katie. I was wrong and I'm sorry. I promise you that I will not kiss you again," I said with as much sincerity as I could. Wolf nodded.

Katie was still another minute while I squirmed, waiting for her response. At last, she nodded, a resigned motion that had me cocking my head to the side.

"You shouldn't doubt yourself, Van."

Relief rushed through me. She was still hurt, but her anger was fading. I hoped the damage I'd caused her would fade soon, too. I said nothing, unsure what I could offer in the face of my colossal mistake and consequent awkward apology.

We sat in silence together for a few more minutes. It was a mostly comfortable silence. Not the kind that drove tense daggers into your chest.

"How's school?" I finally asked. Katie refused to go to public school with the rest of the school-aged pack members. She never explained why, just dug her heels in and flat out refused. We always assumed it had something to do with the past she never spoke of. Instead, Katie did homeschool overseen by one of the local teachers at the high school.

"I actually turned in my last assignment Friday. As soon as it's graded, every high school requirement will be filled, and I'll have my diploma issued."

"Wow, that's great. Congratulations," I said, truly impressed.

She shrugged. "I guess a slightly accelerated program has its perks." Her fingers twitched lightly against her leg. I wondered what had her so tense but was afraid to ask in case I was still the cause.

"Do you know what you want to do next year yet?" I asked, looking for something to say to fill the silence. Katie and I were friends. Good friends. We hadn't really had a choice—she lived with Angus's family after she was adopted into the pack. Angus was not only my cousin but my best friend. We were around each other a lot. As a result, we all knew each other well.

"I don't know yet. I thought about taking a gap year. Try to figure things out," she said softly. Wolf pricked his ears forward.

"That's cool." Wolf rolled his eyes again at my eloquence.

"What about you? How are your classes going? Online schooling a go?" She tossed a piece of gravel off the side of the hill with a little more force than necessary.

"It's going well. I like online learning. It was nice going to campus last year, but it makes more sense with pack life to do it online. The way classes are set up, I have access to the whole course at once. Stuff can be turned in at any time but doesn't have to be submitted until the end of course date. It still gives me the freedom to do all the pack things," I said as the weight of being the Beta of the Hazelton pack settled more comfortably on my shoulders. I might not have brought home the desired Alpha gene with a mate, but I still knew how to be a good Beta.

I hoped.

Chapter 4

Katie

We sat in silence a few more moments. *I promise I won't kiss you again* twisted around inside my head and clung to my heart like tiny grappling hooks embedded in my flesh, tugging and pulling painfully every time Van's words ricocheted inside my brain again. I sighed.

It was a good thing. I didn't need Van to kiss me. Not when things would never work between us. I just needed to get over him and move on with my life.

Whatever and wherever that might be. I found myself chewing my bottom lip and stopped.

"Hey, you wanna go for a run in fur?" Van asked quietly, picking up on my moodiness. That was the problem with people who knew you well. Angus and Emma were the same way. Angus had taken one look at my face last night when he dropped by his parents' house on his way home from the Gathering, and the truth had come out without my permission. Likely Van was here at Angus's insistence, though I thought he'd probably have searched me out on his own at some point.

Sadness lanced my heart once more. Would I never stop loving this boy?

"A run would be nice. It's good weather for it. It might rain later," I said as I stood and brushed off my rear end.

"And I know how you hate soggy fur," Van quipped with an attempt at a smile.

"It's true. Soggy fur is miserable. It drips everywhere, and even as a werewolf, the smell of wet dog gets to me." I wrinkled my nose. Van smiled. "All right. Shoo. I'll shift up here and meet you down the trail by the red boulder."

Van nodded. "Hey, Katie?" he asked softly. Dread coiled at the base of my spine.

"Yeah?"

"Are we good?"

Relief nearly made my knees buckle. I wasn't sure what I had expected him to say, but his words and the sincerity that shone from his eyes nearly brought tears springing to mine.

"Yeah, we're good." I squeezed the words out around the emotion that lodged like a fist in my throat. "But you're still a Sasquatch butt."

He snorted. "Okay. See you at the boulder." He nodded once more then his broad shoulders disappeared into the trees as he walked farther down the trail.

I closed my eyes and tilted my face to the sun for one moment, letting the gentle rays burn away the hurt that still flittered around. I wondered if I'd always love Van, whether I wanted to or not. Shaking my head, I pulled my arms inside my hoodie and took it and my shirt off. Shivering in the chilly wind, I quickly added the rest of my clothes and shoes to the pile, wrapping everything up in my hoodie into a neat little bundle that I could take with me.

Cinching the knot, I stood back up and flung my arms out to the sides, relishing the sharp bite of my fur slicing through my skin, coating me in my brown, black, and reddish mottled coat. My ears pushed out from my scalp, my hair twisting back in and leaving silky fur rippling over my head to my snout as delicate whiskers poked through, quivering in the breeze that brought delicious threads of spring straight to my nose.

My canines jutted from my jaw, filling my mouth before the rest of my snout finished elongating and arranged itself into the shape of my wolf. With a final crack that snapped in the quiet around me, my backbone disjointed, my tail shoving out as I descended gracefully onto four paws. With a tremendous shake, I shook my coat out, exulting in the feel of the fingers of cool air brushing over my ruff and twitching my whiskers.

Snatching up my bundled clothes in my mouth, I bounded down the path, muscles coiling and bunching at my movements. It was thrilling to be in fur. The world looked different from the lens of the animal, and right now, it was what I needed.

Van was waiting as he'd promised, his large sable wolf dappled as sunlight dribbled through the branches and early leaf buds and spotted his coat in sunshine. I dropped my clothes next to the messy pile of his, and we were off.

We ran hard and fast for long stretches through the forest, dodging trees, leaping boulders, dashing up the steep sides of the mountains and skidding, running, and once rolling down the other side.

By the time we pulled up at a clear mountain stream that fed down into a lake, my sides were heaving, and I'd worked up a good lather. The wind shifted, bringing the scent of clay and hazelnuts straight to my nose. I wrinkled mine and bent to lap the frigid water. Even covered in wolf sweat, his scent made me all sorts of giddy.

Van drank beside me, then glanced at me sideways. I had one second of warning before he pounced.

CHAPTER 5

DONOVAN

My muscles ached in the best possible way as cold water slid down my throat. Katie's wolf had lost some of the apprehension she carried in her human form. We needed some levity. I knew exactly how to do that.

I looked up and met her gaze, letting my eyes slant slightly. That was all the warning I gave her. Then I leapt through the air and crashed into her.

She yelped and shoved me off her, rolling with her momentum, trying to pin me. We wrestled a few minutes until both of us were chuffing and laughing too hard to continue. Eventually we loped back to where we'd left our clothes.

Taking turns behind the red boulder, we shifted back and got dressed.

"I'm starving. I'm heading back to the house for lunch. You going that direction?" I asked her as I finished tying my boot.

Her hair was a gloriously wild tangle of black that turned bronzy-red when the sun hit it. She shoved it back into an unruly ponytail. "Yeah. I didn't have much breakfast. Running always works up my appetite."

I nodded my agreement, watching her as she knotted the arms of her sweatshirt around her hips, the material pulling her t-shirt tighter and showing the curve of her waist and unintentionally emphasizing her chest. Quickly, I looked down the path.

"I haven't run like that in too long," I said conversationally as we started down the trail.

"Didn't you run while you were in Rock Falls?" Katie asked innocently as she flipped a piece of escaped hair behind her ear.

A pang sidled through my middle. My feelings about Rock Falls were still all tangled up and confused. I cleared my throat. "No, I did, but it's not the same as running on your own land."

Katie got a far-away look in her eye and nodded. I was about to ask her about it, but she spoke first. "What did you get Emma for her birthday?"

I rubbed the back of my neck. "I'm actually going into town this afternoon. I didn't get her anything before I left for Rock Falls." I grimaced guiltily.

Katie smiled. "You're not late yet. Party isn't until tomorrow night."

"Any ideas on what she wants?"

Katie shrugged. "She'd probably like new books?"

"Angus is going to have to build her another shelf if she gets any more," I quipped. Emma loved her books almost as much as Katie did.

"I don't think Angus minded building the last one." Katie kicked a rock down the trail. It hit a tree and pinged off into the woods.

"What did you get her?" I asked.

"A new book." Katie snorted.

I chuckled. "You got her a book because you get an employee discount at the bookstore."

She smiled. "And because Emma likes nothing better than new books."

"Works out well for you then."

"It does," she said primly.

"Am I going to have to beg you to let me in on what new books Emma wants?" I asked, a teasing whine in my voice.

"You go right ahead and beg, Sasquatch butt," she said, eyes slitted, grin feral.

"I deserved that," I admitted, my gut constricting, uncomfortably tight.

"Come by tomorrow morning instead of going this afternoon. I work tomorrow. I'll have a selection laid out for you."

"Thank you, Katie," I said sincerely. For more than just the books.

"Yeah. I might include one I've been eyeballing, too," she quipped.

"Add two." Guilt was expensive.

CHAPTER 6

KATIE

The scent of the bookstore wrapped around me like an embrace as I opened the door and the bell jingled. I inhaled, taking one second to close my eyes and take in the paper-ink-and-joy scent that flooded my nostrils.

I didn't linger long today. The momentary reprieve the calming scent of the bookstore provided was short lived. My stomach was in knots. For once, not because I'd be seeing Donovan shortly—but because Emma's birthday party tonight had me unable to escape thinking about my own birthday.

Five days.

I had five days to wait on pins and needles to see what happened. I didn't know if a magical switch would flip the second I turned eighteen, or if nothing at all would happen. But I was afraid I didn't have the luxury to wait and find out. If I waited and the switch did flip, people I loved would likely die.

I didn't think I could handle having that on my conscience. I carried enough guilt from five years ago. Even now, as an adult in all respects but age, I knew what happened wasn't my fault, but it didn't stop the memories from eating me alive sometimes late at night as I pondered the what ifs.

I had to prevent the potential disaster heading straight for the Hazelton pack. Tears sprung to the back of my eyes as I contemplated leaving
my refuge. I'd hidden in plain sight among their numbers. But once I
hit eighteen, I wasn't sure it would be enough.

"Katie, is that you, love?" a papery voice called from the back of the
store. *Books & Stuff* was a quaint little bookstore, run by the eccentrically
wonderful Ms. Brisbane, in the picturesque town of Arcadia Bay. She
had owned the store for decades and loved books even more than I did.
More importantly, though human, she knew about werewolves, was
friends with Jesse Hazelton, and didn't mind turning a blind eye and
paying me in cash under the table. The whole pack adored Ms. Brisbane,
and more importantly, she adored me. *Books & Stuff* was only twenty
minutes from pack land, and the place I had called home for the past five
years.

"It's me, Ms. Brisbane. I'm going to gather a few books for an order.
He should be coming to pick them up this morning. Do you want me
to start the coffee first?"

"Oh, that's nice. What sort of books? And coffee would be lovely. I
only just walked in the back with some pastries from the bakery. Go help
yourself. I got you a cherry cheese danish. I know they're your favorite."

"Mmmm," Wolf lolled her tongue as my stomach audibly growled.
"Ms. Brisbane, you're the best. I'll go put the coffee on so we can have a
cup with breakfast. They're more books for Emma, by the way."

"It's so rewarding seeing young people who enjoy reading as much as
you and Emma do." Her weathered face and graying hair popped around
the corner. She was getting on in years but was still sprightly enough to
have a spring in her step. She pushed red frames up the bridge of her
nose. The bright multi-colored pattern of her shirt reflected on the large

lenses. "I've got some paperwork I need to take care of this morning. Just holler if you need anything!"

"Will do," I called back as I headed for the navy-painted door off the back hallway that we used as an employee's lounge. There was only one other girl that worked here, and we rarely worked together since Ms. Brisbane still took an active role in every part of the store.

The tiny kitchenette with the faded green countertop looked charming with the bright landscapes and seascapes Ms. Brisbane had hung up. Rather than looking dated and tired, it was pleasant and earthy in a whimsical sort of way. I took down the coffee, a mouth-watering hazelnut amaretto flavor that Ms. Brisbane had introduced me to and measured out enough for a full pot. It was a more-than-one-cup sort of day.

After that, I meandered down the shelves, picking several books I knew Emma wanted, and one or two that I knew she'd like because I'd already read them. With them stacked neatly on the counter and ready for Van whenever he came, I poured myself a cup of fragrant coffee and brought my danish back to the register where I nibbled and sipped and worried about my impending birthday.

Precisely at nine o'clock, the doorbell chimed again, and the scent of clay and hazelnuts mingled with my coffee.

"Morning, Katie," Van said as the door swished shut behind him. I shivered in my thin cardigan as a chilly breeze swept in with him. "I'm here as promised." He gave me an uncertain smile and my belly clenched.

"Morning, Van. I've got your books—well, Emma's books," I said breathlessly. I quickly took another sip of coffee to cover how my heart beat faster looking over at his tousled brown hair and hazel eyes. It would be so much easier to get over him if he were an absolute troll. But, of course, he wasn't. He was obscenely gorgeous.

"You know I do really appreciate this," he said as he came to the counter and thumbed through the stack of books.

"I got a selection out for you. I know she wants to read these," I pointed to the four books on one side, "and I know she'll enjoy these because I read them already." I let my thumb run down the spines of the other three stacked books.

"Where are the two you picked out for you?"

I glanced up in surprise. "I didn't realize you were serious about that," I said as heat began curling in my gut even as my heart constricted. Memories of his kiss stormed to the front of my brain.

"I was. Go pick out your books." He gave me a crooked grin.

Wolf perked up inside me and I willed myself not to blush. "You sure?"

"Very sure, Katie. Now go. I'm going to steal a sip of your coffee while you're getting your books."

I slit my eyes and swatted his arm. "Do *not* drink all my coffee. I get very cranky without my coffee."

He rolled his eyes and grinned. "You're never cranky in the bookstore. It's your favorite place on the planet." He shooed me towards the shelves as he reached over the counter and snagged my mug.

I didn't protest and turned quickly so he wouldn't see the blush I knew was coming. If he sipped my coffee, the rim of my cup would taste like him for at least a sip. Wolf huffed. Why did I keep torturing myself this way? I knew Van meant nothing flirtatious by his actions. I gave myself a mental shake as I went to retrieve the two books that were on the top of my To Be Read list.

As I pulled up in the driveway of Emma and Angus's modest home, excitement for my friend and dread for myself writhed in my middle and were starting to feel an awful lot like a permanent thing. I took a minute and steeled my resolve. Tonight had nothing to do with my own eighteenth birthday. Tonight was about Emma.

I opened the door to the rush of cold night air and hauled my tail end out of my warm car. Carefully holding the prettily wrapped book so I didn't mash the bow, I dragged myself up the concrete stairs to the house, my legs like lead. Wolf nudged me.

The door swung open, and noise spilled out into the darkening skies. Angus stood there, backlit from the lights inside the house and washed out from the porchlight directly above his head.

"Katie Clay! Welcome to the party! Emma has been waiting for you," he smiled at me.

"Hey, Angus." I gave him what I hoped was a convincing smile. His eyebrows wrinkled.

"You okay? Did Donovan make things right—or at least try to? You say the word, and I'll still skin him," Angus said quietly as the light shined across my expression.

At least my inner turmoil had a cover story.

"No, I'm okay. I mean, if you're going to skin him, let me know. I'll bring the popcorn. He did apologize though. He's trying." I swallowed and attempted another smile.

Angus harrumphed and nodded. His expression cleared and excitement lit his face again as he ushered me in the doors.

"Katie!" Emma shrieked from across the room. She made a mad dash across the room and crushed me in a hug like she hadn't seen me in years.

"Happy birthday," I said, all muffled against her shoulder. Her blonde ponytail swished across my ear as she released me.

"Thanks!" she beamed.

I grinned at my best friend, her excitement infectious. Other wolves from the pack milled around, drinking soda and munching snacks.

"Well, tell me how you've been. I haven't seen you in all of two days." She looped an arm through mine and dragged me toward their tiny kitchen where trays of snack foods had been set out.

I snagged a bright yellow paper plate. "I'm good. Contrary to what Angus might have said," I whispered. She gave me a serious look. "Really. Fine," I protested.

She nodded slowly. I loaded my plate with veggies, little barbequed sausages, and a fruit skewer. "But," I bit my lip as she raised an eyebrow. "I wanted to ask you something later. It's nothing important, so not now. But I'm telling you so we don't forget."

There was no way I'd forget. I could think of nothing else.

"Sure. You know I'm still here for you anytime. Just because Angus and I are married, doesn't mean I don't have time for my best friend."

"I know. Mm. These are delicious. What's in this sauce?"

"I think Grandpa Jesse might have tossed something into the sauce."

I rolled my eyes and chuckled. Jesse Hazelton was our pack's grand Alpha—he was retired. He'd turned the reins of leadership over to his son, Hal, Donovan's father, several years ago and retired to the Alpha house on the back of Hal's property. Jesse Hazelton was a character if I'd ever met one. I loved him for it.

The party launched into full swing not long after. I melted into the sidelines and watched the group of wolves that had become my second family. Donovan winked at me from across the room when Emma spazzed out as she opened his present. I smiled back and took a drink from my cup.

I couldn't let anything happen to these wolves. It was possible I was totally overreacting, but if I wasn't...

I needed to leave to protect them.

Emotion surged to the back of my throat and squeezed my windpipe painfully tight.

CHAPTER 7

DONOVAN

I was hyper-aware of Katie all during Emma's party. I still felt awful about kissing her—not that kissing her had been bad in and of itself—she was an *amazing* kisser. Enough so that I'd been distracted by the memory of the kiss more than once. Wolf chuffed his agreement. But I shouldn't have done it. I could still see the hurt lingering in her hesitancy and her slightly pinched expression. So I gave her space when I normally wouldn't have.

My eyes left Katie and trained back on Emma as she opened her presents. She was overjoyed at each one and made sure she let the gifter know. Emma was like that; a ray of sunshine that shined on you and lit you up in the best way. No one was surprised when she and Angus Claimed each other as mates.

Emma was twenty today. Angus had turned twenty in the fall. I'd be twenty at the end of this year. Most werewolves found their mates by twenty. I shoved a sausage in my mouth and tasted Grandpa Jesse's trademark sauce—he'd probably laced the sauce with some secret blend of herbs and spices when no one was looking, giving it his special flair, and hoping no one would notice before the sausages were served.

Dad was laughing at something Grandpa Jesse said as Emma speared them both with a look that said she knew they were up to something.

I smiled, thankful for such a strong legacy and so many years of good leadership.

But I had to carry it on. I wasn't on a deadline to Claim the next Mrs. Hazelton, but I knew Dad was secretly anxious for me to. It was an added layer of security for the pack to have solid Alpha genes on both sides of the parental gene pools. Sarah had been the perfect candidate. We could have combined packs and become one of the most powerful werewolf packs in the country, jointly sharing the role of Alpha.

It was rare to have a female Alpha or Beta. Nature just seemed to produce more males into those roles, so we sometimes had to look a little lower down the pecking order to find a mate. Unless I somehow randomly stumbled upon my true mate. That would put an end to all this angsty turmoil inside me that made me feel like a hormonal teenage girl. No offense to the hormonal teenage girls I'd known. But man. I was over this. I just wanted a clear-cut path to follow.

A bubble of laughter broke near me, and I turned to politely join in the conversation and promised myself I'd stop being such a downer at Emma's birthday. Sneaking one more glance over at Katie, my resolve weakened. She had the saddest expression on her face that I'd ever seen. It wasn't the sadness that had tormented her for months after we'd found her and adopted her into our pack. It wasn't the sadness that lingered over losing her own family and pack.

It was like a sadness over grief that was yet to come.

My insides froze as I contemplated why she would have cause to look so stricken.

A balloon popped and the whole collective of us twitched at the loud, unexpected noise before laughter broke out at our absurdity. When I looked back to Katie, her face was a wreath of smiles, only the barest hint of sadness left deep in her eyes.

I didn't know if I should ask her about it, or if I'd already done enough damage and should just leave well enough alone.

CHAPTER 8

KATIE

Emma's party last night had been wonderful and dreadful. Wonderful because I loved seeing her so happy. But dreadful because it was at her party that I decided what I needed to do. Both to potentially protect myself and to keep my adopted pack safe from what might come after me. Which was why I was on Hal's doorstep shaking like a pup as nerves coursed under my skin.

I'd come when I knew Van wouldn't be around. I couldn't do this with him there. I'd fly to pieces. With a calming breath and a helpful nudge from Wolf, I rang the doorbell. Footsteps sounded over the hardwood of the hall as Hal came to the door.

"Katie! I wasn't expecting you, come on in." He swung the door wide and motioned with his hand for me to come in and make myself at home.

"Hi, Hal," I said as I politely kicked off my shoes at the door.

"You know you don't have to do that," he said with a fatherly smile.

"I know, but I'd hate to track dirt across your floor." I grinned back as my stomach tied itself in knots.

"Can I get you something to drink?" he asked as he tipped his head towards the kitchen, and we moved down the hall and through the dining room.

"I'd love some ice water."

"Sure. So what brings you to my doorstep when my son is notably absent?" Hal smiled again as I fought to keep my cheeks from flushing.

I cleared my throat as he filled a glass with ice cubes. "Actually, I wanted to ask your permission, blessing, I'm not really sure what the right word is," I said with a grimace that I hoped looked more like a grin.

"You have all my attention," Hal said, Hazelton trademark hazel-colored eyes, a sharp contrast under his silvery hair, focused on me. He slid the glass to me and took a seat on a bar stool at the island. I sat opposite and ran my finger around the rim of the glass as I gathered my thoughts. He let me think, patient while I tried to formulate the words I'd so carefully constructed before I'd come.

"There's something I've always wanted to do," I started, swallowing around the slight tremor in my voice. "And since I'm going to be eighteen in a few days, I was hoping I could make a formal request of sorts." I glanced up at him. His eyes remained focused on me, his head slanted to the side, attentive. "I've always wanted to see the East Coast. I want to go. Go see the other side of the country, go see the Atlantic. And since I'll be eighteen, and I've saved up plenty for the trip, I was hoping I could go by myself. The documentation you so generously provided when I turned sixteen has held up and should be fine for a plane ticket."

That was the rub. I could up and go, but I risked damaging my relationship with my pack—with my current Alpha—because I was technically a ward of the pack. I needed his permission for this excursion. If he didn't give it, I truly hated to think what would become of me if I disobeyed or what might become of the pack if trouble found me. Hal had graciously asked only minimal questions about my past when I'd turned sixteen. Through his contacts, he'd provided me with an ID that had allowed me to work, —though Ms. Brisbane didn't care one way or the other—and get a driver's license, which would hopefully be enough for me to hop a plane and leave the Hazelton pack safely behind me.

Hal pursed his lips, contemplative. My belly roiled.

"Katie, I appreciate that you've brought this to me. Part of me is hesitant—you haven't left this pack to go farther than Arcadia Bay's town proper in the five years you've been here, save a handful of day trips within a group of wolves. The world is a big place. It can be terrifying and confusing."

Tell me about it.

"That is my only reason for hesitating. It's not that I don't trust you, it's not that I don't want you to do this. It's just an awful big adventure for a girl unaccustomed to the rest of the world."

Wolf whined inside. I needed him to agree to this. I needed his support so, someday, if potential things blew over, I could come home. Home to Arcadia Bay and the Hazelton pack.

"I understand your hesitancy," I offered. "But I'm not so completely naïve. I also know how to defend myself, and how to use good judgement."

"You do, Katie. All of those things." Hal tapped his chin. "Let me think on this a day or two. I want you to take the trip, but let me look at all the angles before making that final judgement call. Okay?"

"Okay, Hal," I squeezed out around the tightness in my throat. It wasn't a complete rejection, I reminded myself. There was still hope he'd let me go.

He *had* to let me go.

CHAPTER 9

DONOVAN

Thoughts assaulted my brain as I let the cold wash over me. The day was misty, chilly, and generally miserable in skin. I was going to shift to fur as soon as I hit the tree line outside the Hazelton subdivision. Much like other werewolf packs I knew, we all congregated in one area. It was nice, being home with houses and packmates as familiar as my own name, but it was suffocating, too. I itched to run on four paws, let out some of this frustration that seemed to constantly be simmering under my skin.

I felt weighted down. Weighted with expectations—I needed to find another strong bloodline to mix with. Weighted with self-doubt—no matter how I tried to change my thinking, Sarah's rejection still stung. Far more than I expected it would. It was like a bad taste in my mouth that I couldn't get rid of. If I were being totally honest, I was still feeling weighted down with guilt over how I'd so callously treated Katie, too.

Sighing, I kicked a rock harder than I should have and it went clanging off into the underbrush. A squirrel scampered up a tree, chittering angrily at me. Consumed in my own thoughts, I stewed deeper into the woods. My head was in a muddle, my emotions in a tangle. I was done in skin. And then my shirt got caught on my ears as I yanked it forcefully over my head. With a low growl, I jerked the zipper of my jeans down and shoved the shoes off my feet along with my pants.

With a tremendous shake, I shifted all at once, eager to leave my skin and human problems behind for a time. My paws crashed down onto the leaves and underbrush right as the scent of *human* shot straight into my sensitive nostrils and a scream ripped through the air.

Whirling around, my heart froze in my chest. There, not ten feet away, stood a teenage girl in a yellow sweatshirt, her eyes so wide the whites shown all around her green irises. In horror, I watched as the color leeched from her face, her skin turning a disturbing shade of ashy gray.

Oh, this was bad. Bad, bad, bad, *bad*.

She'd seen me shift. I'd just unwittingly broken one of the paramount rules of the werewolf. *Never reveal yourself to a human.*

Should I kill her? My stomach lurched as my conscience instantly rebelled. As much as maybe I should, I couldn't kill her. I was no murderer. Should I shift back? Try to reason with her? What could I say? What did I do? What *could* I do?

In the end, Wolf made the choice for me. We bolted.

I ran as if my life depended on it. Because it might. The lives of my packmates could be in jeopardy.

If that girl had gotten a look at my face before I shifted, she could identify me. I couldn't begin to fathom the issues that would cause. I ran until I hit the door of my own house. I shifted, not bothering with clothes or modesty, and jammed my way through the door.

"Dad!" I shouted, Wolf anxious, gnashing and pacing still inside me.

No answer. Maybe he was with Grandpa Jesse. If nothing else maybe Grandpa would have an idea what to do.

Shifting back to my fur, I raced over the grass between our home and the Alpha house. Letting Wolf have his head, I scented. There. Dad was here. His scent was fresh. I didn't smell anyone else, but trying to exercise some tiny modicum of caution, since I'd blasted that all to smithereens fifteen minutes ago, I gave a sharp bark.

"Donovan?" Dad opened the door in confusion when he saw me there in my fur. I barreled past him, nearly knocking him over in the process.

"Dad, I'm in trouble. I'm in so much trouble," I gasped, lisping as I started talking before my canines and tongue had gone all the way back to their human shape.

Dad's eyes laser-focused on me. "What's wrong? Are you hurt?"

I shook my head, emotion choking me as the panic I'd forced down threatened to surface.

"Here. Come in, tell us what's happened," Grandpa Jesse shuffled into the room with a robe. I took it absently, twisting the material around in my fists as I stood in the front entryway of the Alpha house stark naked.

"I was headed into the forest for a run. I—I just needed to think, to clear my head. I was so lost in thought, I shifted. And then I realized there was a girl. Not ten feet away from me. She saw the whole thing." I hung my head in shame, Wolf gnashed in frustration inside me. My chest heaved, both from my run and from the anxiety that flooded me and leaked out my pores.

Dad ran a hand down his face, seeming to age twenty years with the gesture. Grandpa Jesse swore softly.

"Did she see your face? Could she identify you?" Dad asked quietly.

"I don't know. Maybe." I glanced down at my hands, started, then jerked the robe on and missed hooking the closure three times in my agitation. Wolf thrashed.

"How could you be so carried away you didn't realize a human was practically standing next to you?" Grandpa Jesse asked, concern heavy in his voice. "You're feeling well, your senses are working the way they should?"

I tugged at the ends of my hair. How did I explain what was going on inside me without making Dad and Grandpa Jesse feel worse about the pressures they unwittingly put on my shoulders?

I swallowed. "They're working. She...she was upwind and I was caught up in my own thoughts. Been thinking some heavy things lately." I struggled to get the words past my lips.

Dad glanced at me in concern. "You need to share? Something else going on?"

"Nothing as crucially important as this."

Dad frowned but nodded. "Donovan, I know you just got back from Rock Falls, but I think it would be best if you left again for a while. If something does come of this girl's accidental sighting of you, she can't identify you if you're not here." He sighed, sadness touching the corners of his eyes. "Send me a mental image of her through the pack link though. I'll investigate and keep a close eye and ears on things. I'll call Indie and see if you can come visit her for the time being."

Indie was Emma's older sister. She'd met her mate two years ago at a multiple pack Gathering and had moved out to North Carolina once they married and joined his pack.

"North Carolina should be far enough away," Grandpa Jesse quipped.

Dad got a far-away expression on his face. "There's one more thing I want you to do."

Chapter 10

Katie

I fidgeted. My fingers twitched, my toes wiggled, my body shook, my eye ticked. I looked massively over-caffeinated and under-rested. Probably because I was.

Even Wolf twitched inside me. She paced and I couldn't stop moving. Not only was I filled with dread for my upcoming birthday—it was tomorrow—I was nervous now because I'd gotten my wish.

Not how I'd planned it though. Hal had called me yesterday afternoon and said to be ready at the crack of dawn to fly to North Carolina. I could see the coast there and visit the Atlantic Ocean. That was helpful—I'd be away from Arcadia Bay and my pack in the event that things went south once I hit eighteen.

Not so helpful that I'd be travelling there with Van.

Just then, the beams of Angus's truck cut through the darkness of the lingering night. Dawn hadn't even broken yet, but I'd already been up for an hour, ready and waiting for Angus to take us to the airport. I hoped my nerves came across as excitement, not the utter dread that had befallen me. I bounced on the tips of my toes and reached for my backpack and tiny suitcase. I'd packed light. In case I had to run.

A shiver of trepidation worked down my spine.

Angus put the truck in park, and Van stiffly climbed out of the passenger side as I exited the house, quietly shut the door behind me, and locked it.

"Hey, Katie," he said. Van's voice sounded rusty like an old man's. And he looked awful. Dark shadows cupped his eyes, even in the dim light from the porch. His face looked haunted. He wore jeans and lightweight flannel unbuttoned over a slightly wrinkled t-shirt. He was far less crisp than normal. I suddenly wondered if Hal had Van traveling with me for more than just an escort.

"Hey. You need a cup of tea for the road? I could put one on real quick. I already drank the pot of coffee," I trailed off. I was rambling. Rambling, nervous, and jittery.

Van smirked. "I'm fine. I'll get something at the airport. Thanks though." He took the suitcase from me and put it behind the seat of the truck next to his own suitcase. "You drank a whole pot of coffee already?"

"Maybe."

"Katie, is this everything? Mom and Dad still asleep?" Angus asked as he gave me a quick side hug.

"Yeah. They got up to see me off, but since it's still hateful early, I told them to go back to bed." I zipped the bottom of my dark gray, nondescript hoodie partway over my shirt. It was chilly. I'd worn my favorite blue t-shirt for luck. The one that had books on it because I needed the comfort of my books. I'd stashed a few books in my backpack, too. Just for good measure.

"Well, that's easy enough then. Up you go," Angus said as he tipped his head to the truck before rounding it back to the driver's seat.

Without thinking, I hopped in the truck, so over-caffeinated and distracted, I momentarily forgot Van was coming with us.

"Am I sitting in the middle, or are you scooting over?" Van asked with a ghost of a smile as I started reaching for the seatbelt on the passenger side.

"Oh," I said inanely. My face flushed. I hoped the darkness covered the color blooming in my cheeks. Wolf squirmed inside as I scooted to the middle of the bench seat, rather ungracefully.

Van climbed in, shut the door, and strapped himself in. He relaxed in the seat, his leg fully against mine from his hip to his knee. My heart pounded. I glanced over at Angus as he put the truck in drive. I couldn't scoot any farther towards him or I'd be straddling the gear shifter. A nervous tremor rocked through me, further unsettling Wolf and ratcheting up the crazy pinging in my chest.

"Strap in there, Katie Clay," Angus said, using my full name as soft strains of some country song wafted from the speakers. Dumbly I buckled myself in, knuckles brushing Van's thigh, and swallowed. We went over a bump in the road and Van's leg jostled against mine. Every nerve ending I possessed was on fire. Why was I so stupidly *aware* of him?

This was going to be a long trip.

CHAPTER 11

DONOVAN

Katie was jumpy like she was spooked. Her leg nearly vibrated against mine. She must have consumed a pot of espresso and have coffee literally running through her veins. I leaned my head against the chilly glass. The action brought memories of the last time I'd been in this truck, returning from Rock Falls, into sharp focus. Regret and a tinge of rejection still nagged at me every time I thought of it. I sighed through my nose and let my eyes drift shut. Wolf nudged me. Katie was still jittery against my leg. I resisted the urge to smile. Maybe she was that excited about the trip.

Dad had told me last night about Katie's birthday request. I wished I'd been a good enough friend that she'd confided her desire to me. At least my willing banishment from pack lands could have one good thing come of it. It would make me happy to help Katie see the Atlantic Ocean. I'd like to see it myself.

I must have drifted off because the next thing I realized, Katie's leg jerked against mine and we were pulling into the airport drop off. We piled out and retrieved our bags.

"Be careful, both of you, okay?" Angus said as he gave us each a hug. I clapped his shoulder once.

"Thanks for the drop off, Angus."

"Anytime, little cousin."

I snorted. Little cousin. I was two inches taller than him now. "Take care of things while we're gone," I said, emotion rising slightly in the back of my throat. Angus would be acting Beta while I was gone. Guilt and shame mixed with those lingering feelings of insecurity. Wolf whined.

"No problem. Katie, keep him in line, yeah?" Angus winked at her, all brotherly concern underneath.

"I'll see what I can do," Katie said with a tight smile. I hoped the tightness was due to nerves about flying, not traveling with me. I thought we were back on fairly solid footing. Maybe I was wrong?

The car behind us honked, even though there were open spaces ahead. Angus frowned in the general direction. "Well, guess that's my cue to leave. Keep in touch. Hope things go well." Katie hopped up and hugged him tight. Smiling, Angus hugged her back, patted her shoulder, then stepped back. He gave us a happy shrug and hopped back in the truck. Then it was just me and Katie with our luggage.

"I think I could use that coffee now," I said as I squinted in the direction of the sun peeking over the rim of the horizon. My eyes felt bleary, even Wolf was staggering sluggishly inside.

"I think mine has worn off." She looped her backpack over her shoulders.

I glanced at her. "Maybe you ought to eat something to counteract all that caffeine you already had?"

She rolled her eyes. "Probably," she conceded. She gave me a hard look out of the corner of her eye and the middle of her cheek sucked in like she was biting the inside again. My insides squirmed and Wolf shook his head uncomfortably. "Why are you here, Van?" she asked softly.

Van. Only Katie ever called me Van. Nobody else in the pack did, not even my own dad. But Katie had called me Van since the day we met on that wet, bloody pass in the mountains.

I heaved a sigh as I grabbed my suitcase and indicated with my chin if she wanted me to get hers. She shook her head and grabbed the handle, still waiting for my response as we trundled to the automatic doors.

"I messed up. In a major sort of way, yesterday," I confessed. There was no reason to keep the information from her, though my heart fell somewhere down around my ankles, waiting for her condemnation.

"What could you have possibly done that was bad enough your dad sent you to babysit me cross-country?" she asked incredulously. There were a few other people milling around. Enough that I didn't want to risk being overheard. I stopped her briefly with a hand on her arm. She stopped, her entire attention fixed on me, her brows drawing down.

I sighed, Wolf shirking against my coming confession. I leaned down so there'd be no chance of being overheard. Close enough that her allspice and maple scent clouded my space. My lips hair's breadth from her ear as I whispered, "A human saw me shift."

Her gasp was audible as her head jerked back, her eyes like giant pools of liquid cinnamon as she stared at me.

"How, where...didn't you know they were there? They catch you watching from up on a peak or something?"

How well I understood her shock. "It's a long story. And she shouldn't have caught me. I was...distracted." Shame curdled in my middle.

A thick red-black brow arched up her forehead. "That's some big distraction," she quipped.

"Yeah. I know. Come on. A line is forming at security. I want coffee and a breakfast sandwich."

We got in line, waiting quietly with the other early morning travelers. Several times Katie's arm brushed against mine. Wolf pricked his ears forward, even more aware of her than usual. The surroundings were new. Even now, the Beta in me wanted to be sure she was all right.

Once we were past security, I glanced at my watch. "We've got an hour and half. I vote we get breakfast first."

"I'm good with that. I could stand to use the bathroom, too."

"Too much coffee?" I couldn't help but tease.

She glared and me and lightly smacked my arm. "Meet you at our gate in twenty?"

"We've got time. We can go together. I mean, you can go to the bathroom by yourself. I don't need to follow you in there." I smirked, trying to cover the sudden rush of embarrassment. I needed more sleep.

To my surprise, color bloomed lightly on Katie's cheeks. She rolled her eyes and adjusted her backpack then took off down the wide path towards the nearest ladies' room.

"You're on guard duty. I'll be out in a minute." She rolled her tiny carry-on next to my suitcase. With a swish of her shiny hair, she was gone.

I leaned against the wall, crossing one foot over the other, tired, worn out, but content to wait.

CHAPTER 12

KATIE

I'd definitely had too much coffee. My bladder was *full*. After an embarrassingly long time emptying it, I felt unbelievably better. Wolf shook herself out, feeling like she could breathe again now that my over-full bladder wasn't seemingly pressing against her.

Now that my pants were fitting properly again, I needed a minute to compose myself. My nerves were jangling around inside me, taut with anxiety and overstimulated from being pleasantly squished against Van's leg all the way here. I washed my hands then hoisted my backpack up on the counter and dug out my brush. A few quick strokes and I at least looked more normal. The light smattering of freckles on my nose and upper cheeks stood out starkly under the ugly white light above the mirrors. I pulled an elastic off my wrist and dragged my hair back into a low ponytail. Replacing my brush, I zipped my backpack and headed out to meet Van. He was leaning against the white tiled wall opposite the bathrooms, looking gloriously disheveled. If it weren't for the shadows under his eyes and the way his shoulders seemed to slump under some invisible weight, he'd have fit right in on the cover of some tall, dark, and ruggedly handsome magazine.

"Ready?" he asked, pushing away from the wall.

My stomach rumbled. Van smiled, his eyes still tired, but teasing. My belly dipped. "Food," I squeaked out. Van chuckled.

Once we purchased Van's sausage, cheese, and egg breakfast sandwich, my lightly toasted sesame bagel with cream cheese, and more coffee all around, we headed to our gate to wait for our plane and eat.

"So," Van started as he took a sip of his plain, boring black coffee. "I didn't know you wanted to see the East Coast so badly. You never mentioned it before." He unwrapped his sandwich while the bite of perfectly toasted bagel turned to ash in my mouth.

I forced myself to finish chewing and swallow the glob of masticated bagel. "Yes. I've always wanted to see the Atlantic Ocean," I said. Inwardly I cringed at how wooden my voice sounded in my own ears.

Van gave me a questioning look.

I shrugged and took a sip of my perfectly sweetened hazelnut cappuccino. It wasn't as good as Ms. Brisbane's coffee, but I did love a good cappuccino now and then. The warm frothy drink slid down my throat. "Well, I guess there really wasn't ever a chance of going until now," I hedged.

"I suppose that's true enough. How does it feel? Being eighteen—well, practically so."

My belly cramped. How did it feel? I didn't know yet. And I was afraid to find out. I shrugged again and offered him what I hoped was an engaging smile.

Van's expression suddenly fell. "You're not planning on...leaving, are you? This sudden desire to travel isn't about wanting to leave the...*area*, is it?"

"No, Van. This isn't about wanting to leave the pack," I whispered as Wolf whined inside me and a fist of emotion squeezed my throat. I never wanted to leave the Hazelton pack. They were the home I'd found once mine had been destroyed. I needed them. Wanted their safety and their wolves like I wanted air. Which was why I had to leave now. I had to keep them safe.

His shoulders relaxed as mine tensed further.

"Good. Anything else on the bucket list while we're at the coast?" He took a bite of his sandwich. I could smell the melted cheese on it.

I sighed. What did I want to do at the beach? "I've heard the Atlantic is vastly different than the Pacific. I want to walk along the shore at sunrise or sunset. Maybe both. I want to look for shells. Just...sit in the silence and be amazed at the vastness of the ocean." The words left me before I'd thought them through, but as I heard them, I realized they were true. The ocean had always been a peaceful though wild place. The Pacific Coast was glorious. I'd heard that the Atlantic was all white sand and warm water where our beaches were rough, tumultuous, and cold a good portion of the year.

"Katie, are you okay?" Van's fingers briefly brushed my arm. All the hairs on it stood up on end as Wolf chuffed a breath.

"I'm fine, Van."

I was not fine.

He knew I wasn't fine. Crap. He frowned and opened his mouth like he wanted to say something, then with a minute shake of his head, ate another bite of his sandwich instead. I nibbled my bagel, both of us lapsing into silence. The TV was on in the corner of the waiting area by our gate. News scrolled through and I tried to pay attention—distract myself from the barrage of thoughts that pounded through my skull and sent anxiety skittering like spiders under my skin.

My heel tapped against the floor in agitation.

Chapter 13

Donovan

I took a swig of mediocre coffee and glanced at Katie from the corner of my eye. Wolf sniffed in her direction. Anxiety was practically dripping off her. But I wasn't sure why. And she didn't seem open to my finding out.

Hoping I wasn't still somehow the cause, I finished my sandwich and tuned into the news as we waited for our plane to dock. Katie fidgeted beside me.

About a half hour later, our plane was ready and waiting. We got up, gathered our minimal luggage, and moved in line.

"Katie, you're practically vibrating. Is this the coffee making an appearance?" I asked her, starting to get mildly concerned.

"The coffee was probably both helpful and harmful today." She gave me a weak smile and shrugged. "Nerves and all."

I'd guess so. We were at the back of the line, so I turned back to the TV screens. They had some garden footage from some historic landmark that didn't really pique my interest, so I started reading the white band of rolling stories at the bottom.

Man catches record breaking seven gill shark. Missing SnowSpace Tech heiress to come forward and claim inheritance. Local girl attacked by feral wolf.

My eyes riveted on the newsfeed. Katie went utterly still beside me. My blood chilled. There was no picture listed with the girl and the feral wolf attack, but I couldn't help but wonder if it was somehow connected to the girl who had seen me shift. Wolf paced.

Katie wrapped her fingers around my arm. They were ice cold. I could feel their frigidness through the layer of my shirt. I covered her hand with mine, gripping her fingers, needing her presence to ground me for a second before the what-ifs rumbled away in my brain. Wolf sat, edgy and alert.

"Van?" Katie whispered. I glanced down and found her eyes wide and her face pale, her freckles standing out more than usual. "I'm terrified of take-off."

The absurdity of her statement sent a ripple of heat through me and shattered the dread that clutched my chest. My shoulders lost some of their rigidity. I moved the handle of my carry-on to my other hand then slid my arm up and captured Katie's fingers in mine, lacing them together.

"It's okay to be nervous." I smiled at her, the need to watch out for her taking precedence over the fear sitting in my gut. She let out a shuddering sigh and turned her body towards me, her forehead momentarily leaning against my bicep. It felt strangely right to have her there pressed against me. I squeezed her hand, my Beta instincts rising up, wanting to comfort her—take care of my pack.

"Boarding pass, please?" the airline employee chirped as we made our way to the counter. I handed her mine. She scanned it and smiled brightly. Numbly, Katie handed hers over, too. "Thanks so much!" the stewardess said again with great enthusiasm. She must have had a pot of coffee before work, too.

I reached back and took Katie's hand again, willing my presence to settle her the way hers had settled me earlier when that news story flashed across the screen. Her fingers were still cold and brittle, but they closed around mine with vice-like tightness.

We weren't assigned seats on our flight, just what we could find when we boarded in our groups. "Here, go in front and pick us two seats together. I'll put the bags up," I said as I nudged her forward, my hand grazing her shoulder since her black backpack covered the rest of her.

"Care if I take the window?" Katie asked, some of her normal, less strained character seeming to resurface.

"Go right ahead," I said, wondering why she wanted to sit by the window if take-off terrified her so much. I wouldn't want to see the ground if it were me.

She slithered into the blue vinyl seat, stowing her backpack under the seat in front of her while I found two open spaces and inserted our small suitcases in the overhead compartment. I felt the front of my shirt come up slightly but didn't have a hand to tug it back down until I had the suitcases situated and the one thing I needed for the trip out of the front pocket of my luggage.

I caught the faintest hint of pheromones dancing in the air.

CHAPTER 14

KATIE

I knew I shouldn't look. But I did. And the little peek of Van's abs between his shirt and the top of his jeans not only did strange things to my belly, but it was the momentary distraction that I needed. I was tired of the stress, of agonizing over things I couldn't yet change. Quickly turning my eyes to the window as Van settled into the middle seat so he couldn't see me blush, I swallowed. My eyes slid closed as he gently tugged my hand from its clenched position in my lap, his larger calloused hand encompassing my smaller one.

He was doing his level best to be kind to me and lessen any fears I had about taking off. I loved him even more for it.

If only that was truly what had prompted those words regarding the flight from my lips. I sucked my cheek in, biting the inside of it as I kept my eyes shut tight for one more minute to collect myself.

"Hey," Van said softly, his voice close to my ear. A shiver worked over my shoulders as his breath tickled the hairs at the nape of my neck. "I thought you might want this. On the plane."

A hard corner nudged my thigh gently and I pried my eyes open.

"Oh!" I was so caught off guard, that for a moment, I forgot everything else. There on my lap was the most gorgeous hardback edition of a book

I'd been dying to read. Ms. Brisbane had special ordered a paper copy for me, but it hadn't come in before we'd left. "How did you..." I started.

Van's grin turned a little sheepish. "I know your birthday isn't until tomorrow, but I thought you might enjoy having this for the flight...Emma suggested you might like this one. I hope it's okay."

Sudden tears filled my eyes. Both at the thoughtfulness of my best friend, and at Van's sweet gesture. I nodded, a happy watery smile on my face. "It's more than okay," I said softly.

"Good, because I pre-ordered the sequel for you, too. But I couldn't get an early copy of it."

My smile returned in full force. Nothing made me happier than gifts of books. Books were my love language, and Van was being the solid friend he'd always been, save the glorious minutes he'd lost his mind and kissed me. Never mind that my heart still went pitter-pat over him.

"Thank you, Van."

He beamed. "Will this help with the take-off jitters?"

"Definitely."

"Hello, ladies and gentlemen," the automated voice crackled through the speakers. I clutched my book to my chest and made sure my seatbelt was fastened properly.

Take-off wasn't terrible. I over exaggerated my nerves for the sake of my blurted explanation earlier, but all considered, it wasn't bad. And Van's arm and leg were pressed against mine in the tight confines of the plane. I didn't mind that either and found his solid presence comforting, even if he had no idea what was really going on inside my brain.

"Are you okay if I drift off for a while? I didn't get much sleep last night." His sleepy words were mumbled near my ear and sent little pin-pricks shuttling over my skin.

"Of course." I gave him a genuine smile. "I'm going to dive into this book someone got me."

He gave me another tired grin then settled his head back against the seat. His muscles released their tension, easing within seconds. I watched him unabashedly as his face lost the lines of worry, relaxing into light sleep. His dark lashes fanned against his high cheekbones, his sandy brown hair flopping to the side. He looked younger, less burdened. Wolf stirred inside me, wanting him. I bit back a sigh. Wanting him despite the fact I knew very well he could never be mine the way I wanted.

I carried too much baggage. Too much brokenness. Too many secrets. Too many enemies. I shook my head to rid it of the dark thoughts and cracked open the book. I took one minute to enjoy the scent of fresh paper and ink. Wolf rose and sniffed, too. Books were a scent we loved.

I didn't linger over the scent now though. Knowing my mind would calm for at least a little while if I lost myself in the thrall of a story, I settled into my seat, leaning more than I really needed to against Van, and let my eyes devour the words on the page.

The hours passed quickly, and by the time we were close to landing, Van was awake, looking more himself, and I wanted to keep reading. But as the plane touched down, I forced myself to reverently close the book, using a stray thread from the bottom of my hoodie to mark my spot, and put it away in my backpack. The second I zipped my backpack, unease started slithering back into my middle.

No. I wasn't going to let it. Wolf snorted and I gave my emotions a hard yank. I *would* be in control of my own emotions...unless they got the better of me. I was not going to dwell on things I couldn't change. Besides, I was literally going across the country. I'd be the proverbial needle in the haystack.

With my mind made up, I tried to be patient for the plane to sidle up to the drop off.

"How was the book?" Van asked as he rubbed the back of his neck.

I could tell my eyes lit as a flood of bookish delight rushed through my veins. "It's glorious. I think I know who the villain is."

Van smiled as the plane lurched towards the gate. "I wish we had a longer layover here in Chicago. I've never seen Navy Pier. I hear it's pretty cool."

"I've never seen it either," I said. "We've got what, a three-hour lay-over? Long enough for lunch and to find our other gate?" I said.

Van's belly rumbled. "Yup. I think that's the last of the breakfast sandwich digested."

The airport was a hive of activity once we disembarked. It was huge. Towering ceilings and people jostling, luggage rolling, and the distant rumble and hum of planes about sent Wolf into sensory overload.

"Wow. This is...bigger than I expected," I said, my grip tightening on the strap of my backpack and the handle of my suitcase.

Van was checking the signs hanging down from the tall ceilings. "Yeah, it is. Come on. I think our gate is this way. I vote we find our gate first, then eat."

"Mm, correction. We're going to find a bathroom, then find our gate, then eat," I said with a saccharine smile. Seriously. My bladder was the size of a pea.

"Yeah, okay. I had coffee, too," Van said with a teasing roll of his eyes.

We used the restroom, and after about twenty minutes of walking, found where our next plane would depart.

"Okay. We passed the food court. What smelled good?" Van asked as we started meandering back towards lunch.

"All of it. I'm starving."

"I'm going for a steak sandwich and fries smothered in cheese." Van licked his lips. I giggled. Van waggled an eyebrow.

"I want Chinese food. Maybe Mexican. Maybe both." My nose wrinkled. It all sounded good. Van snorted.

In the end, Van got his sandwich and fries, and I had half a cheese quesadilla, Cajun chicken, and a side of Chow Mein and steamed vegetables.

"It may take some doing, but any chance you see some place less crowded?" Van asked as he scanned the busy room. "Lotta sensory information here," he said.

"Agreed, "I said. Wolf was pacing, trying to process the onslaught of noise, smells, and bright lights. "Oh, is that a table back there? Behind that newsstand?"

"Yes! Go. Before anyone else gets it!" Laughing, we took off.

We hustled over to the vacant table for two that was wedged between a window and the backside of a shop. The noise quieted immediately as we rounded the corner. It was fairly secluded from the rest of the eating area and had a view of the moving bits and pieces of the airport out the big windows. Faint sunlight trailed in through the clouds.

"This is better. I feel like I can hear myself think over here," Van said as he unwrapped his sandwich. My fingers slithered across the table of their own volition and snagged a sauce-laden fry.

"I saw that. Don't think I'm not eyeing that Cajun chicken." Van speared me with a look. I grinned and nudged my plate closer to him. He nodded and snagged a bite of chicken. "That's not bad," he said as he wiped his lips with a napkin.

The meal passed pleasantly enough. We talked about nothing important, and my anxiety was held at bay. Finally, with full bellies and empty plates, we had nothing to do but go back to our gate and wait.

"Hand me your cup if you're done, I'll go toss it with my trash," I said, standing and gathering the rest of the cartons to toss.

"Thanks." He tipped his cup back once more to finish the last drops. I watched his Adam's apple bob, the tendons in his neck showing slightly. A flush began creeping up my chest.

With no warning, icy power washed over me, drowning me with its potency. Claws of possession slashed at my belly as Wolf rose inside, gnashing her teeth, doubling in size as my birthright suddenly funneled more and more power into us.

"No! *No, no, no, no,*" I whimpered brokenly, the tray I held crashing to the ground as I gripped my head and squeezed my eyes shut.

Terror ratcheted up my spine as my fur threatened to shove through my skin. Power tingled in every cell of my body as bile rose in my throat. Like giant tentacles, my birthright descended, wrapping me in an inescapable hold, choking me and stealing my breath.

"Katie! Katie, what's wrong?" Van's voice was far away and barely registered as tears streamed down my face and my legs gave out. I sank into a heap on the floor, Wolf unsteady on her feet.

We're coming for you. I will find you. You will belong to me. I will break you, destroy you, and you will give me everything.

Alan.

Horror clashed with stark fear and sent a wave of panic shooting through my extremities, threatening to take me under. Black spots danced at the edges of my vision.

Strong arms wrapped around me, and the scent of clay and hazelnuts enveloped me where I huddled on the floor.

The voice in my head quieted, and I knew the moment Van smelled the changes roiling through me. His arms froze in shock, wrapped around me but suddenly rigid. "Katie?" He breathed the word, almost accusatory.

Flinching, a fresh wave of tears leaked from my eyes as a sob caught in my chest.

"They know," I moaned.

"Know what? Who? Katie...*you're a Beta.*"

I shook my head against his shoulder, too chicken to meet his eyes. "They're trying to flush me out." My heart cracked in two. This was why I'd had to leave the safety of the Hazelton pack. The wolves after me would stop at nothing to get what they were after. And I was in their way.

CHAPTER 15

DONOVAN

Confusion thumped against my skull as Katie's changing scent—still allspice and maple, but with an added layer of power and dominance—clouded my brain. Katie was a *Beta*? From what pack? What was going on?

"They want me dead," she mumbled brokenly against my shoulder. That snapped me out of my daze and sent my own Beta sensors flashing on high alert. Wolf pricked his ears forward, straining to pick up any hint of danger. I heard nothing beyond the din of diners on the far side of the corner.

"Who wants you dead?" The words came out cold, calculating. No one messed with my pack. Beta or not, Katie was still my pack. Although, even as I thought it, a new layer of bewilderment surfaced. Katie had never sworn formal allegiance to the Hazeltons. She was like a temporary pack member. She'd been a minor when we'd found her. She'd been too young to join of her own volition. She'd said she needed more time when she reached sixteen—when she could have formally joined the pack, and it just hadn't come up again. She was one of us, but in name only. What did all of this mean, and what exactly did it have to do with what I'd just witnessed?

Katie shuddered against my chest, and I ran a hand over her hair and down her back. "Katie," I said more gently. When she still didn't look up, I carefully tipped her chin. Her cinnamon eyes were swimming in tears, red blotches standing out against the normal paleness of her skin. "Tell me what's going on. I can't protect you if I don't have the facts," I said softly. My thumb brushed along the edge of her jaw before I thought better of it.

She took a trembling breath, her chin quivering as her eyes filled with fresh tears and spilled over her dark lashes. Memories of the first time I saw her crashed down on me. Thirteen-year-old Katie, just as she was shifting from wolf to girl, bruised, battered, and bloodied. Her hair was matted with twigs and dirt, skin streaked red and black, wide cinnamon eyes crusted and brimming with tears as I knelt beside her, blood pooling from gashes across her belly. I shook my head to clear the image, focusing again on Katie.

"Talk to me, Katie," I whispered again.

She blinked, getting a grip on her emotions, and straightened, though she made no move to leave the circle of my arms. It felt safer to have her there, anyway.

"I hardly know where to start," she stuttered, gulping. "I was afraid something might happen on my birthday, but I didn't expect this."

"Becoming a Beta?" I guessed, still shocked with the knowledge myself.

She nodded and sniffed. "I guess that means my brother is dead," she said woodenly. The breath left me in a rush. That was a painful pill to swallow.

"I'm so sorry, Katie."

She shook her head. "He made his choice. He turned his back on me a long time ago when he sided with my uncle."

I hardly dared breathe.

"Do you know anything about my past, Van?" she asked, her voice like gravel under pressure.

"You know I don't. None of us do. You refused to tell anyone anything. I've always tried to respect that." I was prepared to push the issue now though. There were things going on here that I didn't understand, but they had Wolf's hackles raised with the innate need to protect Katie.

A weak smile lifted her lips. "Yeah. I never wanted anything from my past to touch the Hazeltons. I hid in plain sight among your numbers, desperately needing a home, a place where no one could ever find me."

"That's why you refused to go to school in town, isn't it?" The puzzle slowly started to take form in my brain, pieces dropping into a blurry picture.

She nodded. "Yeah. When you and Angus found me on the mountain pass, I knew it was a chance to escape my uncle, and maybe survive long enough to actually live."

My thumb rubbed across her lower back, encouraging her to keep talking.

She heaved another shuddering sigh. "When I was thirteen, a series of events happened that ended with my parents dead at my uncle's hand. He and my brother formed a mutiny within the pack. Their band of wolves slaughtered everyone loyal to my father, keeping their plans and allegiance secret, so that no one saw things coming until it was too late.

"I hadn't shifted before—I was only thirteen—you know most girls don't shift as young as boys, and truthfully, I think that was the only thing that saved my life. The stress of the betrayal, of my parents' loss, it triggered my shift earlier than it would have happened on its own. Nobody was looking for a wolf when they were searching for me. They were looking for a terrified young girl.

"One of them did find me, but..." she paused and swallowed hard, "I won the fight. He died but left me in bloody ribbons. You found me not long after."

My stomach twisted, sick at what Katie had lived through. I'd always assumed it was something bad—likely a pack of feral wolves—but to be betrayed not only by your fellow pack mates, but a blood relative? That was unconscionable.

"Why were they after you? As you said, you were a scared girl. Why did they fear you so much?" I asked as she leaned her forehead against my shoulder. I hugged her tight, sensing the emotions churning inside her.

"I'm my father's daughter. I carry the Alpha gene for our pack. I'm a valuable commodity." Her icy words chilled me—not only for Katie's sake, but because they reminded me eerily of something Sarah had said when I was in Rock Falls. "My brother had sided with my uncle. When my uncle killed *his* own brother, he assumed the mantle of the Alpha. My brother was the closest, oldest relative, so he became the Beta. They would have ended me to remove any opposition I might cause as I grew up."

She raised her gaze to mine once more. Swiping an errant tear, she squared her jaw. "But there was one other thing they hadn't counted on. My father must have known something was happening because he changed his will. He and Mom had told me privately earlier that night. Before...before they were massacred."

Anxiety twisted in my gut. Wolf paced, attuned and alert, ready to defend at a moment's notice.

"I am the sole beneficiary of my father's considerable estate and his shares in his company. I'm set to inherit on my eighteenth birthday. My uncle needs me, or needs my body to present it to collect the money." She looked me in the eye, waiting.

So slowly it was like wading through a quagmire of thick sludge, dots started connecting. Like a lightning strike, the news story from this morning flashed through my brain. *Missing SnowSpace Tech heiress to come forward and claim inheritance.* I recoiled at the absurdity of the thought. Surely not. Could...could it be possible?

"Katie," I asked, my voice verging on being unsteady, "who was your pack?"

She hung her head. "My name's not Katie."

I blew out a hot breath, Wolf thrashing in agitation, waiting for her to confirm my suspicions.

"My name is Kaylee. Kaylee Snowdon. Daughter of multi-millionaire tech genius, Michael Snowdon. Founder and majority stake holder of *SnowSpace Tech*." Her lip tucked between her teeth, and I could hear her heart pounding, even over the blood rushing behind my ears.

"You think your uncle killed your brother so you'd become Beta—to flush you out—because he can't touch your money without you." Saying the words out loud seemed to suck the oxygen from the air around us.

Katie—*Kaylee*—nodded grimly.

"My brother has served his purpose. Uncle Alan always wanted Dad's money but could never get it. I imagine he was quite distressed after he killed his brother, only to realize that neither of his children could touch the money until we reached majority. Ben won't have been able to get any either, even though he's older, because everything is still in my name. I've done some research into it. Unless they produce me or my dead body, they still can't touch the money. After fifty years it all goes to a charity. The money is untouchable without my physical presence and my DNA to unlock the bio code Dad included as a stipulation. I'm guessing this is Alan's newest effort to bring me out of hiding."

My head was spinning. My mouth gaped open and shut a few times, though I couldn't force any sound out.

"Kate—Kaylee," I amended quickly, only to see a hurt expression flash across her face.

She shook her head. "No. I'm Katie. I became Katie Clay the night I left my own pack. I don't want to be Kaylee Snowdon. That girl is gone. It, it wouldn't feel right for you to call me Kaylee." She took a shuddering breath. "Kaylee was who I was with my parents. Katie is who I am with you and the Hazeltons." She tipped her eyes to mine, and the vulnerability I saw there about ripped the heart straight out of my chest.

"Katie," I said softly. "All this going to see the ocean. Was that only a ruse to get you out of Arcadia Bay? Away from our pack?"

She nodded miserably. "I figured there would be some repercussion around my birthday. I couldn't take the chance that Alan would come looking for me and leave a trail of destruction behind him—but I didn't expect this either. I can feel the pull of the pack inside my head right now." She blinked rapidly. "Alan...he threatened me."

"Is he still there now?" Anger and fear rumbled through my chest.

She shook her head. "No. He'll try to intimidate me with fear. He'll link me when he thinks it will do the most damage. But the others—I feel them all in my head." She closed her eyes, wrinkles appearing across her forehead.

"I know what you mean." I tapped the side of my head in sympathy. I felt the mental tethers of each of my pack members. It wasn't a burden, but I could well imagine it would be if I didn't want them there. If I didn't honor the responsibility of carrying them. But Katie, not only had her own pack turned against her, they now wanted *her*—or at least her money. And she had a mental connection to each one of them that must feel like a lead weight dragging her down into the depths. "You can use your link with them as a sort of barrier—to insulate yourself against hearing them. I can teach you," I said, glad there was at least something I could offer her.

My phone buzzed in my pocket. "Sorry. I'll turn my phone off. This is more important." I fished my phone out and my eyebrows lifted. "Hang on, it's Dad. He shouldn't be calling right now." Katie sniffed and nodded.

I answered the call. "Dad?"

"Donovan. Are you all in Chicago?"

"Yeah. We, uh, we just finished lunch," I offered, unwilling to spill all Katie's secrets first thing.

"I just wanted to let you know that we just had some visitors who dropped by unannounced. They wanted to know if you'd brought home a mate—if any new wolves had joined the pack recently after the Lacessere."

Blood froze in my veins as a dozen different scenarios tripped through my brain. "Dad, reception is really bad. I can hardly hear you," I lied.

I hung up abruptly and turned my phone all the way off.

Dad? I called out using our mental Alpha-Beta link.

Son? What's going on? Are you in trouble?

Maybe. Listen, Katie is really Kaylee Snowdon. The missing heiress of SnowSpace Tech. Her uncle killed her parents, and someone just killed her brother about an hour ago. She's a Beta. They're after her. With tech like SnowSpace puts out, I'm not sure using any kind of technology in our own names is safe right now. I'm concerned that whoever came to you might be looking for Katie.

Silence.

Dad?

I'm here, Son. Digesting that bomb you just dropped. I agree. I didn't like the looks of the men who came. Wolves, but shifty, and not in the good way. I improvised and said that the Lacessere hadn't gone as planned. I didn't say much more than that. Are the two of you safe for the moment?

As far as I know.

Dad gave a heavy mental sigh. *Can you drop off the grid? Completely? Do not catch your connecting flight, do not go to North Carolina. If the men do have your scent, so to speak, they'd easily be able to track you through your plane tickets. Which probably means they can track your phones and your computer.* I heard his wolf growl over our mental connection. Mine rose in answer. *You aren't safe on your own either. You need the protection of a pack. Any ideas? If you disappear for a while, we can launch our own investigation here and alert our allies if we find anything.*

A lump formed in the pit of my stomach. *Yeah. I've got one idea.* It wasn't one I was excited to put into action, but my options were feeling pretty limited. Katie's safety was my top priority right now, and that was reason enough to sacrifice any pride I had left. *We'll be careful. I'll let you know what our plan is as soon as we have one here.*

Be safe, Son. Hug Katie—are we still calling her Katie?

Yes. Still Katie. And I'll hug her for you.

"What did he say?" Katie whispered, fully aware that I was having a silent conversation with my dad.

"Phone," I mouthed. I popped the SIM card out of mine. Her eyes went wide then she frantically dug hers out of her backpack, understanding dawning and making her fingers shake as she passed it over to me. Taking her SIM card out, too, I just looked at them in my hands, working through all the strategy I'd had drilled into me since I was a boy.

None of it had been for how to avoid technological exposure.

"We're going to find the post office here at the airport. You okay?" Before I could stop myself, my finger brushed over her cheek, moving an errant piece of hair, and taking the last vestiges of her tears.

She nodded, closing her eyes for a second.

We moved together, rising from our hunched position on the floor, quickly gathered up the trash that had spilled, and took our bags.

Finding the post office, I scowled at the price of packaging materials, but bought a box, foam, and tape. I packed my computer and charger, along with both phones and sim cards into the box, padding it with some clothes from my suitcase, since I knew I'd need to pare down and condense before leaving the airport.

"Here." Katie handed me a wad of shirts from her suitcase, too. I nodded and added those to the box.

"Anything else?"

"Yeah. Take these, too." She handed me a few other articles of clothes that I stuffed in. At least the computer should survive the trip home without me.

Once we'd mailed everything back home to Oregon, I felt I could breathe a little easier. "Okay. Step one, completed. We need to drop off the grid." I quickly filled her in on what my dad had said as we walked towards a cluster of shops.

Katie bit her lip. "I'm so sorry, Van. I didn't want any of this to happen. I don't know how much access Uncle Alan has, but if it's any kind of even basic access, he'll have no trouble tracking you. And if it was him that came to Hal, if he even thinks you *might* have come in contact with me, he won't rest until he's got you in his sights. I can't...I'm so sorry."

"Hey," I stopped us, tugging her over to the edge of the busy hallway. "I know you didn't want any of this to happen."

CHAPTER 16

KATIE

I stood there at the edge of the hall as Van stared down at me. His hazel eyes were flecked with concern and determination. Wolf responded, shaking her fur out, leaning into me for added support.

Fizz erupted in my belly as Van suddenly cupped my neck and the backside of my ear. For one paralyzing second, I thought he was going to kiss me again. But instead, he pulled me into him as he leaned down close, so close his lips brushed the outer edge of my ear.

"Katie Clay, you listen to me. This is *not* your fault. Even though you're not formally part of my pack, I'm still your acting Beta until you willfully leave. And so long as you are, I will do everything in my power to make sure that you are safe."

My eyes slid shut as heat and dread mingled in my middle. Heat at his declaration of service to my safety, but dread that his duty could get him killed...and then disappointment that I was only his duty. Wolf snorted.

He tipped my face so our gazes met.

"You believe me?" he asked quietly. His eyes were shifting, their browns, golds, and flecks of green swirling in intensity.

I nodded. I did believe him. I knew what happened all those years ago wasn't my fault. I just desperately hoped what might still happen wouldn't be my fault.

"Okay. Here's my plan. Tell me what you think."

My belly writhed as Van outlined his strategy. It was smart. I was not surprised on that count. Donovan Hazelton had studied strategy with Hal and Jesse for years. But I wasn't quite prepared for the emotional effect it would have on me.

I'd be confronting the reason Van kissed me.

It didn't matter. Couldn't matter.

Swallowing past the hard lump in my throat, I resolved to shove my unhelpful emotions down. Wolf rubbed her head against me. This was strictly business.

The business of keeping me alive.

I nodded.

Uncertainty flitted over Van's face before he ran a hand through his hair and took a huge inhale. My belly clenched, realizing that Van was nervous about this, too. I wasn't sure how well it boded if Van was uneasy with his own plan.

The girlish part inside me wanted to curl up and wither away. What was Van thinking? Had...had he kissed *Her*? Was he comparing my lips to *Hers* right this second? Was that what his uneasiness was about? Or was he regretting me and all my baggage?

No.

I pushed that thought aside. Van meant what he said. And when he said he wanted to protect and keep me safe, he meant it. He'd go to absurd lengths to protect his own. Although, as he said, I wasn't a Hazelton.

I was a Snowdon.

I was hunted. My jaw clenched.

I refused to be prey.

But better prey in hiding than prey out in the open, prepared for the slaughter.

"Katie, you okay? Did I lose you there?"

I shook my head, shoving it all down, bottling it up to process later.

I nodded. "I've got nothing better to offer." I shrugged, sniffed, and rubbed the cuff of my hoodie over my eyes.

Van blew out a breath and tugged the ends of his tousled hair. "I'm going to need to make a call. I really hope they still have a payphone here."

CHAPTER 17

DONOVAN

Katie nodded. "Here's to hoping they do." She swallowed. Her tears had cleared, replaced by purpose as I'd outlined my tentative plan.

My gut churned, thinking about the next thing I needed to do. "Well, let's go look. There's a directory over there by that candy shop."

Blessedly, they did have a payphone, though it took us awhile to locate it. I'd looked up and memorized the number I'd need before I'd shipped my phone home.

A quick glance at Katie's face and then I cleared my throat and dialed.

"This is Dominic Wolfe," a gruff voice on the other end of the line answered. I swallowed hard.

"Dominic, this is Donovan Hazelton."

"Donovan! What can I do for you?" Warmth seeped into Dominic's voice. Wolf paced inside me.

"Well, I need a place to lay low. Completely off the grid low. I'll have one other with me. We might be bringing some heat with us." I found myself biting my lip as the words left my mouth. There was a moment of silence on the other end. Wolf squirmed.

"You are welcome here at any time. We are allies, and that has not changed. When should we expect you?"

A breath I hadn't realized I'd been holding gusted between my teeth.

"We'll be a couple of days. I'm not sure I can give you anything more specific. Sorry."

"We'll keep an eye out and expect you."

"Thanks, Dominic," I said, every ounce of me grateful beyond words. He grunted and we hung up.

"And?" Katie prompted. Her cheek was indented again. The inside of her cheek was probably raw.

"We're going to Rock Falls." My voice sounded hollow, even to my own ears. Wolf growled in agitation. I'd made friends in Rock Falls, but I was also loathe to go back. Reminders of Sarah and her rejection were still fresh enough they stung. But where better to hide than with the pack that had witnessed it all? After a Lacessere rejection, nobody would expect the rejected wolf to go straight back to that same place. Our formal alliance with the Wolfe pack was new enough it wouldn't be public knowledge yet. Plus, Sarah and Cade should have packed up and gone back to New York and Sarah's pack by now, so at least I wouldn't have to deal with that. And I genuinely liked Sam, Kyp, and Bowen and their mates. Maybe it wouldn't be so bad. After all, they appreciated what I'd done for one of their friends and packmate when I refused my rights and let Sarah Claim Cade.

"Van, are you okay going back there?"

Ugh. Katie was as good at reading me as I was at reading her. "Yeah. Come on. We need to go get cash and do some shopping."

We found an ATM and got out as much cash as both our debit cards and the pack card I had for emergencies would allow us with the daily limit. It was enough to get us where we needed to go at least. Chicago would be the last place we'd be traced to, should Katie's uncle truly be after us.

"Do you want to split up and get stuff quicker?" Katie asked as we entered a square of shops with everything ranging from sunglasses to cell phones to t-shirts that said *Chicago* in scrolling letters and obnoxious colors.

I scanned the area. "No. Not that I don't trust you, but honestly?" I glanced at her, "I'm a little spooked. Let's stay together."

"Awesome. At least I'm not alone in my paranoia." She gave me a smile that verged on a grimace.

"Not over this. Come on." I reached down and she offered no resistance when I grabbed her hand. There was nothing romantic in the gesture, but I felt better touching her, knowing she was there next to me. Wolf was rattled. So was the human half of me.

Even without splitting up, we made quick work of buying questionable amounts of trail mix, jerky, a few candy bars, water, and a black backpack.

"Okay. Let's condense," I said as we found a quiet corner to rearrange our suitcases and take only what we needed and could carry as wolves.

"You're taking the book? Isn't that just going to add unnecessary weight?" I asked, part of me pleased and amused that my gift meant enough to her that she wanted to take it with her.

She glared at me, her eyes slit. "I will *not* wait weeks to get my hands on another copy of this book to find out who the villain is."

I chuckled. "Suit yourself."

She snorted but then looked around. "One sec," she said. "I need a plastic bag. Soggy book is even worse than soggy fur."

"That's a good idea." If it rained, everything would get wet.

"Look, that bathroom down there is being cleaned. There'll be a cleaning cart inside. I'm going to grab some spare trash bags."

"Be careful," I said, realizing the absurdity of telling her to be careful, just going into a bathroom. But I'd never been in a position like this before. Responsibility for Katie sat heavy on my shoulders. Not only was she my pack—someone that as Beta that I was sworn to protect—but she was my friend. The thought of something happening to her sent Wolf pacing, all tied up in knots.

"I will." She squeezed my shoulder lightly as she passed. My eyes stayed riveted on her until she slipped around the corner of the bathroom entry. Then I sat on my haunches, every sense trained outward, waiting for her.

It didn't take her long.

"Any trouble?" I asked as she squatted down next to me and passed over a few plastic bags.

"Nope. But there might have been if I weren't so light on my feet." She winked, though I could see her tension through the gesture.

CHAPTER 18

KATIE

I carefully took stock of the contents of my backpack and my suitcase. Brushing my finger over the picture I'd packed at the bottom of my suitcase, I wondered if I should take it or not. It was a picture of all my closest friends in Arcadia Bay. My new family. I didn't have a single picture of my own birth family. Wolf nudged me as emotion tightened around my throat.

Van gently rubbed my shoulder. "We should mail that back to Arcadia Bay. It's identifying. We can lie if we get caught, but that's harder to do with picture evidence," Van said gently.

I glanced at him, he nodded. I put the picture on the floor next to me and gently inserted my newly plastic-wrapped book into my back-pack—next to the lime green lacey bralette I hoped Van hadn't noticed me shoving in earlier. He knew enough about me. He didn't need to see my underthings, too. Wolf chuffed. I glared at her.

"You have room for more trail mix?" I asked casually, trying to act as if my life and neon unmentionables weren't completely flayed open for him right then.

"Sure, hand it over. I just found a new pocket in the bottom of this backpack," Van said as he held out his hand. His new backpack was a beast. It was easily twice the size of mine. It was good that Van's wolf was bigger than mine, too. I'd have trouble keeping his backpack balanced on my wolf's shoulders. "Need me to carry anything else? I've got a little more room," he said.

"Nope. My books and the rest of my clothes fit into mine since we mailed some back."

"Books plural?" He snorted, the corners of his eyes crinkling slightly.

I put my nose primly in the air and refused to answer.

"Oh, Katie Clay. You're a funny girl. Come on. Let's go find a bus. We'll mail your picture back first."

Van stood and reached a hand down to help me to my feet. His hand felt so good—so right—wrapped around mine. Wolf whined softly inside, just as besotted with Van as the human half of me was. He dropped my hand and grabbed his empty carry-on, totally oblivious to my thoughts. Which was just as well.

Snagging my empty suitcase handle, I followed him, close enough our shoulders brushed.

"Katie, put your hood up."

Van's tone sent shivers rippling over my shoulders as I stopped and flipped my hair inside my sweatshirt and pulled the hood up as far over my face as I could. "What's wrong?"

"Don't look at the screens. The news channel has a composite of what the lost *SnowSpace Tech* heiress should look like. They're not completely right, but it's close enough to worry."

Wolf yelped, tension and anxiety ratcheting my nerves taut. My mouth felt glued shut.

"We're okay. Almost to the bus station. Just keep your head down." My fingers reached for his hand of their own volition. His squeezed mine back, keeping my fingers tight within his own.

I had never been more thankful in my life than I was when I handed over my forged ID, that I'd chosen a name not my own when Van and Angus found me. It had popped out without any other thought. But with my likeness pasted on the newsfeeds, it was more important than ever that my identity not be widespread. Wolf growled as I thought about Uncle Alan. What he'd likely do to me if he caught me.

"Thanks, you're both good to go. Your bus leaves in fifteen, so you just made it," the cashier said as he passed back our IDs along with our change and tickets. I hoped we'd have enough of a head start to lose any trail using our IDs at the bus station might give. With no formal ties to the Hazeltons and my new name, hopefully it would be enough anonymity.

Van handed me a stamp and pointed with his chin to a mail collection receptacle. I threw the envelope with my picture in it, wondering if it was worth the fuss.

"That was close enough. I'm glad we're not hanging around the airport any longer with police sketches," Van muttered as we made our way to the bus.

So was I.

As it turned out, luck was with us. We dropped off our empty suitcases, then dragged our backpacks with us. The bus was close to full, but there were two seats next to each other toward the back of the bus. Van ushered me in to the inside seat then planted himself resolutely on the aisle, like he was daring anyone to even look sideways at us. Even with the stress of the day, it made me smile. Wolf sighed in admiration. I shushed her.

"Sleep if you want Katie," Van whispered as the bus slowly chugged out of its bay. "We're on this bus for hours. It's going to be a long ride. I'll stay awake."

My eyelids were dropping, the adrenaline fading, the caffeine leaving me exhausted in its wake. I nodded, and within moments, I was totally asleep.

Chapter 19

Donovan

Katie slept deeply, leaned against my shoulder. I tried to process the events of the past few days as the bus ate up the highway out of Chicago. Things were fine for the first forty-five minutes or so. But then a burly dude got up and used the teeny tiny bus facility. When he opened the door back up, a wave of stench so powerful my eyes watered and my nostrils quivered slapped me in the face. I wanted to breathe through my mouth, but was afraid I might suck in fecal matter, the smell was so overpowering.

Several nostril-singeing hours later, the bus creaked to a stop and a few people disembarked, while a group of new passengers got on. I watched them like a hawk, Wolf calculating and cataloguing each one of them for any signs of danger.

While some of them didn't scream 'trustworthy,' none of them spiked any of Wolf's baser instincts. I squinted as the sun started setting and light pierced through the windows.

The stop didn't take long, and Katie slept through the whole thing. I was about to need a drink but hated to wake her by bending down and getting a water out of my backpack. Instead, I glanced around at the new passengers, searching them again, hunting for anything I might have missed in the first pass. Long minutes and miles of highway sped past.

The couple in front of us had gotten to their seats quietly and peaceably, but like a switch was flipped, they came to life, fighting, arguing, snapping at each other. I tried to tune them out, focusing on not asphyxiating on the lingering stench and making sure Katie was still resting comfortably. Her head against my shoulder was a solid weight. She was exhausted. And the fact that she could sleep here, now, with her head against me warmed my insides. She trusted me to keep her safe.

Wolf puffed his chest, and I resisted the urge to let my hand rest protectively on her knee.

The couple in front of us was getting louder and more irate. Tension charged the air. Trying not to eavesdrop so obviously, I let my eyes wander to the other side of the bus. Where I promptly witnessed an exchange of rolled bills for a packet of something that was clearly of dubious nature. Wolf snorted.

The surprise must have shown on my face because the man who now had the money caught my eye, boring daggers straight into my brain with his heated gaze.

"You got a problem?" He spat a wad of something brown and nasty at my feet. Wolf growled in my chest.

"No problem," I confirmed and looked straight ahead. Where the couple who had been arguing to the point I wondered if they'd draw blood was now kissing. Passionately. She straddled him in the seat, and he moaned. Loudly. I wanted to throw up. Lust clogged the air, mingling with the still-ripe scent of abused latrine.

"You got a problem with how my sister conducts her affairs?" Money Guy was getting angry. Glancing back to him, I realized his pupils were dilated and his expression reminded me of a wolf too long in its fur after it shifted back to skin for the first time.

This was not going well.

"I've got no problem with anyone," I said again, trying to sound as calm as possible and find a place for my eyes to go that wasn't offensive to someone—me included. I was pretty sure the couple in front of me was rounding to third base while Money Guy was high and had just sold something particularly expensive and decidedly illegal to the small man hovering in the far corner of the vehicle.

"You calling me a liar?" Money Guy stood up, his shoulders thick, his head clearing the window by several inches.

Wolf bared his teeth, and I resisted the urge to sigh. This was not what I had in mind when we got on the bus. Katie's fingers clenched against my forearm, and I knew she was awake and concerned.

"No. I'm just sitting here. That's all I'm doing," I said, again trying to diffuse whatever tension I'd unwittingly caused.

"You're a punk. I don't like punks." Money Guy leaned down into my space. His breath had fish on it, and he needed a new application of deodorant. I stared him back down, unflinching. I could take this beast of a man down in thirty seconds flat. In fur or skin.

"Would you mind backing out of my face, please?" I asked him tightly, ticked off and done with this situation. My irritation was punctuated by gasping from the couple in front of me. Their seats shook and I couldn't help the way my lip curled in revulsion.

Money Guy grabbed the front of my shirt and hauled me to my feet. "My sister doesn't concern you. *Punk.*"

"You need to let go of me. Now." Beta dominance rang behind my words.

The world lurched as the bus screeched to a halt and Money Guy's grip loosened.

"What's going on?" the bus driver asked over the com system.

"Maurice, this punk is causing trouble!" Money Guy hollered back.

Awesome. He was on a first name basis with the bus driver.

"Kid, I don't have time for this. Get off the bus."

I spluttered. "Are you kidding me?" They were going to just drop me off—us, since I wasn't going anywhere without Katie. In the middle of wherever we were as darkness floated over the far edge of the landscape.

"Did I stutter?" the bus driver asked. Money Guy smirked and folded his giant arms across his barrel chest.

Katie's cold fingers clamped around my elbow. I swallowed, counting to ten. Flying under the radar. Right.

Smiling at Money Guy like my teeth were daggers, I grabbed Katie's hand and yanked my backpack up with the other.

The bus was silent as we made our glamourless exit. Just as I turned to go down the steps to make my way out, one part of the amorous couple of us shouted, "Baby!"

I flew the rest of the way out of the bus, Katie hot on my heels.

The bus door screeched shut, and we were left on the side of the road on the sidewalk of some city in the middle of who knew where.

CHAPTER 20

KATIE

That was one of the most appalling, confusing, bizarre events of my life. I had no desire to repeat it. We stood there a dazed second, trying to figure out what exactly had just happened.

Van's mouth opened like he wanted to say something but wasn't sure what words to utter.

"Yeah," I agreed.

Van blew a hot breath out. "I mean, I'm sorry we lost that mode of transportation, but in no way am I sorry to be off that bus."

"I think I'd rather walk than be subjected to any more variations of 'baby,'" I deadpanned.

Van snorted. "That was disgusting. Come on. We've got a long trip."

We started down the sidewalk. It wasn't the best part of town, wherever we were, and night would fall soon.

"Okay. I need to look at the map and figure out where we are," Van said as he glanced around. Wolf was on high alert, though parts of me felt better after sleeping the majority of the afternoon. Thunder boomed in the distance as a crackle of lightning slashed the sky in half.

"Rain. Awesome," I muttered. I hated wet fur.

"We're about halfway to Delaware, I think," Van said. I could practically see his brain calculating. "We're going to get drenched if we stay out here much longer. We need to find a place to stay that doesn't have cameras and doesn't need a photo ID if we're staying off the grid. We're too far inside city limits of wherever this is to shift and travel on four legs."

I winced as I glanced at our surroundings. I could see the landscape of the city change a few blocks down, where a seedier side of things emerged in full force.

"Put your hood up, Katie. Just in case."

I quickly shoved my messy ponytail inside the back of my sweatshirt and flipped the hood up, covering as much of my face as I could without impeding my vision.

"I miss the internet already," Van sighed. Anxiety tripped through my belly and Wolf grumbled. Lunch had been hours ago.

"What do you think we should do?" I whispered.

He groaned. "I don't know any places that don't require photo IDs except places where people like the couple from the bus go for a few hours at a time." Van grimaced.

"Unless we turn criminal and break in somewhere."

"There's that, too," Van conceded. Thunder rumbled across the sky again, raising the hairs on my arms. "Whatever we're going to do, we need to do it soon."

Lightning crackled, and the sky turned angry, black clouds blotting out the rest of the weak sunlight as storm clouds rolled in.

"Walk. There's a group of people staring at us over there, and they don't look like the friendly variety," I whispered. Van stiffened and we started walking toward the more pleasant side of town. "Is that a no on the hourly room then?" I couldn't quite suppress the shiver that worked over my skin. Both at the thought of such close proximity to Van for an entire night—because those sorts of rooms didn't come with nice double beds—and at the thought of all the likely germs in said single bed...

"When we get to the end of this block, take a left. They're following us," Van whispered.

Tension pinged inside as Wolf stretched herself, teeth bared, preparing us to fight. Van slid his hand into mine, leisurely, like we were a couple out for an evening stroll.

We turned the corner.

"Go," Van ordered. We took off, jogging down the sidewalk. There was a massive, age-worn church at the end of the block. Black grime coated the topmost stones and leeched down towards the bottom like inky fingers. Chains crossed the heavy wooden doors, but there was a window partially busted out near the sidewalk.

"How about church instead of a one-night stand for the evening?" I whisper-panted as we neared the building. Glancing back, the group that had been staring at us hadn't rounded the bend yet.

"I think we should try disappearing. Sling me your pack and get up and in there fast."

I slung my backpack at him and quickened my steps, springing easily into the window frame, mindful of glass shards left behind. My shoes crunched against glass and debris as my feet hit the floor.

"Okay?" Van asked quietly from outside. Wolf scented. Nothing in the immediate vicinity besides mold and mildew.

"Clear in here."

Both backpacks came thunking through the window and Van launched himself through a moment after. He whipped around, bracing himself against the wall and glanced out the window, cursing softly.

"I think they saw me come through the window."

"Think they'll care?"

"Considering they're moving like a pack on the hunt, probably."

"Brilliant. Should we shift?" Fear ratcheted around inside my chest, threatening to squeeze my windpipe. Wolf growled, hair standing up along the ridge of her back.

"I vote we run first. No sense in making a scene if we don't have to. Wolves in the city are going to be noticed and reported. Let's go find a way out." Van's jaw clenched as another slash of lightning illuminated his face. The strains of the laughing group coming closer to us raised the hair on the back of my neck. It wasn't a pleasant sort of laughter. "Let's go, Katie Clay."

Van grabbed my hand, and we moved as silently as we could over the busted glass and dried twigs and leaves that had blown in.

"Don't go too far. We're coming in to play!" a voice hollered from the room we'd just left. Van squeezed my hand, and as one, we moved like wraiths down the black corridor into the belly of the building.

Heavy footsteps sounded in the hallway behind us, and we veered off into another hall. Van tensed beside me, my own muscles taut with apprehension. Thunder pealed and seemed to shake the very foundations of the church. Van tried a doorknob. For how run-down the place was, the door was locked fast.

"What you all carrying in them bags? You got something valuable? Let us have a quick look." The sing-songy voice echoed down the hall. More footsteps sounded along with a few curses as feet shuffled loudly on the wooden floors. Anger coursed through me, dousing my fear and clenching my jaw.

Van squeezed my hand again and we followed another twist in the corridor. A row of planks stood against a wall where fading light struggled through the dirty, cracked windowpane. Wolf came to the fore, her ears pricking, listening for sounds of our followers. She smelled at least four other bodies.

Not more than we could handle, but it could get messy.

A train sounded somewhere in the distance as a flash of blinding lightning illuminated the room. I jerked as the light showed me Van's eyes, closer to my face than I realized. He squeezed my hand once and dropped it, going over, and picking up a board, hefting it like an oversized baseball bat. He jerked his head, motioning for me to stand behind him, farther down the hall.

"I know you all are still in here. Just give me the bags and you can go."

The voice was closer. Sweat and arrogance scented the air, and Wolf wrinkled her nose. Soundlessly, I took several paces back as Van readied the board in his hands.

Footsteps crunched a twig on the floor right in front of where we stood. I took one more step backward. With another flash of lightning and a boom of thunder that showed Van's body twisting, just as the thug rounded the corner, Van brought the board smashing into his face. The crack that echoed rivaled the crack of thunder and sizzle of lightning.

He went down moaning, blood gushing from his nose. The scent of blood filled the air, and the lightning momentarily singed my nostrils, blocking out all other smells.

Van turned to me, his eyes growing wide and his mouth opening. Before he could utter a sound, hands grabbed my backpack and jerked me two steps deeper into the darkness. Wolf snarled and fur rippled under my skin.

Keeping my shriek behind my teeth, I let the moves the Hazeltons had drilled into me over the past few years take over. Wolf gave my movements strength as I centered myself then wrenched forward, toppling the would-be thief into me as I stomped the heel of my foot down onto the top of his.

He cursed, but before I could do anything else, Van was in front of me. Grabbing my shoulder with one hand, his other cocked back and flew into the skull of the man grabbing at me. My backpack jerked again as the man let go with another wailed curse.

"Go," Van ordered.

Tripping over the writhing body on the floor, we fled into the belly of the building. The train horn blasted again, closer. Rain pelted outside. Movement and more curses sounded behind us as the rest of the group must have found their injured friends.

Van nudged me. We had reached the back of the church. There was a row of windows facing the blackness outside. Rain pinged hard against the glass, some of it cracked.

"Get ready to run," Van whispered. We stopped at the bank of windows. Grabbing a broken pipe that had long been abandoned on the floor, Van turned his face and backhanded the pipe into the glass.

Shattered glass littered the floor and showered Van as wind and rain whipped into the space. Ignoring the glass fragments he must have all over him, Van clanked the pipe over the busted out window, taking the biggest remaining chunks.

More shouts sounded down the hallway as footsteps pounded toward us.

"Up you go," Van muttered. I took a running leap. Van caught me about the waist and boosted me out, into the lashing wind that drove rain straight into my face. Van hopped out quickly after me.

The train horn sounded a third time, and as I stared through the rain, I could make out its spotlight as it rumbled down old tracks.

"Train," Van and I said at once.

We sprinted, sloshing through puddles, leaping over piles of debris and trash, wind thrashing leaves and pelting rain into our eyes. It wasn't terribly far to the train tracks, but the iron beast was moving fast.

My pack thumped against my back. Wolf put her head down, giving speed to my legs as they ate up the ground. Metal screeched against the trestles as the train slowed. Red lights flared farther down the tracks and the dinging noise of the railroad crossing was nearly lost in the gale.

"Move it, Katie!" Van hollered. We were close to the train now. I couldn't believe we were actually about to do this. But as I squinted through the pouring water, I saw boxy train cars, several with doors in the sides of them, just like in the movies.

Heat from the tracks warmed the side of my face. Van sped up and leaped as only a werewolf could, his arm catching the ladder tracing up the side of one of the cars.

"Come on! I've got you!" He reached his arm down and I strained mine to meet his, my feet struggling in the wet gravel alongside the trestles. "Almost there!"

Wolf growled, bunching our muscles as we prepared to launch.

"Now!" Van yelled.

I jumped with everything I had left. My feet left the ground, and for a minute I was flying, but one second later, I crashed against the rain-slicked side of the speeding train. Panic seized my chest as my fingers grappled for purchase.

"Got you." Van grunted as his hand closed on the back of my hoodie, shoving me back into the side of the train. Clamping my wet fingers around the rung nearest me, I hauled myself in close, toes clinging to the bottom rung.

"Going for the door," Van shouted to be heard over the din of the train and the storm. Wind thwacked my wet hair around my face, stinging my eyes. "You good?"

"For the moment," I hollered back, tightening my death grip on the ladder rung.

Van scaled the ladder, my heart lurching into my throat as he staggered onto the roof of the car. His feet slipped against the rain-slicked surface and a scream launched into my throat, staying there as he righted his grip. Moving to the center of the roof, he flattened on his belly, leaning over so far my heart shrank in fright that he'd topple off and break his neck along the train tracks. His hands fumbled with a lever I could barely make out through the lashing rain as it pelted down unmercifully against me. A shiver wracked over me as wind bit through the rain, chilling me. Wolf trembled with fear and cold inside me.

Van growled, the deep noise reverberating against the thrashing of the storm. Gripping what looked like a small padlock in his fist, his wolf eyes shined briefly in a streak of lightning before he yanked, using the strength of a werewolf, and a metallic screech scraped across my ears. He tossed the lock off into oblivion and turned his attention back to the lever.

Van grunted, his biceps straining under his rain-plastered shirt as he yanked on the lever. With a screech that vibrated into my bones, the door inched open. He gave it another mighty shove and it opened another fraction. Wide enough we could shimmy through.

"Come on," he hollered over the din of the storm.

Fear quaked in my joints. He meant to swing down from the roof into the train car itself. Nausea swirled in my gut. But as I couldn't very well hang onto this ladder that was slicker than hot oil on a glass doorknob all night, my only options were either jump off, or climb up.

Gritting my teeth, I painstakingly hauled my wet carcass up the slippery rungs. Van had moved back and reached an arm down to help me up over the last one. Wind tore at me, whipping my hood back and sending my hair flying around my face as I crested the top.

"We are insane," I shrieked as the wind snatched my words.

"Probably. Come on," Van shouted back.

We crept like spiders clinging to the wet top of the rail car. Fortunately, it was ridged metal, so there were things to grip, even if they were wet and the wind threatened to tear us to pieces for every inch we gained.

After what felt like an eternity, we reached the place where the crack of door was beneath us.

"I'll help you swing down inside, and I'll come after," Van said loudly, close to my ear. I nodded as fear seized my gut and the wind sent another icy blast down my spine.

"Hang on, Katie. There you go. Grip my hands. I'll keep you from going over." Van's encouragement reverberated in my ear as I stiffly maneuvered so I was nearly swinging off into oblivion over the side of the moving train car.

"Please don't drop me," I muttered, unsure if he heard me or not.

For one dreadful, fear-inducing moment, I dangled in the frigid air, tethered only by Van's grip on my arms. Then the world flashed by me in a whirl as the weight of my body crashed me into the wedge of opening in the side of the train car. I landed hard, the breath knocked out of me, as I draped over the corner of a bundle of what appeared to be shrink wrapped t-shirts. Could have been a worse landing. At least it wasn't a bundle of pickaxes or something.

"Katie?" Van called.

"I'm here." Shakily, I stood and quickly slumped off my backpack. Van slung his black pack through the opening. I caught it with an *oomph* as it landed heavy in my gut.

"Okay!" I hollered out.

"Here I come; back out of the way, so I don't hit you," he said, his head popping into view.

I shuffled over to the side to give Van plenty of berth to make his way into the car.

First one leg appeared, then the other, then his trunk. My heart pounded. His feet touched down on the shrink-wrapped bundle. Just then, the train lurched, turning around a corner. Lightning flashed across the sky as Van's foot slipped against the slick shrink wrap. Terror etched across his face as he slid away from the car, his body hanging precariously close to the crushing wheels of the train below.

Wolf lurched inside me as terror propelled me forward. I snatched a handful of Van's wet shirt and heaved with all my might.

We crashed through the opening, Van landing on top of me, sprawled across the bundles of clothes beneath us. We lay there, panting, for several minutes. The terror gradually receded, but my heart still thundered in my chest. My fingers were still curled around Van's wet shirt, frozen with the need to know he was still there, still with me.

"Thanks," Van finally said, his voice rusty as he rolled to flop onto his back next to me. Wolf nudged me. I could hear his own accelerated heartbeat as it marched triple time with mine, even over the clatter of the train.

"Are you okay?" I croaked.

"Yeah. You?" He rolled his head to the side, searching me.

"Just a few years of my life scared off me. Otherwise, I'm good."

He smiled weakly.

My pulse picked up with something other than fear. Van's hazel eyes, shadowed in the dim light that filtered in through the storm, were locked on my face. Slowly, he reached up and moved a wet piece of hair stuck to my forehead. My mouth dried. Only moments ago, his body had been pressed deliciously against mine in a way that suddenly felt intimate. It flooded my memory. Every inch of him, seared into my brain.

I cleared my throat and turned away.

"I'm soaked." My teeth started to chatter.

"And cold." He sat up next to me. "Good thing we wrapped everything in plastic. Good thinking. I'll turn and you can change clothes first. I can hear your teeth clacking together."

I nodded, using my frozen fingers to claw my pack open. It took some doing, but eventually we were both changed, and at least drier, if not warmer. Van stretched beside me, his back popping. He scrubbed a tired hand down his face.

"Van, you're exhausted. Let's lay our stuff out to dry, then you take a nap. I snoozed on the bus. I'll stay awake."

"You sure? It feels...not very Beta-ish."

I smiled at his chagrined expression dimly illuminated in the dark car. The storm still thrashed, but intermittent light poles filtered light into the darkness at intervals.

"Even Betas need sleep."

"That's true," he conceded.

I shivered as I flopped my wet stuff over some additional bundles, hoping they'd at least partially dry by morning. Van laid his out next to mine.

"You okay?" His hand ran up my arm and heat exploded in my core.

"Fine. Just cold."

He nodded. "Come here. I'll sleep but sit next to you. We can share my other jacket, too."

My treacherous heart twisted. I wanted to snuggle with Van. But not because I was cold. I shushed Wolf as she lolled her tongue out at the thought.

In the end, I sat with my back to a bundle, Van's arm around me, and his scent filling my nostrils as he spread his other jacket over the both of us. I tucked my hands into my lap, under the heavy flannel lining of his jacket. He leaned against me. He was cold, too. Every so often a shiver would work through him, so I knew he wasn't doing it just for my benefit, though a part of me wished he was.

It wasn't long before his hand around me went limp and he sagged against me. His breathing evened out and I was left alone with my thoughts, the storm, and miles of railroad track stretching into the black night.

Now that I was still and momentarily safe, emotions I'd been ignoring rose and pummeled me. My eyes stung with sudden unshed tears.

CHAPTER 21

DONOVAN

I slept hard and deep for a time, but eventually, Wolf struggled to the surface, and gradually I became aware of occasional shudders rippling beneath my cheek. I was groggy, like I was wrapped in thick fog and my ears were stuffed with cotton, but eventually the sleepy cobwebs cleared enough to realize that it was Katie shuddering against me. Katie was distressed.

My eyes flew open, senses on high alert, adrenaline pounding through my veins.

"Katie?" My voice creaked like the rusty hinge on an unused gate as I bolted upright.

She sniffed and wiped the back of her hand over her face.

"I'm fine," she quipped. I heard the wobble in her voice though.

Sitting up even straighter and wincing as my back twinged from the unnatural position I'd slept in, I rewrapped my arm around Katie's shoulders, drawing her closer into my side. I didn't say anything, just let her know I was there with her in the dark. I couldn't imagine what she must be handling, learning she was a Beta, that her brother was dead, that her pack of origin was out for her blood, not to mention the wild day of traveling off the grid we'd endured. Shame burned in the back of my throat. I shouldn't have drifted off. I should have realized that Katie would need some support.

Wolf whined and I swallowed.

"They're here. I can feel them. Just at the periphery of my awareness." She gulped a breath.

"Your pack?" I asked softly.

She nodded, the weak glare from passing lights shining through the crack in the door illuminating her splotchy skin and tear-stained cheeks.

"It's terrifying. All those wolves inside my brain. Knowing I can't acknowledge them or give them any sway in my mind."

"You're afraid they'll find you if you do?"

She nodded.

I didn't have words for that, so I let my hand rub up and down her upper arm. "I'm sorry," I whispered after a few moments of silence. I wished there was something else I could do to help her—lift the burden she carried.

"I don't know how long Alan will look for me. If he can't find me...what will he do?"

"I don't know. But my dad is on things. He'll be doing everything he can from his end. Our job is to lay low and keep you out of sight." I hoped my words sounded of conviction.

She drew another shuddering breath and nodded.

"I didn't mean to wake you," she mumbled.

"It's fine. I should have made sure you were okay before dropping off. That was my bad." I shook my head. I couldn't afford to be off my game like this. Not with Katie in the balance.

"You needed it."

"I need you to be okay more."

She turned, light slashing across her wide cinnamon eyes, glassy from her tears. Wolf perked his ears forward but then she dropped her gaze and sighed.

"You should go back to sleep. I'm okay."

I squeezed her shoulder. "It's okay to not be okay," I told her softly. She gave me a weak smile.

"Go back to sleep while you can, Van. I'm awake for now. You only napped about an hour. I slept a lot longer than that on the bus. For which I'm profoundly thankful, based on what I woke to."

I snorted. "Be very, very glad, Katie." I grimaced at the memory. I wanted to stay awake to make sure she really was all right, but my eyelids dragged downward.

"Sleep, Van," she whispered, smoothing her hand over my hair once.

Sleep claimed me as I relaxed against her.

I woke to frigid dawn light seeping through the crack in the door. Katie nudged me.

"I'm awake," I mumbled. Kinks and crimps studded my backbone, and I only just kept the groan behind my teeth as I straightened my spine.

"The rain has finally stopped, though I'm not sure for how long. Also, it's getting lighter every minute. I think it might be time we jump off, so we aren't caught and have uncomfortable questions asked when this train stops wherever it's going."

I glanced at my watch then out at the wooded landscape whipping past us.

"You're probably right. I guess we should see if our clothes dried."

They were still damp, but we made short work of rolling them up and stuffing them in our packs.

"We're going to want to lay those out before they mildew," Katie groused as she zipped her bag shut and rubbed the heel of one hand against her eye. Her shoulders drooped.

Thunder rumbled in the distance and Wolf shivered inside.

"More rain. Wonderful."

"Did you dry out all the way from last night?" I asked as I flipped and snapped the top of my pack.

"Mostly." Her belly growled.

"Let's get off this iron dragon and find some food."

"I won't complain about that. Particularly if it means missing more rain."

I poked my head out the crack in the door, wind chilling me and sending a shiver working over my shoulders. I tugged my pack straps tighter.

"There's a bend coming. It'll have to slow some. No civilization I can see in either direction. You ready to tuck and roll?"

Katie gulped. "Here's to super-fast werewolf healing."

I snorted, muscles coiling and bunching, ready to leap.

The train's wheels screeched as it slowed to take the curve. It didn't slow much. This was likely going to hurt. I spied a plump looking tuft of vegetation, took a breath, and leaped, Wolf giving height to my trajectory.

I hit the ground hard, the wind knocked from my lungs and the jarring impact with the ground reverberated up my legs and jumbled my innards around.

A quick shriek ripped through the air, and I glanced up in time to see Katie sailing through the air. She executed a perfect roll as she tucked her limbs in and turned across the ground.

Crawling and clawing my way back to my feet, I unsteadily made my way to Katie. She lay sprawled on her back, chest heaving.

"You okay?" I asked, bracing my hands on my knees, and quickly cataloguing her for injuries.

She grunted. "My eyeballs are still jiggling in their sockets. I officially hate trains."

I snorted. "Come on. Let's hit the tree line before the rain soaks us a second time."

She reached her hand up, expression still a mask of annoyance until it broke into a grimace as she stood. Her shoulder popped loud enough I winced.

"I'm fine," she quipped before I could ask. "You missing any appendages?" she asked as we traipsed to the brush.

I wiggled my fingers. "Think they're all accounted for."

"Uh oh."

"What?"

"I just felt a big fat raindrop on my forehead."

Lightning flashed and the burned sensation lingered in my nostrils next to damp earth and vegetation. Thunder rumbled and it felt like the ground quaked beneath our feet.

"This is not good. We're going to attract as much attention wandering around in a downpour as we would if we were wolves running around in back packs," Katie grumbled as she glanced at the sky.

We picked up our pace, hitting the trees as rain drops pattered down, splatting heavily against the ground.

"Look for shelter," I said, my eyes scanning. There were rocky crags not terribly far away through the trees. "Over there," I said, pointing and changing course.

The rain fell harder, coming down erratically through the trees, but hard enough that I felt the wetness seeping into my clothes. My breath puffed. It was chilly. We needed to get out of the elements.

We dashed through the tangled underbrush, dry leaves and dead twigs snapping under our feet.

"Van, I think that's a cave. At least an indention in the rocks." Katie paced ahead of me until we came to the rock face. Sure enough, a shallow cave opened into the side of the cliff face. It wasn't deep, but deep enough that we could wait out the rain and stay dry, and wide enough we wouldn't be overly cramped.

"Five star hotel, right there," I said as I pushed her in and followed close behind right as the sky opened up and water poured in a torrential sheet, obscuring even the trees not ten feet away.

"Wow," Katie said. She flung her arms out, flicking off some of the water, and backed up a step. The water ran off the side of the cliff, creating a partial waterfall over the cave opening. If it weren't so cold and miserable being wet, it would have been pretty epic.

"Okay. I'm sopping. I need dry clothes." I glanced over and saw a shiver ripple over Katie.

"Did you ever get totally warmed up last night?" I asked as I shrugged out of my jacket. The chill breeze hit my damp shirt and I shivered, too.

"Not completely." She pursed her lips, looking into her bag.

"What?"

"I'm debating fur or sweater."

"Why don't you shift so you're warmer and take a snooze. We can trade naps while we wait out the storm. We can't be that far from

Delaware. We were on that train a good six or seven hours at least and headed in the right direction. We'll wait for the rain to stop then figure out where we are. And get a hot meal if possible." My belly growled and Wolf licked his lips at the thought.

"That works. Trail mix is getting old." She shivered again. "All right. Turn around so I can shift and lay my wet stuff out to dry. Again."

"Sure."

I heard the rustling and wet suctioning sound of her clothes peeling off, and heat suddenly flooded my cheeks. Why, I had no idea. This wasn't something we hadn't done around each other and the pack a hundred times before. Why was I suddenly reacting to this girl who'd been one of my closest friends for years? Memories of our kiss floated to the front of my brain. Wolf snorted. I blinked and shook my head, willing the shame I still felt about it to simmer back down. Guilt. That had to be it. I *did* still feel guilty about what I'd done. Katie deserved better than that.

Popping and creaking sounded behind me, and she yipped once. Glancing over my shoulder, I saw she'd draped her clothes out as best she could and was now shaking, fluffing her fur to rid herself of any lingering damp.

"Okay. Fur definitely sounds warmer," I conceded. "But first," I hesitated. "Happy birthday," I whispered before flipping around and yanking my shirt off, goosebumps prickling my skin.

Katie chuffed through her nose.

CHAPTER 22

KATIE

Happy birthday.

The words stirred all sorts of emotions inside me. Instead of focusing on those, I shut my thoughts down and stared at the boy a scant few feet from me in the cave. Wolf might have drooled. Van's back, his wide shoulders that tapered to a trim waist, were to me. I did not want to be so aware of him—so ridiculously attracted to him. It wasn't fair. I could never be with Van without putting a bullseye on his chest. What we were doing together now was bad enough. Who knew what Alan would do to Van if he caught us together? It'd only be that much worse if we were *together*. I shuddered, ripping my eyes from Van's form, ears twitching as I heard him undo the zipper on his pants.

Yep. Time to turn around.

Thoughts of Alan and his vengeance weighted me down like stones on my chest. I was tired. Exhaustion rested in my bones. Maybe the oblivion of sleep would let me escape my tangle of thoughts—worry, anxiety, attraction, uncertainty, fear, all squirming in my belly.

Without realizing it, a soft whine escaped.

Van's wolf turned to me, eyes wide and focused on me. I shook my shaggy head, not meaning for him to overhear my inner turmoil. Swallowing hard and refusing to think any more on heavy things, I picked a spot towards the back of our makeshift shelter and circled three times and laid down, wrapping my tail around my nose for warmth, and to hide any anguish that might show on my wolf's face from Van.

He nudged me gently with his nose and I felt him settle in front of me, blocking the occasional wind that whipped in around the water still cascading over the roof of the cave. I bit back the whine that tried to surface and screwed my eyes shut. I didn't need Wolf to cry. I'd done enough of that last night.

The ground was cold and hard, but thankfully, my fur buffered against both well. It was amazing how much more at home I felt as a wolf, in the cave. I was soon warm and toasty, my fur doing its job nicely, and sleep pulled at me.

Shadows lengthened and fear burbled in my belly, spreading to my limbs like rot. I thrashed, desperate to get away but rooted to the spot. My mom screamed, and dad cried out. I wasn't fast enough. I couldn't move. Could only watch as Uncle Alan brandished his claws like knives and ripped open my dad's abdomen. Dad's insides spilled out into the chilly night, steaming lightly as bile burned the back of my throat and my eyes went hazy from the tears that poured down my cheeks.

Mom howled, fur erupting through her skin, splitting the seams of her clothes. Alan didn't wait. Pitching up to his hind legs, he swiped his claws again, slashing across her throat. Sticky red blood spurted across the room, dousing my uncle, the floor, soaked into the carpet.

Fury, anger, grief, loss, and terror overrode my senses where I hid behind boxes in the garage. Hidden, I watched my parents' slaughter through the gaping back door as grief struck me numb. Cool night air whispered over my sweat-chilled skin. The garage door was up. I had to move. Had to force myself to get away. But I couldn't. I could only stare at my parents' mangled bodies and wail inside as grief tore me apart.

"Ben, where is your sister?" Alan said.

Ice snaked down my back as my lungs froze, unable to draw breath.

"She's not in her room. I don't know. I'll find her." He curled his lip at the pile of abused flesh that had been our parents moments before.

My brother.

My brother.

Ben.

Some unseen tether in my brain snapped. I fell to all fours behind the boxes as panic and convulsions ripped through me. My skin shredded apart, tearing, stinging, slicing. I bit down, cutting into my tongue, to keep from screaming out in pain. Blood filled my mouth as my back shattered into a thousand pieces. Surely, I was dying.

Agony rent my heart as claws mashed through the skin of my fingers. Teeth, jagged and sharp, filled my mouth.

Pain, hot, potent, and a welcome distraction from the anguish inside my heart, gutted me. For three seconds, I wheezed silently, sweaty on the cool garage floor...and furry.

Understanding hit me like a baseball bat between the eyes.

I shifted.

This was my wolf form.

Too soon. Too early to be in fur.

Wolf shook her head. She was there. Present. Outside my body, no longer just inside my head. I could protect myself. I was a wolf.

Run.

Run, run, run.

Get away.

Protect.

Live.

CHAPTER 23

DONOVAN

Katie thrashed in her sleep, legs beating the air, grunting as she shook her head. Concern ratcheted up my spine. Angus said she had nightmares sometimes. I wondered if this was one of them. She'd certainly had plenty of fodder over the past few days for nightmares—new and old—to make an appearance.

Should I wake her?

Carefully, I nuzzled her. She calmed, whining, tears streaming over her muzzle.

Katie, I called to her over my mental link. It didn't do any good as she wasn't officially part of my pack, but I tried nonetheless. She rolled toward me, her chest hitting my legs. She stilled more as I nosed her cheek. Her breathing was coming in tight pants, but still the dream held her. Nudging her harder with my paw, her eyes flew open, and she sat up with a harsh yelp.

I barked softly, letting her know she was with me. Her gaze scattered frantically around the cave before settling on me. I whined softly, trying to sooth her, dipping my nose to her cheek again.

She lay back down, covering her face with one paw in embarrassment. I ran my nose over her ruff, trying to let her know she didn't need to be embarrassed about bad dreams. Eventually, I stepped over her and settled behind her, resting my chin against her ruff, draping one paw over her protectively. If we'd been in skin, we'd have been spooning.

The thought made me pause curiously. I mentally shrugged. It wasn't meant romantically. My only intent was making Katie feel as safe as possible. Her body pressed back against mine, the heat between us welcome against the falling temperatures. Before long, her breathing evened out and I knew she'd fallen back to sleep.

I laid there against her for a long time. I ran over what had happened in my mind several times. I didn't think we were very far from Delaware. We could likely be in Rock Falls within a day's journey.

The thought brought new emotion curdling in my insides. Shame surfaced. I wasn't sure why. While in Rock Falls, I'd done nothing to be ashamed of—quite the opposite, in fact. I'd chosen to let Sarah be with the wolf of her choice, rather than shackling her to me and increasing both our packs' bloodlines. Some likely thought it was a foolish move, but I saw the way she looked at Cade, and knew she'd never be able to look at me the same way.

But it still felt like major rejection.

And that sucked.

I liked Sarah—had liked her a lot. And I'd started getting my hopes up that she was the wolf I would take as mate. She fit the bill on every particular—down to being smart and gorgeous. And it hurt like first shift that she didn't want me.

I shoved the uncomfortable thoughts away. I didn't want to dwell on what felt like a confused mistake. Fortunately, I wouldn't have to see her or Cade in Rock Falls, as they'd have gone back to Sarah's pack in New York by now.

That was at least a relief.

But I'd still see the rest of the Wolfe and Kypson packs. I knew them well enough to call them allies—maybe even teetering on the brink of being friends with a few of them, but I still wasn't eager to go back to Rock Falls.

Katie twitched against me.

But Katie was worth the discomfort. I had to keep her safe at all costs.

The rain didn't let up. At one point, I paced to the front of our small cave to make sure we weren't in danger of being flooded. The water sluiced down from the top of the rock wall with force into an age and weather-worn ditch where it was shuttled away to parts unknown.

Stretching my legs out, I walked back to Katie, settling in behind her once more, one paw around her, my chin on her ruff. Just as I'd settled, Katie stirred, her head rising as she looked around sleepily. I pulled my paw back, sitting up and giving her some space, though I liked being that close to her.

It was warmer.

That was all.

Katie shook her ruff out, raising some dust, and I sneezed. She chortled deep in her throat, and stretched, her back and hind legs coming off the ground. She stood fully and took two steps forward to check her clothes.

Facing me again, she yipped. I obediently shut my eyes and covered my face with my paw. She snorted. With a sigh of long suffering, I rolled all the way over, smiling to myself. Katie was fun to tease.

Again, I was acutely aware of the sounds of her shift, of the soft noises her clothes made as they brushed over her skin, of the zipper on her jeans. Heat kindled in my belly, and I was profoundly thankful that my fur would cover any color that rose in my cheeks.

What was wrong with me?

"Okay, I'm dressed."

I turned to see a shiver work over her shoulders. I cocked my head, curious why she'd go back to skin if she was obviously already cold in her clothes.

She cleared her throat. "I," she began. She swallowed hard. "The dreams leave me unsettled. I'm sorry you had to see that," she whispered.

Quickly I got to my feet and nudged her arm with my nose.

"Still. It...I hate them. I need to distract myself. And I still have a book and a half in my bag."

I chuffed. Only Katie would rather freeze in skin to read her book than stay warm and dry in fur. I sobered. But I could understand the desire to escape her dreams. Angus told me they weren't pretty, and the one I'd witnessed hadn't looked like a walk in the park.

"Besides," she continued, "I've had a nap. You're probably ready for another one. I'll stay up and read while you sleep." A sheepish grin stole over her lips. "Although if you and your fur wanted to lay on my feet to keep them warm, I wouldn't object."

I snorted, whapping her lightly with my tail.

She grabbed her books and a bottle of water and bag of jerky out of her bag and slid down the wall of the cave, book angled toward the weak light filtering in through the water. I grabbed my dried-out jacket from where it was laid out, nose wrinkling at the smell of *train* coming off it, and brought it to her.

"Thanks." She shivered again and slipped her arms into it. She looked good, swimming in the oversized fit of my jacket.

Shaking my head, I stretched once before curling around Katie, covering her feet and some of her legs with the bulk of my wolf's body.

"There we go. A regular portable heater."

I flipped her with my tail again before drifting off to sleep to the sounds of Katie turning pages.

The rain lasted late into the next day before finally petering out and leaving a thick fog in its wake, the ground saturated like an over wet sponge. Water lay puddled all over the forest floor in the dying sunlight.

We were both in skin, having shifted to eat a meal together and break the silence. I'd taught her how to put up a mental block against her pack's link over the last bits of a chocolate bar. We'd practiced. She hadn't liked it but was grateful that it was keeping the worst of the voices out.

"You want to wait it out one more night and take off in the morning?" I asked, peering into the woods.

"I guess so?"

I glanced back at her. She crept to the edge of the cave near me.

"I mean, I guess travelling in daylight is preferable. But honestly, without that waterfall coming over the front of the cave, it's just a little bit creepy out here in the dark." She shivered.

"We'll be okay. We'll sleep in shifts, just like we have been doing. We're built for this. We've got teeth and claws and thick hide."

"I know. You're right. It just...I've never really been one for camping, you know? It's fine in a pack like when we're all back home and head out for an overnight together or something. Emma and I have had some fantastic marshmallow roasts and runs through the hills on those nights. But this is different. Knowing someone out there has it out for me," she finished softly. "Being away from the rest of the pack," she said so low I nearly missed it.

"Katie," I started, taking her hand, "I am going to do everything in my power to keep you safe."

She turned her wide cinnamon eyes on me.

"But that's just it, Van. I don't want you to need to keep me safe. I can't handle the thought of what my uncle might to do *you* if he caught up to us."

"You're still part of the Hazelton pack by extension. Even if you weren't my friend, that would be reason enough."

"Would it be weird to ask for a hug?"

I smiled. "No. Never weird. Come here."

The entrance of the cave was just tall enough we could stand fully as I wrapped my arms around her. She laid her head against my chest. For long minutes we stood there, reminding each other that we weren't alone.

CHAPTER 24

KATIE

As it turned out, both of us had trouble sleeping. And even more ironically, we were both likely anxious about going to our destination.

The idea of Rock Falls scraped along my skin like shards of broken glass. The idea that I could be coming face to face with the girl I knew Van wanted—the girl he'd seen when he'd kissed me—tied me up inside and made my anxiety over my family situation about a thousand times worse. Because while the threat of Uncle Alan and his pack—my pack—of betrayers was a constant weight on me, it was still distant. It wasn't staring me in the face like meeting the famed people from the Rock Falls packs...one of them in particular.

I'd forced Angus to tell me details. Reading between the lines, Sarah Thornehill was perfect in every possible way. Except that she loved some mangy wolf dude named Cade and not my Van.

Who wasn't *my* Van.

I yanked on the sleeves of my hoodie. I was both intensely relieved and annoyed with the illustrious Sarah for rejecting Van—because what wolf girl in her right mind would reject him—and equally annoyed with Van for wanting her, and still more annoyed at myself for allowing my insides to be tied up in knots I had no hope of detangling.

In short, I was a hot mess.

I don't know if Van was picking up on my nerves or having nerves himself about going back to Rock Falls, even though Angus said everything else went all right, or if he was feeling my own agitation.

Regardless of the reason, we left in fur before dawn light fully lit the skies, backpacks strapped securely to our wolf bodies and sliding strangely against my fur as we trekked through the quiet woods.

The first few hours went well. We skirted a town, still leery of civilization, but were able to pinpoint our location, and the going wasn't too terrible. There was a lot of forested area where we could blend and not be seen. Things went well until we stumbled upon a scent that prickled the hairs all along my back.

Bear.

I whimpered and tossed my head. Van paused and scented, his ears perking forward as he picked up the smell of the large mammal. There were two of us, and likely only one bear, so the odds were in our favor, but no one ever wanted to tangle with a bear if it could be avoided. They were mean, nasty, temperamental, and had enormous claws and teeth. And only base animal instinct.

Van and I backed up, moving away slowly, on high alert.

The bushes rustled. Dread crept up my spine.

A little growl, and the most adorable, fuzzy headed little cub rolled out of the bushes and sneezed at us.

Van yipped and terror fueled my tired limbs. We sprang into action, running as far away from that cub as quickly as possible. Where a cub was, mama bear wouldn't be far behind. And we reeked of *predator.*

Unfortunately, that held true. Loud grunts and snorts sounded behind us. I risked a glance over my shoulder and wished I hadn't. A gigantic black bear pounded the earth behind us, gaining.

The she-bear roared, sending my adrenal glands way past over-drive.

Van barked angrily toward the bear, nudging me to move quicker. I didn't need the encouragement. I shot forward so fast I nearly left my fur behind. The backpack jolted against my shoulders, slipping and sliding and throwing my normally smooth gait off kilter at a time I desperately needed all the speed I could produce.

The bear bellowed behind us, and fear rippled over me like an electric current. She was too close, and not giving up her pursuit.

Van barked, indicating that I should move ahead of him. I was already going as fast as I could, encumbered with my bag. I yipped back, terror making my bark a shrill echo in the forest.

We ran for what felt like eternity. Eventually the mother bear gave up the chase, content enough to amble back to her cub now that she was satisfied the danger was far enough from her offspring.

Even after the she-bear stopped her pursuit, we ran hard. At last, we staggered to a stop near a creek, sides heaving, legs rubbery. We wheezed, catching our breath, lapping up the cold creek water in between heavy pants.

Sides heaving, my gaze connected with Van's. Wordlessly, our wolves moved toward each other, rubbing noses, ruffs, faces against each other in the typical Hazelton greeting. It was comforting, soothing, and calmed me. I let my head lean against his ruff a moment longer than I needed, soaking in his scent and the way his larger wolf's body made me feel safe. Van rubbed his cheek against my side and I knew I needed to step back before I made a fool of myself by rubbing against him overmuch and looking like a love-struck idiot. Instead, I planted my butt on the mossy creek bank, surveying and trying to regulate my breathing. I wasn't out of shape, but the massive adrenaline rush and the heavy weight of the bag on my shoulders had taxed my endurance. And Van's nearness often had that effect as well.

Van nudged me, his nose cold from the creek. I nodded, nudging him back, letting him know I was alive. We sat another minute, listening to the woods. At length, Van yipped, and I turned. I heard his skin crackling back into place as his fur receded.

"I'm covered."

I turned, and nearly swallowed my own tongue. He was only *barely* covered. Instead of fishing around his for clothes, he was simply holding his oversized backpack in front of his pertinent parts. Technically, he was every inch as covered as if he'd had a pair of shorts on, but the fact was, it was only a backpack slung in front of himself keeping me from all-out ogling. I swallowed, trying to get a grip on myself.

Thankfully, Van seemed totally ignorant of my tongue all but hanging out of my mouth. His defined abs glistened with sweat from our run. I yanked my brain from his muscles and back to his words.

"...check the map. We ran north away from the bear, but we couldn't have gotten too far off course."

I nodded dumbly and ripped my face away as he rummaged through his pack for the map.

"It might take me a minute if you'd rather be in skin," he said absently. "I can stick my pants on," he offered.

I barked, face still turned away, pretending I was keeping a look out. I'd much prefer my hot-and-botheredness kept secret in my fur rather than broadcasting it via bright red skin.

CHAPTER 25

DONOVAN

Katie was acting all weird and jumpy. Maybe the run in with the bear had her more on edge than I realized. My heart had galloped into my throat, terrified that bear was going to catch us. Wolves were predators. And nothing came between a she-bear and her cub if it wanted to live.

We had. But we'd lived.

Barely.

I shivered as a chill breeze whipped over my sweaty skin. I hadn't bothered to put clothes on since I wasn't planning to stay in skin long. The cool felt good on my naked skin after being so worked up on the run.

I consulted the map. I couldn't be sure where we were, but I had good instincts and a great internal compass thanks to my wolf, and I thought we were only about forty miles away from Rock Falls.

While I was more than ready to be done with this leg of our journey, my belly crawled thinking about going back and seeing all the things from the Lacessere—where I'd lost Sarah—that still haunted me.

"If we're close to where I think we are here, there should be another town about five miles southeast of here that should be on our way to Rock Falls. Want to stop for breakfast?"

Katie yipped. I glanced up and realized her back was still to me. I looked down and smirked.

"I'm still covered. You're good. But I could use some scrambled eggs, maybe some bacon. Sausage. Toast. Biscuits and gravy..."

Katie barked exasperatedly. I chuckled.

"Okay. I'll change back to my fur, and we can shift about a mile from the town and go in on legs, yeah?"

She yipped again and I took that as my cue to put my skin away.

A small eternity later, when my belly was growling audibly, I finally scented the first hints of civilization. I nudged Katie in the ribs, making her squeak. My wolf grinned. Even in her furry form, Katie was ticklish. She swiped at me half-heartedly with her paw. I barked and nodded in the direction of the town.

Scenting, I knew Katie picked up the industrial smells, too. We turned and shifted to our skin, rummaging around our packs for clothes that weren't wrinkled beyond recognition.

"Ugh. I cannot wait to have access to a washer and dryer," Katie lamented as I heard her zipping her jeans. The sound sent my blood thrumming a little quicker in my veins. I shook my head. There was something wrong with me. This long in the bush had addled me some-how.

"It would be nice to have a shirt with a few less wrinkles," I conceded as I held up a t-shirt with more wrinkles than fabric.

"You decent? More *decent* than you were earlier?" Katie asked, an edge in her voice that I couldn't quite decipher.

I chuckled. "I was totally covered. And yes, I'm decent." I finished putting my shirt on as she turned.

"Holding a bag in front of your man bits is not *decent*," she groused.

"Noted. I'll take the time to fish out clothes and drag them on next time."

She rolled her eyes at me. "I'm starving. You ready?"

"Yeah, let me put my shoes back on." I bent down to tie my laces and was momentarily distracted as my eyes snagged on Katie's legs. Even in rumpled jeans, her legs were noticeably long, and as I was thinking about them, flashes of her in shorts blasted behind my eyeballs. Clearing my throat gruffly, I wrestled my eyes back to my shoes and quickly finished.

"Let's go find breakfast." Before I could think any other stupid thoughts. Clearly, I needed food.

We popped into a truck stop to use their shower facilities so we didn't terrify the civilized masses with our unwashed state. Hot water had never felt better. And while my clothes were still a rumpled mess. At least my skin was clean, and the stench of unwashed dog was gone. Slathering on an extra layer of deodorant, I hurried, anxiety still rippling under my skin with Katie out of sight.

I'd only been away from her ten or fifteen minutes, but the time stretched out like a small eternity I couldn't quite grasp. Wolf bristled.

Something felt wrong.

CHAPTER 26

KATIE

I made quick work of washing all the dirt and wilds out of my red-black hair, twisting and wringing it out as best I could since I didn't have a towel. I had three clean shirts in my bag and one clean pair of pants. I eyed my options and dried off with a tee shirt. It didn't take me long, and I didn't dawdle. Part of me wanted to stay under that shower spray until the water ran cold, hidden away from the world. But the world was on the other side of that door, and that knotted up my insides. Because aside from Van and the Hazeltons, I wasn't sure who else in the world I could trust right now.

My world had been shaken to its foundation the night Alan killed my parents. But half my known world had crumbled once I realized he'd killed my brother, too. I knew in my bones he was trying to flush me out. He didn't want me. If he could kill Ben, who was loyal to him, then the only possible reason he could want me was the money my father left me.

The joke would be on Alan though. Beyond a generous allowance once I turned eighteen—which I could access now, I supposed—I couldn't touch the actual money until I was twenty-one. And if he killed me before then, all that money would go to various charities in my father's name.

Bitterness burned like gall on the back of my tongue.

I rammed my legs into my pants and quickly laced on my shoes. Slipping my zip up hoodie on over my shirt—it smelled the freshest of my outerwear—I walked out of the bathroom to wait for Van.

I was surprised to find that I cleared the bathroom before he did. Leaning against the wall, I scanned my surroundings. There weren't many people milling about. Two customers. One looking at the candy bars, the other eyeing the energy drinks. One worker at the counter. As I watched, the clerk reached up and clicked on the TV in the corner.

"Reward for any information about the *SnowSpace Tech* heiress." The woman on the screen wore red. My heart thundered. This was a national news channel. In the next instant a sketch of what the missing heiress might look like flashed across the screen.

It wasn't completely accurate, but it was far too close for comfort. Immediately, I tucked my quickly braided hair down my back, and flipped the hood of my sweatshirt over my head, pulling it low.

Van walked out at just that minute, took one look at my face, grabbed my hand, and bolted us toward the door.

"What happened?" he asked as soon as we were out in the chilly morning air, his eyes skimming the area, on high alert, searching for hidden threats.

"News broadcast. They flashed a sketch. Van. It was a *national* news channel." Panic rose in my belly and for a second, I thought I was going to puke right there outside the gas station.

"Okay. We're going to eat on the road." He glanced at my face again. "You need something more than trail mix. I do, too. Especially if we're going to keep going until we hit Rock Falls. I don't want to stop again if we can help it. We need to stay off the roads and stay hidden. Luck is with us. Look. There's a payphone. I'm going to call Dominic, and then you're going to wait there in the tree line while I get some breakfast sandwiches. Then we'll move."

I nodded, too numb to do much else.

Van fished some change out of his pocket and placed a call in the ancient-looking payphone. I was surprised there was even one still around. Everyone had a cell phone now. Except two run-away kids who needed to hide from the world.

"All right. Thanks, Dominic. I really appreciate it. Yep. See you there."

"And?" I prompted as Van swung his bag back over his shoulder.

He nodded in the direction of the tree line, just a few yards from the gas station.

"There's another town about four miles west of here. Dominic thought it would be safest for us to meet there. Some of his pack work in that town, and he has good relationships with several of the locals, should anything arise. His wife, Mary, is going to meet us there in an hour and a half. So, we'll have to move at a decent clip, going through the brush, but we can do it."

I nodded again, processing.

"And now. The most crucial part of the entire morning." Van's eyes were dead serious, and my belly clenched. "What do you want on your breakfast sandwich?"

My shoulders relaxed and I mock punched him in the shoulder.

"Turd. Load me up on the protein. And the biggest coffee you can carry. I'm having caffeine withdrawal."

"Yes ma'am. Cream and sugar, right?"

"Lots of both."

Van smiled. "We'll make it through this, Katie Clay. We're almost to Rock Falls, and then we can hunker down in a place with real beds, and hot coffee every morning. And safety in numbers." He moved in, wrapping an arm awkwardly around my shoulders, the straps of my backpack forcing his arm at a strange angle. All the same, he squeezed me to his chest, and I took a shuddering breath against it.

"You smell a lot better than you did two hours ago."

"You still smell like maple and allspice." Then, to my utter shock and delighted horrification, he scented me. Ran his nose right up the side of my neck.

Goose bumps erupted over my skin, and I was too dumbfounded to respond. He pulled back, totally oblivious to the way Wolf and I were practically drooling, winked, then adjusted his pack.

"Be back in a few with hot chow. Stay hidden."

My face was probably glowing hot enough it rivaled a flare. My blush was sure to attract airplanes, but sure. I'd stay hidden.

Breakfast sandwiches had never tasted better. We munched as we walked. Caffeinated coffee was a glorious thing I had desperately missed while we stayed in the cave.

We made good time, and Van easily found Mary Wolfe parked on the back edge of the local supermarket parking lot.

"Donovan, it's good to see you again. You must be Donovan's friend," Mary said with a smile as she held her hands out to me. Suddenly unsure of myself, I held mine out in return.

I cleared my throat. "I'm Katie. Thank you for letting us come."

Mary made a *phshaw* sort of noise and Wolf immediately warmed to her. "You were right to call us. Dominic would have come himself, but he had a meeting with his firm that he couldn't miss." We hopped in her gray car, buckled up, and she pulled out of the lot. "Though I would like to apologize. We would be more than happy to have you stay at our house—it's so quiet now with Sam moved out—but we had a pipe in the upstairs bathroom burst yesterday. It's made an unbelievable mess. Unfortunately, the guest room, the hallway, and the bathroom all need work done and are in no shape to be used. But Steve and Amalie Rivers said you all are welcome to stay at their house for as long as you need. Since Raven and Cade are both gone, too, they've got the empty nest as well. I think they felt this was one small way they could repay you for what you did for Cade, too," Mary finished softly and glanced back in the rearview mirror where Donovan sat.

"Thank you so much. We're grateful," Donovan said. Wolf shifted uneasily inside me at the stiffness of his tone. A little piece of my heart broke off as I could only guess what he was thinking.

CHAPTER 27
DONOVAN

"Donovan!" Steve Rivers called as he stepped outside his house onto the stoop. My heart stuttered painfully against my breastbone. He reminded me so much of Cade—of the reason the sting of rejection still dogged my steps. But he and his wife were essentially sticking their necks out for us, so I shoved the uncomfortable feelings back down and clasped the man's arm.

"Thanks for letting us stay, Steve. It's good to see you again."

"Not as good as it is to see you. You are welcome here any time."

I introduced Katie as Amalie came out.

"You all just come in and make yourselves at home. The beds are all made up and most of Cade and Raven's things are already moved with them, so you can spread your stuff out however you need. Katie, I've put you in Raven's room, and Donovan, Cade's is on the other side of the shared bathroom. Will that work for you all?"

"Definitely. We really appreciate it," Katie said.

Just what I wanted. To live in Cade's old room. Wolf snorted, feeling the sting of it, but reminded me not to be petty.

"Sam told me this morning that they're doing a bonfire over behind his cabin tonight. You all are welcome to come," Steve said.

At least it might be a good distraction from wallowing in Cade's scent. It would be good for Katie to get out, too. Maybe distract her from everything as well.

Sam and Megan's place wasn't far from the Rivers' house, and Katie and I walked over after a delicious dinner of Amalie's pork roast, mashed potatoes, and vegetables.

Katie was quiet, and so was I. Wolf paced inside. I was nervous. Stupidly so. I tried to remind myself that there was no reason to be anxious. It was just the past coming to haunt me. And my past was far less complicated than Katie's. I had nothing to complain about.

The scent of a group of wolves met us, the musky tang a welcome scent among allies. I started identifying them as we came closer.

Megan and Rachel were chatting about something off to one side. Kyp, Rachel's chosen mate, was over there. Bowen, Kyp's Beta, added another log to the fire. Another wolf couple I faintly remembered…Jake? I couldn't remember the girl's name. Raven, Cade's younger sister, entered the circle of light from the shadows; Bowen's head immediately shot up and zeroed in on her, his lips twisting upward. A shiver worked over my spine as I took a deep inhale, smelling the combined scents of the Wolfe and Kypson packs.

I scanned the few other heads then stopped short.

A sucker punch to my solar plexus would have left more air in my lungs. I stood there, just outside the ring of firelight, Wolf completely at attention inside me as a pale blonde head appeared, the mere sight of her carving my heart up into tiny pieces.

Wolf bristled as a black head appeared next to her, both of them coming through the group of wolves gathered around the fire pit behind Sam's cabin.

Sarah.

And her mate. Cade.

Wolf whined, his ruff lying down.

What was *she* doing here?

What was *he* doing here?

Why weren't they back in New York together, starting their lives together? Why were they *here* where I'd have to see them, have to relive each second of the shame and leftover desire that I was feeling right now? I prayed my unruly pheromones weren't leaking out through my skin.

"Donovan?" Sarah said, her voice showing her surprise as her eyes landed on me. She wasn't unhappy to see me. She was as beautiful as I remembered, light green eyes, blonde hair hanging in soft waves rather than the straight way she usually styled it. She wore confidence like a queen would wear a regal robe.

"Donovan!" Cade broke away from his mate, stepping forward and clasping my arm. His face was wreathed in genuine smiles as he clapped me once on the back. "Hey!" He released my arm and stepped back toward Sarah. She came forward and gave me a quick hug. Cade looped his arm loosely around her waist and she leaned into him.

"Hey," I said back, unsure what else to say. "I expected you all would be back in New York by now."

"Nah, we're going to finish out the school year here then move after graduation," Cade supplied. Of course, they were. "But what about you? You're here, in Rock Falls. Everything okay? What are you doing here?" Cade asked, concerned and not at all put out with my presence.

"Um, we hit a slight snag," I started before clearing my throat. Fumbling, I reached behind me for Katie, tugging her to stand next to me. I wanted to keep hold of her hand—wanted to grip it like a lifeline to ground me to myself, but I forced myself to let go. I didn't want to make things awkward for her—at least not any more than they already were. Although, likely, they were far more awkward for me than they were for her.

"This is Katie. She's from my pack," I couldn't help the pride that snuck into my voice. Even if she was pack in name only, she was one of mine, and I was incredibly proud of her for how well she'd held up under the strain of things the past week. "We'll...be staying in the area for a while," I said vaguely.

"And you're welcome any time," Sam offered with a smile as he came through the others gathered. "We're glad to have you both. Why don't you all come over by the fire. We can all talk, catch up, introduce everyone who hasn't met."

"Megan and I made cookies," Rachel chimed.

"Only four kinds," Kyp teased her quietly. The look he gave her was filled with so much adoration my stomach literally flipped. Rachel's face was radiant as she slipped her fingers through Kyp's and squeezed.

The air was choked with pheromones from multiple wolf couples. At least any of mine wouldn't be distinguishable.

I think I preferred the she-bear.

CHAPTER 28

KATIE

My insides withered on the spot.

That was Sarah Thornehill? Well, Sarah Rivers? Thornehill-Rivers? *The One*? It didn't matter what her last name was. Nothing mattered when you were perfection like that.

Beautiful, flawless skin, gorgeous blonde hair in perfect waves, eyes the shade of celery, feminine curves that meshed with her athletic build to make her unapproachably fierce. She was every inch a would-be Alpha.

Compared to her?

I *couldn't* compare to her. I couldn't even come close. I was her complete opposite in every way I could see. Tears pricked the back of my eyes. No wonder Van wanted to see her instead of me when he'd kissed me. All the old pain and doubts crashed down on me. Wolf whimpered inside me, trying to bolster us for all the good it did. I wanted the earth to open up and swallow me down.

Van's hand fumbled for mine as he drew me parallel with him. I wished he'd keep hold of it. He dropped it like my skin secreted acid. I bit the inside of my cheek to keep the tears at bay.

"This is Katie. She's from my pack," Van said. Wolf pricked her ears forward. There was an unmistakable note of pride in his words that attempted to thaw the frozen block of emotions sitting in my chest.

I found myself being herded along with everyone else to the sizable fire pit dug into the earth and ringed in large stones. A log crackled, sending shoots of orange sparks into the dusk falling around us.

"I'm Raven," a black-haired girl with wide blue eyes introduced herself.

"I'm Katie," I rasped, wishing my voice came out smoother.

Raven smiled. "I'm Cade's sister. We're all really grateful for what Donovan did. Any Beta who will put his own claims aside like that is someone worth following. I'm glad your pack has a good leader." She smiled, her eyes crinkling just slightly at the sides.

"Yeah. He *is* a good leader," I said. He was. Despite his failings, he was one of the best men I'd ever known. All the Hazelton men were—Van came from a long line of honorable men who did the right thing. It left a curious sensation of longing, pride, and loss burning inside my chest. I shoved thoughts about my pack of origin and my adopted pack back to process later, when I wasn't making a debut entrance to two other packs. "Are, are you part of the Wolfe pack?" I hedged as Raven handed me a plate piled with cookies.

Raven smiled shyly. "I was. Bowen is my mate. I'm officially Kypson pack now." She nodded her head to the tallest of the male wolves who had congregated on the far side of the fire. He was a big guy and exuded power. I was slightly surprised to find he was a Beta, rather than an Alpha.

"Katie, it's so great to meet you," the red-haired girl bounced up beside me, curls flying loose around her face. "I'm Rachel. Obviously, you've met Raven. This is Sarah," the blonde goddess smiled, and my heart fell to my toes, "and this is Megan, Sam's mate."

"Can I get you some hot chocolate or apple cider?" Megan asked, her face open and friendly.

Wolf nudged me. There was nothing but acceptance shining from each of these girls. Even Sarah. No questions. No hesitation. Just welcome.

"I'd love some cider, thank you."

"I think the guys are all going to play corn hole. Girl chat?" Rachel suggested. For the second time that evening, I found myself herded. This time to a cluster of logs set up near the crackling fire. Sitting next to Raven, I nibbled a cookie. Cinnamon, white chocolate, and a hint of orange exploded in my mouth.

"This is really good," I said.

"Oh, do you like it? I was afraid there was maybe too much cinnamon. Rachel and I are trying out a few new recipes," Megan said. "Rach, what do you think? Too much cinnamon, not enough orange?"

Rachel bit into hers. "Consistency is perfect. Personally, I like the stronger cinnamon flavors. All right, Sarah, Raven, you take a bite, too, let us know what you think."

And just like that, I was sucked into their circle. At one point I mentally stepped back, studying each girl and marveling just a little at how quickly they had ensconced me within their circle. No questions, no rude stares, no concerns about what Van and I might be running from. Maybe it was the sharp contrast it provided to my childhood pack, but slowly the awkwardness I felt started to dissipate. Until things progressed from baking, school, and college plans...to romantic topics.

"Is everyone still clear next Saturday for dress shopping?" Rachel asked. I glanced around. They were all dress shopping? Spring formal, maybe? I'd never gone to any high school dances. They felt too public. Too much out in the open. "Katie, I don't know how long you're in town, but we're all going wedding-and-bridesmaid-dress shopping next weekend." Rachel's smile about split her face as she held out her hand with an impressive diamond sparkling in the firelight. She babbled on, "We're having the full traditional human wedding right after graduation. I don't want it to be awkward for you, but you are absolutely more than welcome to come with us. It's no fun to be stuck in a new place with no friends on the weekend. You should definitely come if you're still around."

"Oh," I honestly didn't know what to say to that. "Thanks. I'm not sure how long we'll be here, but I do appreciate the offer." My eyes tracked to Van. His shoulders had lost some of their rigidity as he held a glass bottle of purple soda and laughed at something Kyp said.

Rachel didn't miss my glance. She leaned in. "So, are *you* the reason Donovan gave Sarah up so easily?"

Sarah choked on her cider.

"Rachel," Megan said, rolling her eyes.

"I have eyes, thanks very much. Just looked like Mr. Hazelton's lingered on you a little longer than average," Rachel winked at me.

A hot flush crept up my neck and I attempted a nervous chuckle. "Ha, uh, no. No, I'm not the reason. That was all Van." I smiled weakly.

"And it was a truly selfless act that will never go unremembered," Sarah cut in. She nodded to me before her gaze cut to Cade. An expression of such love washed over her that I had to look away. I hoped my feelings for Van weren't so loudly broadcast. I didn't think I could stand it if they were.

"You, you all are all with your mates?" I tripped over my words, desperately trying to turn the conversation back to someone—anyone—else.

"Yes," Megan said. Her eyes lit up. "It's been an interesting few months in the Wolfe pack and the Kypson pack. Actually, all of us have found our mates within the past six or seven months."

"Really? Who found who first?" I asked as I realized I was the only girl among us who hadn't chosen her mate yet. It was an impossibility. Something I desperately wanted but could not have. Especially not now that Alan was out for my blood. I suppressed a shudder and refused to think what he'd do to any mate of mine if he caught him.

"Sam and I were first," Megan continued then glanced to Rachel.

"I got myself in a spot of bother and Kyp came to my rescue. Though he had to turn me into a werewolf in the process," she cleared her throat, "I'd already had a crush on him, but after that, we just fell in love. I knew I never wanted to be with anyone else." She glanced at Raven.

"Bowen and I had...an unusual first meeting," Raven said with a rueful grin. "I'm not sure how much you know about the pack wars that concluded just before Sarah's Lacessere, but Bowen was on the opposite side. We're true mates, and I wasn't too keen on that at first."

My eyebrows lifted. And I thought my life was a tangled mess. Raven looked to Sarah.

"And then there was me. Cade and I were attracted to each other long before we ever admitted it. As I'm sure you're well aware, I wasn't supposed to like Cade. I really couldn't help myself. Anyway, we made a few less-than-stellar decisions, and that led to the Lacessere, but you probably know all about that as Donovan is the real hero in that story." Sarah took another sip of her drink, contented.

"Anyone special for you back in your home pack?" Raven asked innocently.

"No. I'm not sure I'll ever take a mate," I admitted, surprising myself.

"Nothing wrong with that either," Megan offered, watching me closely.

I wasn't sure she believed me.

CHAPTER 29

DONOVAN

I glanced over to where the girls sat, clustered around the far side of the fire pit. Sarah's blonde hair caught the firelight, but Katie's dark hair shined like black flames. I caught my breath, looking at them both, nearly side by side.

Sarah was cool, calculating collectiveness, gorgeous, ethereal.

But Katie...Katie did nothing in half measures. Katie was heart and soul. She was warmth, light, fire, intelligence, and passion. She was breathtaking. Wolf nudged me.

Like a flower opening itself to the sun, I realized two things in that instant. I liked the *idea* of Sarah. She was pretty, had everything on her pedigree that she should—everything I should want in a mate.

But Katie.

Stirrings began in the pit of my stomach as I casually watched her. Katie knew me. Katie had been a fixture in my life for years—and I took her for granted. Wolf nudged me again. I wanted Katie. Emotion flooded me—there was no denying that I felt something deep and greater than friendship as I stood there sipping a grape soda while letting my eyes trace the curve of Katie's cheek, the wisp of hair that had escaped, the tilt of her chin...

Katie also had Alpha genes, same as Sarah did.

WHAM

The impact of that realization hit me like a board between my eyes. Katie.

The thought was so impossibly obvious I nearly smacked myself in the head. I'd been so focused on keeping her safe, on getting her out of the line of fire, I hadn't stopped to think about any ramifications beyond that.

Katie had Alpha genes. If Katie and I took each other as mates, not only would I be able to offer her better protection, stability, and a husband who would cherish and respect her, but she'd bring the genes the Hazelton pack needed.

With Sarah out of the picture, I hadn't realized I had other immediate options. As I looked at the girls now, I wondered how I could ever have wanted Sarah when there was Katie. Maybe I'd been too intent on the pedigree I felt pressured to pursue. If Katie was an option…a giddy little bubble of desire fizzed up my esophagus. If Katie and I Claimed each other—we'd solve a huge chunk of both our problems, as well as fulfill what I now realized I wanted, with one little mutual nip. Mind and heart racing uncomfortably fast, I tried to tune back into the conversation.

"Your turn, Donovan," Bowen said and tossed me a beanbag. I nearly dropped it in my stupefied excitement.

The Rivers had a fantastic upper story porch, accessed from the end of the hall, rather than one of the bedrooms. After the evening full of unexpected and unwanted confrontations, revelations, and general lingering exhaustion, my emotions felt a little worse for wear, though it hadn't been as strange as I thought it might have been.

Truthfully, I felt like my eyes had been opened a little wider. I needed space to think, clear my head, strategize about how to present a mutually beneficial Claiming to Katie. Because I wanted her. I was in no doubt on that point. I needed to make myself attractive to her as a mate.

The night air was brisk and cool on my face as I shut the door quietly behind me. Allspice and maple tickled my nostrils.

"Katie?"

"Sorry. I'll go." Her voice was tight, and I wondered if I'd inadvertently made another misstep. She rose from one of the chairs off to the side of the deck.

"No, don't. Stay. I'm sorry. I didn't mean to invade. I didn't realize you were out here." Silence stretched as she sat stiffly, her hands clenched tightly in her lap.

"Katie? Are you okay?" I gingerly eased myself into the chair opposite her. My knees lightly brushed hers and tingles spread to my toes.

That was new.

Katie sighed. "It was a long night."

"Too much? It looked like you were getting along well with the other girls."

"I did. Better than I expected." She blew a short breath out.

I was quiet, trying to read between the lines. I wanted to touch her.

"Did you kiss her?" Katie finally broke the silence.

I tipped my head back, looking at her in confusion. "Who? Sarah?"

Katie nodded, her lips a thin line and barely illuminated in the moonlight.

Regret curdled in my belly. This was about what I'd done. How I'd hurt Katie. Guilt pierced my chest.

"No, I didn't kiss Sarah."

"But you wanted to?" she pressed.

I shrugged, unsure what to tell her besides the truth, though I was afraid saying it out loud may only wound her further. That was the last thing I wanted. But Katie deserved my honesty. "At the time I did. She's pretty; I was attracted to her—the idea of her—and for a while, I really thought she and I would be mates." I swallowed. "But I don't want her anymore. Not just because she's off limits. But because she was never meant for me. I realize that. I'm so sorry that in my confusion, I hurt you. I should never have done what I did." Thinking about it brought the bitter gall back to my throat. I needed to lighten this moment before I suffocated under it. "You're an exceptional kisser though," I blurted. Wolf winced inside.

Katie snorted and slashed her sleeve over her right eye. "You're still a Sasquatch butt."

The mood less oppressively heavy, we sat in silence. I studied her unabashedly. She was lost in her own thoughts, the moon streaming down onto her red-black hair, lighting it in little silvery patches.

Katie was beautiful. Exquisitely so. Wolf concurred. Pawing once inside me, I gave into the wolf's nature and looked at Katie with new eyes. My pulse tripped double time.

Swallowing hard once more, I had yet another revelation. Maybe I'd stopped being attracted to Sarah because I was much more attracted to someone else. I'd just ignored it in pursuit of the one thing the pack needed most from me.

CHAPTER 30
KATIE

Sometimes honesty sucked.

But I was glad of it, nonetheless. It was hard to hear that he'd wanted to kiss her, but some strangely warped place inside was fiendishly glad he hadn't. Mostly so that he couldn't compare his kiss with me to a kiss with her, even if he had been thinking about her while he kissed me.

It was also good to know that at least I wasn't a bad kisser. The thought that maybe some part of Van had liked the feel of my lips against his filled me with a satisfied sort of pleasure, but also twisted with the awkwardness and bitterness of the whole situation.

"Katie," Van said after a long stretch of silence. I glanced at him. He licked his lips and fidgeted his hands. "I've been thinking."

I lifted an eyebrow, unsure where he was going.

"If, we were to, if you," he raked a hand through his hair, standing parts of it up on end, and giving him an even more rakish appeal than usual. Blasted werewolf genes. "I'm not saying this well." He blew a hard breath out. "If we were to Claim each other, you'd fall completely under Hazelton protection, and the Hazeltons would have exactly what they needed, too."

A deathly quiet stole over us for a full minute.

The weight of what he suggested settled over me like a burial shroud. How could everything I'd ever wanted bring such pain and darkness to me?

I loved Van. But I didn't want a political alliance. I didn't want to be an obligation, a box to tick off, a means to an end. And even if that *was* acceptable, I couldn't bring a mate into my own quagmire of a family situation. So many uncertainties, so much ruthless hate and blind ambition. Uncle Alan would rip anyone or anything to shreds if he felt threatened. And if I had a mate that could be used as leverage?

Nail the lid of my coffin down right now.

I'd move heaven and earth to keep someone I loved out of harm's way—especially if I was the cause of it.

No. Even if I were more to Van than a political match, I could not Claim him. A part of my heart broke off, turning to ash as it disintegrated. My eyes ached with unshed tears.

"No." The word strangled past my lips. Without waiting for a response, or to see his reaction, I rose and went back into the house, shutting the door to Raven's room behind me. I made sure the door to the bathroom was firmly shut, too, then I sank onto the floor by the bed, drew my knees up, and sobbed silently into the denim of my jeans.

CHAPTER 31
DONOVAN

I sat on the deck in the crisp spring air, dumbfounded.

If I thought Sarah's rejection stung, Katie's about ripped my heart out. She didn't even consider my proposition.

No.

That was it. No questions, no discussion, no excuses. Just *no.*

I knew Katie well enough to truly think she'd at least be interested in talking about the possibility of Claiming each other. I knew she liked me—Angus said she'd loved me for years. On some level I knew that, too. Katie had always been a good friend—one of my best.

And recently, I'd been thinking about her. As maybe more than a friend. Tonight's revelations had shown just *how much more* than a friend. Wolf's realization that Katie had the perfect genes had been the icing on the cake. It was like a dam had burst inside me, and a huge tangle of emotions and excitement had poured out.

I wanted Katie.

I wanted Katie.

Awe started to overtake the rejection still coursing hotly through my veins. I needed to sort this out. Conviction gripped me. Wolf stood, shaking out his coat in solidarity.

We wanted Katie.

Katie and no other.

I needed help.

Angus.

Donovan? What's wrong?

Nothing. Everything. Sorry. I have no phone. I need advice.

Let my heartrate go back to normal. Go ahead. What great problems plague you that I can help you solve?

I asked Katie to Claim me.

You WHAT?

Even through the link, the words were shouted.

I sighed. *She turned me down flat. No explanation, no nothing.*

I'm not sure if I'm surprised by that or not. Any great declarations of love? Flowers? What exactly have the two of you been doing while you were supposed to be fleeing for your lives?

I paused. Then winced. I'd approached our Claiming like a business transaction. Wolf snipped at me, and I could have growled at myself.

No...I could have handled it better.

That's likely an understatement.

Thanks so much for your support, Angus.

Anytime, Cuz. What do you need from me? It sounds like you've botched things again. You need to woo her. I can't believe I'm saying this. This is like you asking to date my little sister. I might be ill.

Oh, shut up, Angus. It's been a crap week, just tell me what I need to do to woo Katie. How would Katie best respond to my advances? How could I show her that I wanted *her, needed her*? Her genes were definitely an added perk. But even without them, I admitted to myself, I still wanted Katie the girl and Katie the wolf. It had to be Katie.

I could hear Angus whistling through his teeth. *Well, maybe start with why she turned you down? It can't be because she doesn't love you. She does. She always has. Have you tried talking to her?*

I winced again. *Not just yet.*

I'd start there, Angus finished dryly.

Right.

And maybe do some soul searching first.

It was a restless night. I didn't sleep well. Not only did I feel bruised because of Katie's rejection, I was torn up that I'd messed up so colossally again where she was concerned. Would I never get anything right with this girl?

I went over and over in my head, all the reasons that Claiming Katie was a good idea. It *was* a good business transaction. It was smart for both our packs. She got the protection she needed; I got the genes the Hazelton pack needed. I got her. Logically, it all made perfect sense.

But then I went down the avenue of my feelings and dared to let myself explore those.

Wolf chuffed at me, calling up a randomly invented image of Katie with my cousin Connor, a Beta of his pack in Britain, and the first eligible wolf that came to mind. My blood pressure about spiked through the roof.

Not because Connor wasn't an excellent guy, but because he wasn't *me.*

I was intensely jealous of the thought of Katie with another wolf. It was practically a visceral reaction. That...was interesting. I admitted to myself that I wouldn't be that jealous if I hadn't started getting invested. This was different than what I'd felt for Sarah.

I tried to call up Sarah's light blonde hair and green eyes, her fierce determination, her natural beauty. It was still there, but like it was veiled. It didn't shine as brightly. I didn't want Sarah.

I wanted Katie.

I scrubbed my hands down my face and rolled over in the bed for the umpteenth time.

Angus said to woo her.

For all my skill with battle tactics, I wasn't sure what tactics to employ for *wooing*.

CHAPTER 32

KATIE

When I woke for the third time in as many hours, I finally rolled out of bed. I shrugged on a sweatshirt and padded softly downstairs. The warm scent of coffee tantalized my nose, and I gravitated into the kitchen.

"Good morning. You're up early. Morning person or trouble sleeping?" Mrs. Rivers was pouring a mug of the fragrant brew as I paused in the doorway of the kitchen.

"Um," I stuttered.

She turned and smiled at me, getting down another mug from the cabinet. "Coffee?"

"Please," I replied gratefully. She filled the extra mug. "It wasn't my most restful night," I admitted.

"I'm sorry to hear that. At least you should be able to relax and take it easy today. There's movies, snacks, books, the kids have one of those video game things in some closet. You're welcome to use it if you can figure out the cords." She smiled as she passed the mug to me. "Cream or sugar?"

I took a rapturous inhale. "Just black today, thanks."

We sipped in comfortable silence for a few minutes.

"Well, I'm going to need to head out the door. I apologize for being such a poor hostess this week, but one of the organizations I volunteer with is having a big fundraiser this week, and I'm in charge of coordinating a few of the cogs and wheels, so I won't be around much, and Steve is working a job a few counties over, so you'll mostly have the house to yourselves. But please make yourself at home. Let me know if there's anything you need, or anything we can do to help." She smiled, whisking a few stray wisps of her nearly white-blonde hair off her shoulder.

"Thank you. Truly, Mrs. Rivers. Opening your home to us like this," I drifted off, not having the words to adequately express the deep gratitude I felt.

"Amalie, please. After what Donovan did for Cade, this is certainly the least we could do to repay his kindness." I smiled, though my belly clenched at the mention of her son...because he brought unwanted images of perfect Sarah swimming to the front of my brain.

After Mrs. Rivers—Amalie—left, I leaned against the counter, sipping my coffee, willing life to return to my limbs.

Van had asked me to Claim him last night. And Amalie's words had just reopened that fissure of uncertainty and inadequacy in the middle of my chest. I could not reconcile those two things together. Claiming Van? How many hundreds of times had I daydreamed about doing exactly that? But equally, how many times had I despaired when I thought about his kissing me—but imagining I was Sarah?

I shook my head, Wolf grousing inside.

As much as I wanted Van, there was no way I could Claim him now. I'd always wonder if I was second best. Wonder how I compared. Wonder if he'd rather be with *her*. The idea of Claiming Van felt tainted. Then there was the small issue of my dear old uncle who wouldn't hesitate to disembowel Van if he thought it would gain him what he wanted. And Claimed, Van only presented a wider path straight to my heart.

I'd die before I let Uncle Alan near Donovan Hazelton.

Wolf perked her ears up as I finished that ferocious thought. Van was shuffling down the stairs. Muscles stiffening, I wasn't sure if I should stay and suffer the awkwardness that was surely coming, or if I should run.

I sighed. There was nowhere to run to save back to Raven's bedroom. I grit my teeth. Best have it over with.

Van hesitated in the doorway of the kitchen, much like I had.

"Morning," he said hesitantly.

I cleared my throat. "Morning."

We stared uncomfortably at each other for a full minute, neither of us knowing how to diffuse the awkward tension between us.

"I suppose last night is another massive mark on the Donovan is a Sasquatch butt tally."

It was so unexpected, I nearly spat my coffee out as I snorted.

His face lightened as some of the tension cleared the air.

"I...I'm sorry. What I said last night. I meant it, but it came out all wrong." He tugged at the ends of his hair. "I seem forever to be saying the wrong thing to you. I would gladly Claim you, Katie. But not because you have great genes. Not because you need my pack or we need you. But because you're you." He swallowed hard. "I'm sorry it came out sounding like a business transaction. That wasn't how I meant it."

The air was heavy with a different kind of tension now. It was almost painfully sweet. Still more painful than sweet, but in some strange way, it was gratifying to hear those words come from his mouth.

Finally, I nodded. I didn't trust myself to speak just then, with a fist-sized clump of emotion squeezing off my windpipe.

CHAPTER 33

DONOVAN

Katie didn't say anything about my explanation, and by some mutual unspoken agreement, we put it behind us and went about our day of relaxing. We watched a few movies. Katie found a book or two she thought she might read from among the shelves in the basement Mrs. Rivers had pointed her toward. I nearly went stir-crazy.

I didn't wait gracefully. I wanted to go out, run, take action, do something active to get us out of our current predicament. As it was, I didn't even dare get onto a computer for fear what I'd search for would ping something and somehow alert Katie's uncle.

In short, it was a long day.

I was worked up enough, it was a relief to see Cade's face pop up on the other side of the window near the door.

"Hey!" he said as he walked through the front door. "Several of us are going for a quick run before dinner. You guys want to come?"

"Yes," burst from my lips. "I'll see if Katie wants to come, too." Although, belatedly, I realized Wolf wouldn't allow me to leave Katie out of my sight for so long. Not that I thought something was going to happen to her here, I just couldn't bring myself to take the chance.

"Katie," I called. She looked up from the window seat at the back of the house where she was reading. "You want to come for a run? A few of the others are going, and we've been cooped up here all day. Might be good to get some fresh air."

A tiny smile played at her lips. "I'm actually quite comfortable, thanks, but clearly you need a run."

Dread pulled at my stomach.

"Yeah," I said slowly. "I'll just stay here if you are."

Katie rolled her eyes and shut her book. "Oh, come on, let's go." The smile grew as it toyed at the corner of her mouth.

"You sure?" I felt compelled to ask, even though I was sure I'd leap out of my skin if I had to sit still much longer.

"I'm sure. The least I can do for sucking you into my family drama is to let you run without worrying about me, though I think I'm perfectly safe for the moment, and feel quite comfortable taking care of myself."

"Thanks," I said gratefully. I let my fingers brush her elbow as she passed in front of me, wafting allspice and maple as she did. She twitched slightly, and I knew she'd caught me scenting. I grinned a little. Good. Let her know my interest in her wasn't purely business. Maybe flirting was part of wooing. I knew how to flirt. Maybe it was time I tried it with Katie.

Intentionally.

CHAPTER 34

KATIE

I was nervous about running with the other wolves. I'd never have admitted it in a million years how knotted up my insides got just thinking about being in fur next to Sarah. The thing was, I liked Sarah. In the time I'd spent with her, I'd found her nice, kind, and open. And hemorrhaging pheromones anytime she looked at her mate.

But she was also everything I wasn't. Everything a good Alpha girl should be. It was hard not to make all the comparisons, because for all intents and purposes, Sarah and I should have had the same role in our packs. Even though I was currently an unwilling Beta, I still saw in her what I should have—could have—been. When I looked at the two of us side by side, I found myself lacking. I stuffed my feelings back down and rolled my eyes at myself as Wolf nudged me.

"You guys do okay at the house today?" Cade asked conversationally as we walked along the well-worn path from the Rivers's house toward Sam and Megan's cabin where we'd had the bonfire last night.

"Sure. It's quiet," Van laughed.

Cade smiled. "Sometimes quiet is nice. Sometimes it gets old real quick."

Van nodded. "Also true."

We were silent a few minutes.

"So, how have things been, since, well, since I left?"

I couldn't tell if Van was asking out of politeness or if his voice was strained.

Cade's face broke into the stupid grin of a wolf completely in love.

"Good. Really, *really good.*"

Van laughed again and something passed between them I didn't quite understand.

"And no hard feelings?" Cade asked as the cabin came into view.

Van glanced sidelong at me with a look I could only describe as smoldery, and Wolf suddenly stood at attention. My cheeks flushed and I nearly tripped.

"No hard feelings at all," Van said, hint of a smile in his words. Cade raised an eyebrow and chuckled.

I wanted the earth to swallow me whole, even as a curious tingle slid into my middle. What game was Van playing?

Stupid Sasquatch butt.

With the cabin just ahead, mercifully, we made the rest of the short walk in companionable silence, though my insides were stewing with pent up emotions. Suddenly, I thought maybe I was the one that needed the run. My slitted eyes chanced a quick glance at Van. His shoulders were relaxed, his gait comfortable.

How unfair was that? Why was I the one suddenly tied all in knots? I was out here on this run for him, not because I needed it.

Cade's phone buzzed.

"I'll catch up, yeah? Give me a sec." Cade said as he swiped open his phone.

"Sure," Van said, totally unperturbed.

I growled. Wolf smirked. I growled at her, too.

"Katie, you okay?" Van asked.

Oh, fur on fire, tell me I didn't just growl out loud.

I cleared my throat. "Fine." My voice squeaked. I could have perished of mortification on the spot.

Van reached out and laced his fingers through mine. It's possible my mouth dropped open. I mean, he'd held my hand a fair amount over the past week, but this was different. This wasn't about making me feel safe or comforting me. This was...something else. And I didn't dare explore that too closely.

"What are you doing?" I hissed.

"Making sure you're fine," he whispered back.

"I am perfectly fine," I snarled, tugging my hand to no avail.

Van squeezed my hand gently, refusing to let go. Part of me relished the contact and that he insisted holding my hand. "What's wrong, Katie?"

What was wrong? Everything. Nothing. I had no idea. I stopped struggling, and Van's grip on my fingers gentled, his thumb brushing over my knuckles.

"You're going to give everyone ideas if you keep holding my hand like this," I finally said.

Van shrugged. "I'm okay with those ideas. Are you, Katie Clay?"

I stared at him, at the gorgeously infuriating grin that curled the right side of his mouth.

"Van, what are you doing?" Suspicion laced my tone, even as Wolf wanted to cozy up next to him.

"Hopefully showing you that last night's conversation was more than a business offer."

Words fled. He was *what*?

Before I could process the quagmire of emotions that ripped through me at his words, a large reddish-brown wolf loped over to us, followed by a white one, a silver wolf bringing up the rear. Immediately, Wolf identified them as Megan, Sarah, and Sam, respectively.

"Hey, guys," Cade called, jogging to catch up to us. "We can shift in the trees over there or in the cabin, whatever you're more comfortable with," he told us. Sarah's white wolf rubbed her head over Cade's side, his fingers stroking over her ears.

My heart flipped. Van showed no signs of anything bothering him at all. His hand still held mine loosely. What had come over him?

"Katie?" Van turned to me.

"Um, trees?" I struggled to bring my mind back to the present.

A few more minutes, and I had a moment of privacy to shift. Before I did, I closed my eyes and took a deep inhale of the piney forest. Spring was on its way, even though the chill of winter still tinted the air. Wolf nudged me.

I stripped, shivering as the cold bit into my naked skin. I let a shiver carry my fur through my skin. It rippled in the breeze as my bones creaked and cracked, sinews stretched, tail extended, and muscles corded.

Whiskers poked through my upper lip as it extended into my snout, scents of the woods filtering into my nostrils and sending messages to my Wolf's brain as the last shreds of my human skin dissolved into fur. My claws dug lightly into the turf beneath the tree where I stood on four paws.

With a mighty shake, I gave Wolf her head. She threw back her head and howled. The noise undulated up my throat, flowing past my lips and canines into the early evening air.

Donovan yipped, suddenly next to me then in my space, rubbing his shaggy head over my ruff and under my chin. Wolf relaxed a little in the familiar gesture of the Hazelton pack, letting Wolf scent Van and reciprocating. His cold nose nudged my cheek and I glanced at him sidelong. He nudged me again, tongue lolling, twinkle in his wolf's eyes. I thought he was flirting with me.

Audacious canid.

I curled my lips back slightly. Van chuffed and nudged me with his nose again. I rolled my eyes. The other wolves joined us then, and we spent a few minutes familiarizing our scents with each other. It was strange, but oddly pleasant to meet other werewolves. I'd not met any outside the Hazeltons since I'd fled my own pack of origin.

We ran. Even though I'd been in fur for the better part of our travels, I hadn't realized how much I'd craved the presence of other wolves. The little band of us ran along the river, dipping and leaping over ditches and rocks, divots along the river's edge. We were quiet, the only noises those of the forest, and the occasional chuff of breath and crack of branch under paw. The wilds soothed me, bringing relief to some of those rough, jagged parts of my spirit.

When we finally returned to the fire pit behind Sam's cabin, I felt lighter. We shifted back, said our goodbyes, and then Van and I made our way back to the Rivers's house.

A few steps into our meandering pace, Van took my hand again.

"Are you making this a habit?" I asked, still unsure how I felt about things.

"If you'll let me," he quipped.

I didn't have a retort for that but blinked curiously as Van let go of my hand, only to claim it again and lace our fingers together, his thumb sliding over the inside of my wrist. A shiver of pleasure worked over my shoulders. I did not want to be so attuned to him, but truth be told, I'd always been aware of Van. Ever since the second he and Angus had found me, bloodied on that pass.

He felt safe. And as soon as I'd recovered, he'd felt like something else. And now here he was, holding my hand of his own volition—I think romantically intended—and I didn't know what to do with it.

"Van, I can't Claim you," I whispered, emotion surging to form a tight knot in my throat.

His steps slowed. "Why?" He glanced at my face, his eyes unreadable.

"I don't want to be a transaction. And beyond that, if Alan knew I'd taken a mate, he'd use that to carve my heart straight from my chest. I won't do that to you. I won't do it to me, either."

He was quiet a moment but didn't release my hand.

"I don't want this to be just a transaction, Katie. We are not going to let Alan win. He can't have you. I won't allow it."

He didn't press the point, and I let it go, but his words tumbled around inside my brain.

CHAPTER 35

DONOVAN

The next two days stretched out in front of us as we hunkered down and tried to wait out the storm her uncle was brewing. I tried to be more intentional in my actions toward Katie. She didn't seem to believe me when I told her she was more than a business deal, so I determined I had to *show* her. I touched her more. Let my fingers brush her elbow. Held her hand. Touched the small of her back as I let her pass in front of me. Put my arm around her across the back of the couch as we watched movies. Her actions toward me didn't change. She held herself carefully in check, never letting herself relax into me. She never dissuaded me from my increased attentions, but she was careful not to encourage them either.

It was maddening.

I brought her coffee. Watched for ways I could do things for her. Surprisingly, doing those little things for her, and seeing her cautious reactions, increased my feelings for Katie in a major sort of way. I saw Katie's beauty. Her spirit. Saw things in her that I'd never appreciated. She got lunch for us every day. She did my laundry without asking. She watched sports with me and hollered when the opposing team scored. She ran in fur next to me each night.

I wanted to let my hands linger on her. Feel her skin beneath the pads of my fingers. I wanted to hold her. I wanted to Claim her.

But worst of all, I desperately wanted to kiss her.

And that was the one thing I'd promised her I wouldn't do. I wouldn't break my word to Katie. Not when I'd already messed up so many times with her, and not when memories of our one kiss were so tainted. The next time I kissed her would have to be her idea. But the waiting was hard.

I linked Angus again on Wednesday night, needing advice again, as Katie was still holding me at arm's length in terms of advances.

Angus.

You guys safe?

For the moment. I need more advice.

Angus groaned through our link. *This is so awkward for me. I hope you appreciate that.*

Yeah, yeah, I know. I rolled my eyes. *Look, I'm trying to woo her like you said. She's not reciprocating. She's not turning me away, but she's not responding, either.*

It's only been a few days.

I rolled my eyes again. *I know that. But what else can I do?*

You need to court her. Show her you're serious, Angus said.

Yeah. Thanks, I grumped. *I'm still getting called 'Sasquatch butt' thanks to the last round of your advice. I don't even know why I'm asking you,* I muttered.

Because I give excellent advice where the ladies are concerned. And who else would you ask? He snorted through the link.

I smirked.

But she's not pushing you away, is she? Emma's voice broke into my thoughts. I winced.

Emma? Are you there, too?

Of course, she answered sweetly. *Angus is telling me everything.*

I groaned.

Angus chuckled, the sound reverberating inside my head. *Emma says it's not all bad. If she's not pushing you away, there's still hope. Hang in there, little cousin.*

But do show her you're serious. Only if you are. You've got to be all in, Emma intoned, threat implied in her tone as she broke in again.

How did I manage to get both of them tangled up in my non-existent love life?

All in. Show her. Got it, I quipped. Not really. I had no idea how to show her I was serious. That I wanted her, not just to save her and make a political alliance. Claiming her would do all of those things, and maybe that's how my desire to Claim her had started, but those weren't my reasons now. I didn't know what else to do to show her I was serious.

You can do it! Grandpa Jesse hollered through our link. *Just do it better than last time!*

Grandpa? Seriously, is the whole pack there just waiting for a play by play? I asked, half expecting the entire pack had gathered there in Emma and Angus's house, awaiting the next installment of their favorite Beta soap opera.

Oh, quit grousing. He's over for dinner, Emma chided as if she'd been able to overhear the entire conversation.

Well, thanks for the support, guys, but I think I've had all the fun I can stand for now, I said to all three of them at once. Perk of being a Beta. I could communicate with more than one wolf at once, where they were limited. Wolf rolled his eyes, tongue lolling happily as the people I loved threw their support at me—however awkward it was.

Keep us up to date! Grandpa said. I could hear the smile in his voice.

CHAPTER 36

KATIE

I didn't know what to do with Van's new-found determination to…I wasn't even sure what he was doing. I liked it. So much. He *saw* me. Maybe for the first time. Whatever it was, his eyes followed me, and his fingers usually trailed after, raising gooseflesh all over my arms. I liked nothing better than to feel his hands brush over my elbow or my back. To have his arm come around me along the back of the couch, leaving the open invitation to curl up against his side.

And I wanted to. Badly.

But I couldn't.

I was convinced he wanted to Claim me. But I wasn't convinced it was because he wanted *me*. He liked me. I knew that. We were friends—and had been for years. He wanted to save me from my uncle, and my genes were everything the Hazelton pack could want, though my pack of origin left a few things to be desired. But we were playing a different ballgame now.

Now the stakes were higher—deadly high.

I had enough self-respect to want to be loved if I was going to be Claimed, and I had enough common sense and self-preservation to not give into the temptation of Claiming Van. Until Alan was stopped, I couldn't think beyond that. Until Alan made his next move, I didn't know what mine should be either. A large part of me hoped he'd make his move soon, and it would all be over, one way or the other. The part of me that was still that scared girl I'd been the night Alan had murdered my parents, still cowered in fear, quaking in the dark recesses of my mind.

I was at an impasse. Some weird juxtaposition of living in the past, being stuck in the present, and still unable to move forward into the future.

My emotions were in a tangle, and I was a hot mess.

CHAPTER 37

DONOVAN

With nothing but another long day stretching out in front of us, I riffled through Cade's old closet. I hoped he didn't mind too much. A smile quirked my lips when I found a few old board games tucked away in the very top of the closet behind some dusty boxes.

"Bingo," I said softly, then sneezed as a shower of dust rained down on me.

"Do you want a sandwich?" Katie called from the kitchen as my footsteps sounded on the stairs.

"Sure. Hey, I found our entertainment for the afternoon!"

I plopped the games down on the coffee table and walked to the kitchen.

"Ham and pepper jack today," she said as she handed me a plate.

"Looks good. Come on. Let's eat in the living room." I indicated she should go first. Wolf rumbled lightly inside as her spicy scent drifted up as she passed me. I kept my eyes locked on the back of her head, lest they wander father down where they really wanted to go.

"You found games!" The excitement in her voice melted some of the tension that seemed to constantly simmer in my middle.

"Yeah. I thought it might be a nice break from all the TV. Since it's raining, and neither of us particularly enjoy wet fur, I thought maybe we could play a few."

"Thanks, Van." She smiled up at me. And then a glint appeared in her dark eyes. "Now, prepare to be annihilated."

I chuckled as she moved an ancient game box towards me. A ship and crashing torpedo graced the top of the box.

"You're going down, Van." She smiled ferally as her eyes slit playfully.

"That's what you think, Katie Clay," I smirked. Katie was competitive to a fault. She always had been.

After tossing down our sandwiches, we moved to the floor and stretched out. The game took a lot longer than I remembered, but we were enjoying it. I was ahead by one torpedo shot, and she'd just bombed the first hit to my last ship. We were neck and neck. Whoever landed the next hit was going to win the game.

"A-9," she said, her eyes intently sweeping her board.

"Ha! Miss!" I crowed. Katie growled and shoved in a white peg hard enough her whole tray moved.

I consulted my pegs on the top of my game board where I had meticulously recorded each hit and miss. I had two options. One of them would win me the game, the other would likely allow Katie to win. Propping my cheek on my elbow, I stretched myself over the hard floor, contemplating my options. My hip was starting to get stiff against the carpet. I chewed my lip and resisted the urge to peek at Katie's game pieces. One more move and I could win.

"I-2."

"You Sasquatch butt!" Katie exploded. "You just sank my last ship!"

A laugh burst from my chest as Katie grabbed for a throw pillow to launch at my head. She was too close, and I grabbed her wrist instead, the pillow *thwapping* harmlessly against the floor behind me. An expression of irritated amusement flashed over her face, and in two seconds, she pounced.

"I almost won!" she hollered as she tackled me.

We laughed together, rolling around on the floor, wrestling like two pups, and scattering game pieces beneath us.

"I can't believe you won! That was an hour of my life! I was *sure* I had you beat," Katie said with a playful snarl as she rolled hard, pinning my back to the ground with her knee to my chest. She glared down at me triumphantly from her winning perch.

"You haven't won this, either." I snorted.

Jabbing her ribs where I knew she was the most ticklish, I grinned as she yelped and flinched hard enough her knee dislodged. Laughing and exulting in my momentary upper hand, I danced my fingers up her ribs and she squirmed and squealed, trying to get away. I snatched her around the waist and rolled us again, pinning her under the weight of my body, her hands trapped underneath my chest as I caged her in.

The atmosphere went from playful and carefree to crackling with electricity and awareness in less than a second. Breathing hard, I stared at her wide cinnamon eyes, fringed by dark lashes. Desire flashed through me, kicking my heart rate up and sending Wolf thrashing. Her lips parted and her quick breaths ghosted over my face. I swallowed hard, every part of me excruciatingly conscious of her curves smashed beneath me. I shifted so I wasn't crushing her, but hovered, bodies brushing together.

"Van," she whispered haltingly, though she made no move to get away.

My eyes trained on her perfect pink lips. Curse the promise I'd made her. Letting my gaze float back up to her eyes, I slowly traced the pad of my thumb over her bottom lip. A subtle tremor ran through her body, still against me, igniting every cell in mine, though still she did not try to wiggle free. I let my fingers whisper along the curve of her jaw, gently touching the place where her pulse pounded behind her ear, down her neck, my fingers raising gooseflesh over her skin. Softly running my fingers back up her neck then tangling them into the hair at the nape of her neck, I leaned in even closer, letting my nose skim her collar bone, the side of her neck, the outer shell of her ear. My thumb rubbed lightly at the throbbing pulse behind her ear as I scented her deeply. My eyes dilated, Wolf nearly beside himself as her allspice and maple scent filled my nose and pheromones clouded the air around us. Clenching my eyes tight, I took another deep inhale at her neck then pulled back only far enough to see her face. Her red-brown eyes were ringed in her wolf's yellow ones, her body quivering against mine, her want etched clearly in every line of her face.

"Claim me, Katie," I whispered, heart thundering in my ears. Wolf pushed me to Claim her first, but I knew it had to come from her. I wanted Katie for my mate. *I am in love with her.*

The realization struck me solidly between the eyes.

"Van, don't." She squeezed her eyes shut and shook her head slightly as if trying to rid it of a bad thought. My heart fell at yet another rejection, but I wasn't deterred. Not yet. She spoke again before I could offer resistance. "It's not real. It...it's just lust," she shoved the words from her lips as her eyebrows slanted together and her expression turned anguished.

My eyebrows shot up my forehead. "I'm not going to lie. There's plenty of lust right this second but give me enough credit to have lived long enough to know the difference. Does this feel like lust to you?" I gripped her palm, pressing it to my chest where my heart beat heavily against my ribs. "I want *you*, Katie. And I know the difference between lust and—"

"Get off me," she said, fear and hurt lurking in her eyes. I was so stunned, I toppled to the ground like a dried leaf when she pushed against my chest. She jumped up like a shot and fled the room.

I smelled blood. A lot of it. My heart catapulted into my throat, every sense on high alert as I leaped to my feet. Was Katie hurt?

Did *I* hurt her?

CHAPTER 38

KATIE

I ran to the bathroom. It was the closest form of refuge from the living room, but as soon as I crawled out from underneath Van and stood, I knew there was another reason I needed to make a beeline for the room.

Ugh! I wanted to beat my head on the side of the sink. Instead, I gripped it, a woozy sensation blurring my vision. I took a deep breath as my vision cleared. Wolf whined.

Well. This was fun.

"Katie!" Van pounded on the door and my nerves scattered, pulse jumping.

"What?" I yelled irritably, embarrassment and stupid lingering desire flushing my cheeks.

"Are you hurt?" he demanded through the door.

"What? No. I'm fine." My voice sounded strangled even to my own ears. Emotionally scarred for life? Probably.

"Katie, I smell blood. Are you hurt?" he repeated.

I rolled my eyes and let my forehead slide into my hands. This just kept getting better and better.

"No, Van. I'm fine. I just got my period two weeks early."

I almost snorted at the immediate silence that descended on the other side of the door. I supposed that was one way to put off any thoughts of Claiming. Wolf ducked her head.

"Is that normal? You...you're, nothing's wrong?"

I shook my head, heat radiating from my flushed cheeks.

"Too much stress. Stress triggers extra cycles for me sometimes," I said, wishing we could just be done with this conversation.

He cleared his throat. "Do you need anything?"

That was at least a useful question. "Actually, can you bring me my backpack and drop it right inside the door?"

His footsteps marched away from the door.

I blew a hot breath out my mouth and tried to collect myself.

Nothing like more awkwardness to add to our already strained relationship. I checked the damage. This one had started hard and fast. I needed fresh clothes. With elastic in the waist. I was bloated, a headache was brewing, and right then, cramps seared through my low belly. A heating pad would be great, too. Maybe I'd just take some ibuprofen and try for a nap.

Van knocked softly on the door. It was amazing what the word *period* did to a guy.

"Katie? I've got your backpack. I'm not looking, swear, just opening the door and dropping it in to you. Is that okay?"

"Yeah. That's fine," I said, cowering where I sat on the toilet behind the sink anyway. The door clicked open, and my black backpack came swinging into view and dropped unceremoniously into the middle of the tiny bathroom, right onto the blue fuzzy rug. The door shut.

"Van," I called before his footsteps echoed down the hallway.

"Yeah, Katie?"

I bit my lip. "Thanks," I said softly, knowing he would still hear.

"Sure. I'll be in the living room. Let me know if you need anything else."

"Okay," I whispered.

Mercifully, I still had a change of clothes that included my fuzzy gray sweatpants and everything else I needed in my bag.

I cleaned up, changed, and felt better once my jeans weren't cutting into my swollen belly. Instead of joining Van in the living room, I detoured to the laundry room and started a load with my dirty clothes.

I sighed again. I should probably go find Van. I wasn't exactly ignoring him, and I wasn't exactly embarrassed by what had happened…just…a little weirded out. That wasn't the sort of conversation Van and I were used to having.

But at least it superseded the awkwardness of whatever it was that had transpired between us on the floor. A hot flush rocketed through my body. I had never been in that position before. Literally or figuratively.

I almost believed that Van wanted me.

I still wasn't convinced I was anything other than a replacement for Sarah—my genes swapped for hers—a way for him to somehow assuage his wounded pride—but there had been something else in his gaze. In the way his body hovered over mine. In the way he'd scented me. In the way he'd immediately gone to get my bag and asked if there was anything else he could do. I shook my head and ran a hand down my face, struggling to right my emotions. Wolf paced inside, keyed up, jittery, and unsure.

In a weird sort of way, it felt like there was a new level of intimacy between the two of us.

I didn't know if that was safe.

CHAPTER 39
DONOVAN

Man, did I ever know how to make a situation worse. I scraped my hands through my hair and plunked back down on the couch. At least in my defense, I had been worried that something was seriously wrong with Katie. I guess things kind of *were* seriously wrong if Katie was stressed enough that it triggered her body to do whatever it was doing when it shouldn't be.

I really hoped it wasn't my fault—that I wasn't the cause of the extra stress. At least, I was relatively sure I wasn't the *only* cause of added stress.

I cringed at my next thought but swallowed down my pride and used my link.

Emma?

Donovan? You scared me to death. Wasn't expecting you to use your link. What's wrong? Emma replied concernedly in my head.

Hey, Emma. Sorry. No phone is very inconvenient. Um, I stammered, *Katie doesn't look like she's doing super well.*

What's wrong with her? Panic laced her voice.

She said she's really stressed and she's having an extra period.

Oh.

I charged on ahead, fumbling for the right words. *Sorry, I would have linked someone else, but you're the closest thing I've got to a sister. I...is there anything I can do for her? She sounded pretty miserable. She's still in the bathroom. Should I be worried?*

I could almost hear Emma smiling at me all the way in Oregon. *Van, sometimes you really are sweet. Yes. Listen up and take notes. You need to go get her a glass of water and some ibuprofen. If you've got hot chocolate, make her a cup of that, too. Any chance you've got a heating pad?*

I haven't seen one here. Not sure where to look?

If you can't find a heating pad, you can get a sock and fill it with rice. Knot the end and stick it in the microwave for about thirty-five seconds.

Okay. I can do this.

I know you can. The smile was back in her voice.

Anything else you can think of? I asked her as I made my way into the kitchen.

Read her body language. Be thoughtful. This is a great chance to practice those wooing skills.

Got it. Thanks, Emma.

You bet.

I did not 'got it,' but I'd do what Emma suggested. I found the bottle of medicine, got that, a glass of water, and a mug of hot chocolate together on a tray and put it on the end table and went to go find a sock.

I was just putting the rice sock down on the couch next to me when the bathroom door cracked open, and Katie exited. For whatever ridiculous reason, my heart rate kicked up. The door to the washer opened and soon I heard water going through the pipes. Slowly, Katie's footsteps came through the kitchen and into the living room. I turned to look at her from where I sat on the couch. She'd changed into sweatpants but still looked uncomfortable. Her right arm tracked to her left, sliding up and down her forearm as her eyes looked everywhere but at me.

"Hey, you okay?" I asked, a little uncomfortable myself, afraid that I'd made things more awkward with my attempts to check on her after my near-declaration and the most intense romantic encounter I'd ever had. Her eyes strayed to the side table.

"Is that hot chocolate?" she asked, her eyebrows raising.

"Um, yeah?" It came out sounding like a question.

A ghost of a smile flitted over her lips. She nodded and came around to the other side of the couch. "Did you seriously make a heating pad out of one of your socks?"

I couldn't tell if she was pleased or mocking me.

"Yeah," I answered again slowly.

She plopped down on the couch, and I think surprised us both when she threw her arms around me and hugged me. My arms slid around her, cradling her gently, Wolf lapping up the attention. A shudder trickled over her back, and she sniffed against my shoulder.

"Katie, are you crying?" I tried to keep the alarm out of my voice.

She sniffed again and pulled back. "Sorry. I don't mean to be. I'm irrational."

I smiled then and looped my arm around her shoulders again and tugged her back into my side. She cocooned herself under my arm, against my ribs and snugged up to my shoulder.

"How about I put a movie on, and you can drift off if you want to," I said.

She nodded against my chest as another errant tear streamed from the corner of her eye.

CHAPTER 40

KATIE

Raven dropped by later that evening. Most of my cramps had subsided, and I was feeling tired and worn out, though at least most of the awkwardness from the earlier game had also dwindled.

I was reading a book, curled up in the window seat at the back of the Rivers's house when Raven popped her head in the room.

"Hey, Katie."

"Oh, hi, Raven. I didn't hear you come in." I'd been completely and willfully absorbed in the book.

She smiled. "They guys are having a pick-up game of basketball. The girls are going to sit on the sidelines and finish up homework, though, truth be told, we'll probably do very little homework and mostly sit and talk. You wanna come?"

Did I want to go? I honestly wasn't sure. I still had an inferiority complex every time I saw Sarah, and I still felt like crap. But on the flip side, fresh air would probably be good for me, and it would get Van out of the house. He'd taken to pacing this evening, which told me he was going stir crazy. Maybe *I* was just driving him crazy. And probably not in the way he'd like.

"Sure," the word tumbled from my lips before I'd fully decided.

"Awesome! It's not too cold, but you'll probably want a jacket."

I put a slip of paper in to mark my spot between the pages and swung my legs over the edge of the seat.

"Katie?" Van called. Heat rushed to my face without my permission. "Do you want to go?" he asked, likely assuming Raven had provided the details.

"Yeah. Sounds good," I offered. His whole face lit up and my belly twinged. He was so handsome when his eyes sparked like that. I blinked. Thoughts like that would do me no good.

"Great! I'm going to go get my shoes. Want me to grab your hoodie while I'm upstairs?"

"Thanks." The twinge intensified. I secretly loved it when he was intentional about doing things for me.

We made it to the old concrete court not far from the Rivers's house and Sam's cabin, and it wasn't lost on anyone that Van was holding my hand when we approached. Wisely, he'd let my hand alone until we were nearly there, just within sight range of the others, before he snatched up my fingers. I wasn't expecting it, and by the time I realized what was going on, yanking my hand back would have only made things more awkward. I glanced up at him, accusation in my eyes. Van smirked and had the audacity to wink at me as he squeezed my fingers. When I turned back to the other assembled wolves, Rachel's eyebrows hiked up her forehead and a grin curled the corner of her mouth.

Van tugged me closer and whispered against my ear, in full view of everyone, "I'm probably going to get my tail handed to me in this basketball game. Cheer for me anyway?" His breath brushed the fine hairs against my ears and a shiver worked down my spine.

"Only if your team mascot is a Sasquatch," I retorted, pulling away. My nerves were on fire that close to him.

Van snorted, squeezed my fingers again and released me into the knot of girls clustered near the side of the court.

"No. He's not interested at all," Rachel quipped as I awkwardly fidgeted with the hem of my shirt.

"Yeah. I think it's a recent development," I said dryly.

"I don't know that it was all that recent," Sarah said.

I looked at her sharply. She smiled. "Rachel wasn't wrong when she said he was looking at you at the bonfire."

What exactly had Sarah noticed? And why was she looking that closely at Van? Jealousy and insecurity warred within me, tying my insides into gigantic knots I had no hope of detangling.

"Did anyone think to bring a blanket to sit on?" Megan asked, directing my dizzying thoughts toward her, and giving them a place to settle that didn't involve a stupidly handsome werewolf.

"Guess it's just the grass then," Raven said.

We made our way over to a patch of mostly dead grass, the green of spring not quite ready to take over things, and sat in a cluster. The guys checked the ball, and Cade started taking it down the court.

"I actually do have some homework," Megan said ruefully.

"What are you working on?" Raven asked.

"It's English. We just finished *Pride and Prejudice*, and I've got answer guides to finish filling out."

"Oh, I love the story of *Pride and Prejudice*," I said. Books. Books were safe. I could talk about books without things being weird.

"I love the back and forth between Darcy and Elizabeth, and I like how they are basically in love with each other before they even realize it," Rachel said as she pulled a notebook out of her bag. Her eyes flitted to me before training back to her notebook. My cheeks burned.

"Is that The Wedding Notebook?" Raven asked as she leaned over Rachel's shoulder.

"It is." Rachel giggled.

"Did you settle on your dress style yet?" Sarah asked. She leaned back, her long legs crossing at the ankles.

"I know I don't want an empire waist. And I think my hips are too big proportionately to look good in a mermaid-style skirt." Rachel chewed her lip as she consulted her notes.

"You can always try on all the styles on Saturday to see what you like," Sarah said.

"True. I don't want to make everyone wait on me the entire day though. I'm sure the dress-trying-on will be long enough as it is." Rachel grinned ruefully.

"Rachel, this is *your* wedding. You're the only one among us to have the *full* human wedding experience. Try on *all* the dresses. We want to do all the human wedding things with you," Megan said with a smile.

I glanced around the circle of girls. "None of you had a human wedding?" It wasn't unusual for werewolves to skip the human formalities, but a lot of us still wanted them. I didn't think Megan had been a wolf all that long—a curiosity in and of itself. I assumed she, at least, would have wanted all the trappings.

Megan grinned again. "I sort of did. Sarah did, though it was fairly last minute and not as big an affair as Rachel's will be."

Rachel grinned like she had a mouth full of pie. "I'm the first of three daughters to get married. My mother is just a little bit excited. And she's using it as an excuse to make Joanie—my sister who had some issues last year—re-enter our family circle. It's helping her, and we're all really happy about it."

"We're happy about it for and with you," Sarah said.

"Okay, was it Wickham who went after Lydia, or did Lydia go after Wickham first? Or is this a trick question? Too many other things happened while I was reading this, and I can't remember," Megan glared at her paper as she twirled her ink pen.

Ah, something I could weigh in on with some authority. "I think Wickham ran off with Lydia because she was willing. Wickham is likely the instigator, but also likely received ample encouragement from Lydia. She desperately wanted to beat her sisters to the altar, and as the youngest child, she'd been coddled and spoiled, possibly beyond redemption in their social circles. Together, they made an explosive combination."

Four pairs of eyes stared at me and that uncomfortable wiggle in my gut let me know I'd likely gone too far in revealing my bookish obsessions.

"Wow. You're amazing. May I quote you on that?" Megan asked.

"Of course," I laughed nervously.

"Where did you learn all that?" Raven asked.

I shrugged, uncomfortable being the center of attention. "I've always loved books. I've read most of the classics, and because I am that nerd, I've researched a lot of them, too." Since I'd done most of school as some weird hybrid of homeschool via the public education system, I'd had the time on my hands to indulge my love of books. They were my escape from reality. And I had needed them.

"That's awesome. I love books, but I don't like the classics as well as I like modern fantasy and paranormal," Rachel confessed.

"I read plenty of those, too," I said, my shoulders relaxing some of their tension.

"Give me a solid murder mystery," Sarah said.

We chatted books for a time, which did wonders for my nerves. I loved talking about books. Eventually, the conversation turned toward some things that were going on at school, and I tuned out and turned back to the boys still playing on the court.

Bowen and Cade were taking on Sam, Kyp, and Van. It was obvious they'd all played basketball at some point, but Cade and Bowen far outmatched the others, though they were no slouches. They twisted, turned, dribbled, and shot. The ball bounced off the rim, slapped against the old concrete, and sailed through the air and through the net.

Of their own volition, my eyes strayed to Van. He was smiling, a light sheen of sweat beading on his forehead, enjoying the camaraderie with the other boys. Cade faked and spun around Kyp, only to be picked up by Sam. Cade dribbled around him with some fancy footwork and pivoted to shoot. At the last minute, Van broke free and came up to block the shot. Cade didn't stop, and the two of them collided with an audible thud that made me wince. Both Van and Cade staggered back, nearly toppling over. Sarah fairly radiated a growl and Wolf's hackles rose.

Van looked at Sarah, who was looking at Cade, and memories of Van kissing me, but wanting Sarah, crashed through my brain. All the confidence that had built up over the evening talking with the girls about books fled. I was suddenly reminded how bloated, unattractive, and un-put-together I felt. I was aware enough to realize my crazy hormones were affecting my judgement, but it still sucked. I sighed.

CHAPTER 41

DONOVAN

My head smarted where I'd collided with Cade. Sarah's quiet growl rippled over my skin and my eyes flew to hers, suddenly aware that my status as an outsider, ally or no, was secondary to her ties to her mate. I realized it was probably a knee-jerk reaction from her wolf. I'd have done the same thing if someone had bashed into Katie, and she wasn't even my mate. I just wanted her to be.

"Ow," Cade laughed as he rubbed his shoulder. "I think that was a foul. Let me just go sink these two shots and win the game." His trademark cocky smile was back on his face, and I snorted.

"You just need an excuse to save face, so we don't beat you," Sam said. His blue eyes twinkled as he stretched his back.

"Hate to break it to you, but we're still ahead," Bowen said with a smirk.

Cade sunk his two shots, then the game halted as we migrated toward the girls by some unspoken agreement. It was true, Bowen and Cade had still won, but we'd had fun, and until I'd accidentally annoyed Sarah, it had been a great time. Wolf shifted his weight inside, wanting to double check that our status with our allies—friends—was still solidified. The human part of me was sure that there had been no real insult given, but it reminded me that I was here as a guest. And that I could potentially bring a very real threat to the Rock Falls packs. I needed to be sure I didn't outstay my welcome.

Sarah laced her fingers with Cade's as soon as they were close enough. I didn't miss the way her eyes quickly assessed him. He grinned crookedly at her. Cade was not offended. And I was reasonably sure Sarah's reaction was a wolfish one, not because she was legitimately concerned I had it out for Cade. I didn't. Not at all. I may have been bitter when I first got back to Arcadia Bay, but I felt no lingering anything beyond polite friendship for Sarah.

My eyes tracked to Katie. Just the sight of her red-black hair sent my blood pumping quicker. She rubbed the toe of her shoe in the grass. Her face was pale, but twin spots of red stood out high on her cheeks and Wolf sat up in alarm. She wasn't sick, was she? All thoughts of Cade, Sarah, and alliances fled as Wolf stood up in alarm, all my focus homed in on Katie. I desperately wished I could ask her if she was well using the link, but because she'd never officially joined the Hazelton pack, that wasn't an option.

Instead, I decided to make an executive decision and remove us both from the situation.

"Thanks for the game, guys. See you around?" I said, casually letting my hand graze Katie's back to subtly turn her back in the direction of the Rivers's house.

"Sure! Maybe we'll play another round tomorrow," Cade called back. I nodded and waved to the group.

"Oh! Katie," Megan called, "I was going to tell you and then we all got sidetracked with everything else. Saturday night is the Spring Concert in the Park. They do it every other year at the fairgrounds. We're all going after Rachel's big day of wedding shopping."

"And you should still definitely come wedding dress shopping with us," Rachel interrupted.

Megan smiled at her friend before turning back to us. "If you guys want to come, we can all go as a group. I checked the weather, and it looks like things will be nice and not too cold."

"Yeah, maybe," Katie said noncommittally. "Thanks for inviting us."

"Sure. See you all tomorrow?" Megan said.

"Probably." Katie smiled—a small smile, but still a smile.

We said our goodbyes then turned to walk back. Katie was quiet and kept her arms folded against her chest, intentionally keeping me from holding her hand. Wolf paced inside, antsy and a little achy with her repeated rejections.

"Katie, talk to me," I finally said once the Rivers's house was in view, and we were alone.

She sighed. "I don't know what there is to say."

"Why are you...I'm not sure if you're sad, or angry, or miffed at me, or if you're sick. I want to help you, Katie, but I don't know what's going on right now."

She stopped walking, pausing to look out at the river not far from where we stood. Water rippled over stones and the soft noises of it were soothing.

"I'm hormonal for one thing," she said at length.

I cringed at that new territory I had no idea how to navigate.

"I'm stressed about Alan and the rest of the pack." She was quiet, but a storm still brewed behind her eyes.

"What else?" I prodded gently. I was fairly certain *I* was part of what was bothering her, but I didn't know the particulars. I wanted to crush her in a hug as tears filled her eyes and hung precariously on her bottom lashes.

"I'm in this no-man's land. I can't move forward; I can't go home. I hate the way you look at Sarah, even though I can't do anything about it. I know part of me is being irrational, but the other part of me hates it. You say you want to Claim me, but I'm *not* a substitute for Sarah. I won't Claim you. Regardless of how much I might want you, I refuse to be second best. My parents—for the time I had them—raised me with more self-respect than that. This," she waved her hands between us, "isn't a replacement for what you lost with Sarah. I'm not Sarah. I won't ever be Sarah."

Her words about broke my heart. How did I make her understand what she meant to me? "I *know* you're not Sarah. I don't *want* you to be Sarah. I want you to be *you*." Wolf paced inside me. "I can't help it if I occasionally see Sarah if she's in a group with us. But that doesn't mean I'm looking *at* her." How did I make her see that I *couldn't* look at Sarah now, even if I wanted to? Not only was she Claimed, mated, and happily married to Cade, but I *only* wanted *Katie*. Frustration boiled inside. Wolf pawed in agitation. "Does it help to know that I get jealous every time you talk to one of the other guys?"

She sniffed. I tugged my hands through my hair.

"Do you want me, Katie?" The words dropped out of my mouth.

"I've *always* wanted you, Van," she snarled, angry and teary.

"Then is it so impossible to imagine that I might want you back?" I asked her as Wolf howled in frustration inside me. "Why won't you believe me when I tell you that I don't want a political alliance, I don't want your Alpha genes, I don't want all the trouble your uncle is going to bring, but I *do* want *you*?" My chest heaved as I dragged my hands through my hair again. I wanted to throttle her and kiss her. I couldn't decide which I wanted to do more.

She said nothing, just gaped at me, her eyes wide.

"What is it about me you don't want?" I finished on a broken whisper.

CHAPTER 42

KATIE

"What is it about me you don't want?"

At Van's whispered words, the tears smarting against my eyes spilled over. I wanted *everything* about Van. But a part of me still wasn't convinced he understood—what Alan would do to him if I Claimed him, and that I wasn't Sarah. The part of me that always felt lesser than roared to life as a sob choked out.

"It's not that I don't want you, Van. It's that I can't have you." I shrugged, not sure I could explain it any more clearly than that.

"Yes. You can." Suddenly, he was in my space. His hands locked around my waist and brought me gently against his chest. "Claim *me*, Katie. I want nothing more than to belong to *you*."

"What do you see when you look at me, Van?" I said, expecting a response about genes and bloodlines and a desire to protect me. I struggled to read his expression through the tears still welling. My hands found his chest, felt his heart beating steadily but quickly beneath my fingertips.

"I see fire. A girl who does nothing in half measures. Who loves deeply. Who holds herself in check because she's scared someone else will get hurt if she doesn't. A girl who protects the pack that took her in by any means she has. Even if it means leaving their collective safety and putting herself at risk. I see a girl whose heart is kind and generous. A girl who is so beautiful it takes my breath away." He dipped his head, so he was whispering in my ear. "I see the girl I want to make my mate."

Gooseflesh broke out over my skin as Wolf practically shook with pent up tension and not a small thread of desire. Van pulled back just far enough to look me in the eyes.

"I want to kiss you really bad right now, Katie," his eyes dipped quickly to my lips before darting back to mine, "but I promised you. And that's important to me. I don't want to mess things up worse than I have already. But you should know that just looking at you turns me on. And before you accuse me of being all lustful again, I'm grown enough to know the difference between lust and emotion." He leaned down to whisper in my ear once more. My toes tingled, anxious and anticipating his words. "Sarah never once turned me on the way you do." Lightning struck my heart, electrifying every one of my cells.

I was utterly speechless. Van pulled back and searched my face a moment more before speaking again.

"Sarah is beautiful. She's a lovely girl. She's got all the right genes, all the right pedigree, she's smart and will probably make an excellent leader. But she's not *you*. You are heart and soul, fire and passion. Being with you the past few weeks has made me realize how much *you* matter to me. I've always valued your friendship. Never more than I do now."

We stared at each other for a long minute. My heart pounded so hard against my breastbone, Van could likely feel it reverberating in his own chest. My mouth was dry as his words tumbled around inside me. A tiny spark of hope flared to life. I knew I should quash it but couldn't quite bring myself to do it. I'd loved this boy so long. Searching his face, I saw no trace of doubt behind his words. Nothing to indicate that he wasn't looking at and seeing me. Me—Katie Clay, Kaylee Snowdon—it didn't matter to him. It dawned on me then. He knew my entire story. Knew what had happened to me, to my parents, what my uncle and brother had done. But he hadn't run. He'd stayed beside me every step of the way. Faithful and true. Wolf settled. It still didn't erase the problems my uncle posed.

But if Van meant what he said, and he still wanted to Claim me, then the new possibilities that opened up were equally terrifying and exhilarating.

My eyes flitted back to his, searching, questioning, daring to hope.

"Take your uncle out of the equation. Would you consider my offer then?" Van's hazel gaze drilled into me. My heart thudded. If Uncle Alan and his pack of misbegotten dogs weren't a threat to me, what could my life be then?

I blinked. I'd honestly never thought about my future in those terms. Ever since I fled the Snowdon pack, my life had been consumed by dread of them. Of what would happen to me if they found me, and then later, what might happen to me once I turned eighteen and reached majority.

Van lightly traced the pad of his thumb down my cheek before lightly rubbing an errant piece of hair between his fingers. It was hard to breathe with him looking at me like that—like I was the sun and his world revolved around me.

"Your uncle will not be a factor forever. We are going to figure out a way to keep you safe and take him out. After that, then what? Would you consider me then?"

I had never considered anyone. Wolf nudged me. But I had daydreamed. And every single daydream had included Donovan Hazelton.

I balanced on the edge of a precipice. Was it possible that everything I wanted was within my grasp?

I held the female Alpha gene. By rights, with my parents gone and my uncle my enemy, who I Claimed was *my* decision.

Did I...*could* I consider Donovan Hazelton?

The earth seemed to stop moving as silence blanketed us in a bubble of our own creation. We stared at each other as thoughts, hopes, dreams, and nightmares tumbled inside my head.

I nodded slowly, afraid my voice wouldn't work.

A smile broke out over Van's lips. His perfect lips. His hand cupped my face as his other, still at my waist, tightened, thumb brushing over my hip.

"Would you let me court you? I'm sure I'll make plenty of mistakes, and you'll probably call me Sasquatch butt more times than I can count. But please. Give me this chance." He smiled fully and I couldn't stop my lips from crooking upward. "Let me in, Katie. Don't hold me at arm's length."

"Van," I breathed. I wrapped my arms around his neck, and screwed my eyes shut as more tears leaked out. His arms came around me, nearly crushing me against him. Nothing had ever felt so good. Terror and desire pinged around inside me with the utterance of one word.

"Okay."

Chapter 43

Donovan

"Okay."

Okay. Okay? *Okay!*

"Katie," I whispered against her hair as my heart grew wings and Wolf threatened to erupt through my skin in his excitement.

"Slowly, Van," she murmured against the side of my neck. Her lips innocently brushed my skin as she spoke and sent a shiver racing down my back.

"Slowly." I strangled on the word. Relief, excitement, and desire tingled across the tops of my shoulders. She pulled back, and reluctantly, I let her ease from my chest, though I kept my hands draped loosely on the tops of her hips. Magnificent curves. Her hands rested on my biceps, and I barely resisted the urge to flex them.

"I...this needs to go slow Van." She swallowed. "You can court me, but I need to be able to call the shots. I need to know this is what *I* need. I can't let you and your cloud of pheromones come in and make me forget everything I need to do."

A stupid grin tipped my lips. "I have a cloud of pheromones that makes you forget yourself?"

She glared. "Shut up. I've been aware of you from the second I met you."

I snorted and pulled her back in for another hug.

"You call the shots. But I think we've established that I'm not a mind reader. If you need something, you need to tell me."

"I'll try to."

I let my hand brush down the length of her ponytail.

Later that night as I stretched out on Cade's old bed, I linked Dad.

Dad, Katie is officially letting me court her.

Our Katie? I didn't know you were interested.

I am now. I grimaced, wondering how often I'd unintentionally hurt Katie by not reciprocating her feelings, though I knew we'd always relied on each other's friendship. Still. If she'd felt even a fraction of what I felt for her now, I knew my lack of deeper feelings must have stung.

What brought on this change? Dad's voice broke me from my thoughts.

I think spending time with Katie while we were on the run made me appreciate her more than I ever have.

That's good, Son. Speaking of being on the run, once things are cleared with Katie's uncle, you all should be safe to come home. Nothing has come of the girl that saw you shift. I did some digging. She has a history—she won't be a reliable or credible witness. Even if she has told anyone, no one would take her seriously.

That's at least a relief. We were quiet a moment. *Dad, you approve of Katie, don't you?* I felt the need to ask outright.

As a mate? I think she'd compliment you well. I'm just surprised to find that you have an interest in her since you never seem to have before. It certainly doesn't hurt that Katie has the right genes.

I winced as Dad's comment, though perfectly logical and something any werewolf Alpha would consider, it brought my first attempt at approaching Claiming screaming to the front of my mind.

I think it's just been slow in coming. But she wants to be sure I'm what she wants—and I think the whole thing with her uncle needs to be completely resolved before she Claims me, but my heart is set on Katie. I want to make her your daughter-in-law.

Dad chuckled through the link. *I'd like nothing more, Donovan. Good luck.*

Thanks, Dad.

Now. To deal with the uncle. Because now he was the thing standing between me and my desired mate.

Wolf snorted inside, ready to take on this new challenge.

CHAPTER 44

KATIE

Fortunately, the next two days passed peaceably. My stupid extra cycle ended, my body felt better, and my erratic hormonal emotions calmed. Things were quiet. Van and I played more games, watched more movies, and we talked. Openly. About what we each wanted. Both now and for the future.

It was a sort of healing balm that sparked a new level of intimacy between us. While I still hadn't let him kiss me again—I wasn't kidding when I told him I needed to take things slow—he hadn't once pushed me.

I didn't go dress shopping with the girls on Saturday, but I was looking forward to the concert in the park. I figured there'd be enough people there to get lost in, in the unlikely event I needed to. Van wasn't concerned, especially considering we were all going together with the group.

The girls got back from dress shopping and came straight over to the Rivers's house, bursting with tales of tulle, satin, and lace, ready to whisk me away to Rachel's house to get ready for the spring concert.

"She'll still be on pack land. The rest of the guys are meeting us there in an hour." Rachel smiled sweetly at Van as he protested their enthusiasm as they practically man handled me out the door to get ready at Rachel's house with them.

"Katie isn't going anywhere without me," Van said, a hint of dominance in his voice as he followed us out onto the stoop. "If she wants to go, I'll come, and just stay out of your way." He wasn't budging.

Wolf snorted at the insinuation that I couldn't take care of myself. The human part of my shushed her, knowing his overprotectiveness wasn't a belief in my weakness, but a belief in the vileness of my uncle, and his desire to protect me—the way a mate would. That thought curled pleasantly in my belly.

"Might as well come on then," I said with a shrug that likely looked more casual than I felt.

Van sat silent and resolute the whole way over, crammed into a car full of she-wolves.

"I'll just stay in the living room," Van said wearily once we got to Rachel's house. He sounded so exhausted that a chuckle wiggled its way from my throat. He smiled ruefully at me as he sat on the couch.

"Come right in here to the kitchen, and make yourself at home, Donovan. Kyp will be here soon, too, and you two can visit about all the manly things," Rachel's mother enthused. I bit back a snort as Van's smile turned plastered on and his eyes got large.

"She's harmless," Rachel whispered conspiratorially as we headed up the stairs.

We spilled into Rachel's room, and I realized the other girls had bags they were plopping down. Megan kicked her shoes off and wiggled her toes before she pulled her sweater off over her head, leaving her in jeans and a sparkly cami.

Glancing around, Raven was pulling out a change of clothes, too. The feeling I was about to commit a social faux pas hovered near my backbone as my fingers grazed over the thin layer of shirt covering my abdomen.

"Bathroom?" I asked, suddenly needing an excuse to leave the room for a few minutes.

"Sure. One door down to the left," Rachel said.

I took a minute in the restroom, collecting myself in the silence before reentering the fray.

Rachel didn't miss a beat. "You are going to have so much fun tonight. They don't do this every year like they do HarvestFest, more like every other or so, but it's such a lovely, romantic time. Music, food trucks, beverage stands, crafter booths, and then a concert. It's going to be stellar," Rachel enthused, her green eyes sparkling as her red curls bounced with excitement all their own.

"You've just got romance on the brain," Sarah teased, looking pointedly at Rachel's ring finger. The diamond seemed to sparkle all the brighter upon inspection.

Rachel's laugh was a tinkling of bells. "I mean, it's not like you can blame me." She shrugged and wiggled her fingers, ring catching the light again. "I *do* rather have wedding *everything* on the brain. Katie, I wish you could have come today. I think I found The Dress. We're going to one other dress store next weekend that we just couldn't squeeze in today, but I think the one I found today is the one I want." She whipped her phone out and showed me. It was gorgeous. The silky white bodice cinched in around her waist then gently flared over her hips to rest against the ground in a beautiful silhouette. Tiny rhinestones glittered in a tasteful but elegant pattern over the top and trailed over part of the skirt, leaving a froth of fluffy tulle peeking out from a part in the silk overskirt.

"It's beautiful—*you're* beautiful in it!" I said even as a curl of self-consciousness unfurled in my stomach as I took in what the other girls were wearing. Sarah had on a pink sweater and a skirt. Rachel wore a black dress with a smattering of red cherries on it and a matching red cardigan. The whole outfit looked like it came straight out of an updated 50's magazine. Megan and Raven had on jeans, at least, but both had on tops that could have easily passed for dressy casual.

"Sarah, before I forget, did you happen to get notes in Jadel's class today?" Megan turned the conversation.

I had on jeans and a literary-themed t-shirt. And a ratty old zip up hoodie.

Was this concert a dressy sort of affair? My fingers twisted into the hem of my worn cotton t-shirt.

Rachel caught my eye and tilted her head slightly toward the hallway. I followed her out the door.

"Don't take this the wrong way, and please don't be offended. But do you want to borrow a dress or a shirt?" Rachel smiled kindly.

Appreciation swelled in my chest. "Are you sure you don't mind?"

Rachel chuckled. "Megan is already wearing one of my shirts. And this is her cardigan." Rachel winked. "I don't mind at all. What strikes your fancy? You know, I have this green dress that would look amazing with your hair. It would look super cute with a denim jacket, then you won't freeze when the sun goes down."

In the end, I had on Rachel's dress, Sarah's denim jacket, a pair of Raven's booties still somehow in Rachel's closet, and a silver hair clip from Megan that I used to pull back the front of my hair, leaving the back down and straight.

I felt pretty as I stood in front of the mirror in Rachel's bedroom. My freckles dusted my cheeks and nose, a rosy flush that looked attractive rather than embarrassed kissing my skin. I had on makeup for the first time since I left Arcadia Bay. I hadn't realized how much I enjoyed—and had missed—looking girly.

Maybe it was because I knew there was a certain wolf downstairs that I wanted to impress. My cheeks darkened. Wolf chuffed.

"Donovan is not going to be able to take his eyes off you. You're practically sparkling." Raven smiled as she took in my ensemble. "Here. This is the perfect shade of lip gloss." She passed me a tube. Popping the top off, I ran a quick coat over my lips, liking the soft color they added. Nothing over the top, just a little enhancement.

"Thanks," I said, handing it back.

"My money says that lipstick gets taken off by someone else's lips tonight," Raven said with a smile and quick elbow tap.

I snorted. "I'm not sure we're quite there yet." Although the thought of kissing Van again made my knees weak and my belly quiver.

"He might change your mind once he sees you. He looks at you like you're the only girl in the world. Add a raised hemline and some flirting, and he'll practically be a puddle at your feet." Sarah smiled as she finished her assessment, and in that moment, she somehow ceased to be my competition. She was rooting for me. For me and Van. Heat that had nothing to do with the blush staining my cheeks flooded my chest.

Male voices tumbled up to Rachel's room as we finished our final preparations. I stepped down the stairs after Sarah, ready to leave. Wolf puffed her chest out, immediately aware when Van's gaze locked on us. I glanced up, meeting his stare.

Sparkles erupted inside me, fizzing and whirling in my belly. He drank me in like parched ground soaking up water. To my own jealous satisfaction, Van didn't even notice Sarah in front of me. His eyes stayed trained on me the whole way down the stairs.

Conversation and greetings circled around us as the other girls found their mates in the room, but time stopped in the bubble surrounding Van and me.

"Wow," he murmured.

I couldn't stop the curve of my lips. It was *good* to be seen.

He let his eyes slide over me and I fought to keep my skin from flushing as Wolf preened. I didn't wear dresses often, but if Van looked at me like this, I'd wear them every day for the rest of my life.

"You guys ready?" Bowen broke into the bubble surrounding us. My skin did flush then as I caught the hint of a knowing smile curling his lips.

"Yes," I muttered, wishing my pale skin didn't show my embarrassment as easily as it did.

"Have a wonderful time," Mrs. Crumb came to walk us out. "Rachel, I'm not sure if Joanie is feeling up to going tonight, so I think we're going to stay in," she said softly, not realizing that every werewolf in the room could easily hear her words. "But you go and have a wonderful time." The older woman smiled at her daughter, her hair once the same shade as Rachel's, now graying at the temples.

"Rock out to whoever that new-fangled band is that they brought in." Mr. Crumb's face broke into a smile and his eyes creased at the corners. He crossed the room and looped an arm around his wife.

"Daddy," Rachel laughed. She quickly hugged her parents.

"Take care of our girl," Mr. Crumb said to Kyp, clapping him lightly on the shoulder and squeezing slightly.

"Always," Kyp answered with a smile, though seriousness rang in his tone. Mr. Crumb gave Kyp a quick side hug. Kyp smiled again, patting his soon to be father-in-law on the back.

"You all enjoy the concert," Mrs. Crumb said as we tumbled out the door.

Van threaded our fingers, the callouses on his hands sending tingling little fireworks up my arm. His thumb rubbed the inside of my wrist once and Wolf nearly collapsed in a heap, tongue lolling.

Had I really agreed to let this boy court me?

Wolf nudged me. Why didn't I just Claim him already?

Because I was still scared he'd be ripped from me like the rest of my family.

But...maybe I didn't have to let fear rule me.

CHAPTER 45

DONOVAN

Seeing Katie in that dress, her collarbones peeking out from the neckline of green material that fit tight over her chest, the way it draped around her hips...

Bottom line, I was turned on.

Very. Turned on.

Wolf puffed his chest out as a dozen scenarios to get Katie alone dazzled through my brain. Not that it would have mattered. I gave Katie my word that I wouldn't kiss her again, though I loathed myself for it now. I wanted nothing more in the world than to plant my lips on hers and never surface for air again.

"Hey, Donovan."

I yanked my mind from those thoughts to Cade, trying to register the words he was saying.

"...thought you might need a vehicle. Use mine." Cade tossed me a key. I caught it more from reflex than anything else, and then stared stupidly at it for a sec as my thoughts bounced from Katie in her dress to Cade's truck. I was really glad I still had my driver's license.

Because Katie. In Cade's truck. With me. Alone.

A slow smile curved my lips.

"Thanks. Follow you guys to the fairgrounds?"

"Sounds good!" Cade called back. He ushered Sarah into a white car next to an older truck.

I opened the door to the truck and nodded for Katie to get in. I let my fingers brush her elbow and couldn't quite keep my eyes from sliding over the curves that passed my face as her skirt swished into the front seat.

"You all the way in?" I asked innocently, my hand resting on her ankle, right above the short boots she wore. Her eyes grew wide, though I thought I could see the beginnings of sparks in their depths.

Good. Maybe my hormones weren't the only ones in play. I gave her a saucy wink and let my fingers slide up her leg a few inches before reluctantly breaking contact and shutting the door.

I traipsed around to the other side, rocking up into the truck and sticking the key into the ignition. I turned it over, then glanced at Katie.

"You ready?" Meaning, would she rather go somewhere, just the two of us, and make out?

Katie leaned over, innocently exposing a glorious valley of shadow between...I jerked my eyes away and back to hers.

"You're smelling all pheromoney again," she whispered, a wicked smile crinkling her lips.

I swallowed hard.

"You look hot." I shrugged.

She rolled her eyes, though the smile stayed on her lips as I pulled out of the driveway and followed the caravan of werewolves towards the fairgrounds.

CHAPTER 46

KATIE

Wolf exulted in the scent of the chemicals Van was giving off. If I'd been in doubt of his attraction to me before, I wasn't anymore. The air in the cab of the truck was thick with pheromones. Van was doing nothing to rein it in either.

I allowed myself to admit that I didn't want him to. There was something unbelievably sexy about knowing the boy I loved found me attractive. Part of me was starting to believe there could be a real chance to Claim Van. If I survived the confrontation I knew was coming.

I was reaching the end of my limits. I was done being afraid. Afraid I couldn't protect everyone I loved. Afraid my uncle was coming after me. He was—it was fact. There was nothing I could do about it. Donovan Hazelton wanted to be with me. Despite what was coming.

Glancing at our fingers, Van's clasping mine lightly on the center of the seat between us, I let myself fall into the familiar daydream of my future.

Years from now, I wanted a quiet life. A safe life. A life where I spent my days in the bookstore but spent my nights with Van. Where I shared my life with him.

I drew a shuddering breath. Van's fingers squeezed mine once. He said nothing, letting me be still. Wolf nudged me. He knew me well enough to know I needed time to think. In fact, I doubted anyone knew me better than Van did.

That thought drew a tendril of comfort over my shoulders. Emma might understand me better, and Angus and his parents loved me like one of their own, yet...

I glanced at Van. He took his eyes from the road a split second to meet my gaze and smile. The corners of his eyes crinkled, his look soft as his gaze caressed my face before turning back to the road.

Was I ready to believe that Van loved me unconditionally? He hadn't said the words. But all his actions leading up to us sitting here in the middle of a borrowed truck said he felt them.

Leaning back against the seat, I flipped my palm up, letting our fingers lace together. I stared out the window at the passing woods on the edge of the road. Most were still stark and gray, barren from the cold of winter that still lingered. But every so often, there was a flash of green. A hint of color that suggested not everything was dead. There was hope yet—life ready to spring up and crack through the dead casement shrouded in the darkness.

My heart beat steadily in my chest. Maybe I was like those trees. I'd been dead and barren, hiding in my fear for so long that I'd forgotten how to live. My blood stirred as Van's thumb brushed the outside of my palm. Maybe there was green life inside me yet. It was time to let the dead break away and fall to rest.

It was time to live.

And I wanted my living to include Van.

The fairgrounds were bordered on three sides by ancient trees, thick with age and hung with mystery. And twinkling fairy lights. The lights twisted up trunks and into the canopy of branches and truly turned the fairgrounds into a fantasy paradise.

"It's beautiful," I said as Van pulled into the grassy meadow that served as the parking lot. There were already dozens of vehicles parked in front of us.

"So are you," he said softly. I glanced at him. He smiled, his hazel eyes bordered by thick lashes, his lids at half-mast.

"Thank you," I whispered, suddenly flustered. Raven's words about letting someone else take the lipstick off me floated through my brain.

That could be a fun possibility to explore.

"I'll get your door."

"You just want to feel me up again," I retorted, the teasing words feeling familiar on my tongue. Truthfully, I hoped he'd touch me so carefully again. Goosebumps popped over my arms at the thought.

"Say the word," he said with a grin and a wink.

I snorted as a rush of bubbles set loose inside me. Van had always been a little bit of a flirt, but I liked it now that it was solely directed at me.

Van opened the door, and gazed pointedly at my legs, visible from my knees to Raven's adorable ankle booties.

He looked up at me through the dark fringe of his lashes, his expression positively roguish. My breath caught as his fingers grazed my skin.

"Just how far should I feel you up here, Katie Clay?" His voice was playful but low and throaty as his fingers grazed my ankle, and slowly dragged up my shin.

"And here I thought you were a gentleman." The words scraped from my throat.

He lifted an eyebrow and trailed his fingers two inches higher. "Very gentle," he whispered with a delicious teasing smirk. My tongue froze to the roof of my mouth.

I felt it when my eyes dilated. Wolf was practically in ecstasy. Van's hand closed over my knee, his exploration of my skin halting before it crossed into inappropriate territory. My heart pounded against my ribs as my mouth dried. He leaned in, his face entering my space. Blood roared in my ears as his lips neared my cheek. If I turned my face a fraction, our mouths would meet.

Before I could move, Van whispered in my ear. The hush of his words spangling across my skin and teasing the hairs at the base of my neck. "Now who smells all pheremony?"

I squeaked as he squeezed my knee, his thumb hitting the sensitive spot on the inside, tickling me. He stepped back and I didn't know if I should glare at him, slug him, or kiss him.

"You play dirty, Donovan Hazelton," I said, finding my voice. I slit my eyes at him for good measure, even though I wasn't put out with him. His quick squeeze had jolted me back to my senses.

Van quirked an eyebrow, ridiculously handsome smile curling half his lips.

"I'm playing for keeps, Katie Clay." He winked as he took my hand, unnecessarily helping me down from the truck.

At least out in the open, there was enough air and other smells from food trucks, kettle corn, and the jumble of other bodies to dampen the scent of *attraction* that was probably lingering on every inch of my skin.

"Is that an axe throwing booth?" Megan asked, her voice tight as we paused inside the gates to put on our admission wrist bands. Sam pulled her into his side.

"It's not archery. It's fine." He smiled at her.

Megan rolled her eyes and muttered. "It had better not be archery."

"Oh. Sad day. No kettle corn unless there's a worker shift change," Rachel said mournfully.

"Why not?" I asked, glancing at the stand set up not far from us. The buttery sugar-coated popcorn scent wafted over, and my mouth watered.

Rachel leaned in conspiratorially to whisper. "We always try to watch out for Tobias. That's him in the glasses with the bright orange hair stirring the kettle. Try not to get too close to him. He's one of the nicest people on the planet, but he's horrendously allergic to dogs. He sneezes like his life depends on it when we get near him. Poor boy."

I snorted. I couldn't help it. "That's awful."

Kyp nodded, rueful expression on his face. "Awful for him for sure. I didn't know that when I first moved here. I sat next to him in one of our classes. He had to leave the room, he was so affected. Eyes swelled up, snot running. It was gross. I felt terrible."

"It's not like you knew," Rachel said, leaning into him adoringly.

"True, but still."

At least the group I was with probably wouldn't notice if I made googly eyes at Van, they were all so besotted with their own significant others. Wolf's chest swelled. I wasn't the outsider in that department now either. I glanced at Van. He hadn't let go of my hand since we left the truck. My belly flipped in a sweet sort of excitement, realizing that for the first time, I could call someone mine if I wanted to.

If I allowed myself to.

"I'm going to go find us a spot and spread our blankets out," Megan said as she looked over toward the pavilion where prime spots on the grass in front of the outdoor stage were quickly filling.

"I'll come, too. You guys go get your food, then we can switch off," Sam said to the rest of us.

This must have been common practice as the other wolves passed their blankets over to Sam and Megan without a pause.

We scattered to get snacks and drinks before the show started. There was an amazing looking taco truck—complete with a giant rotating taco on the top. Van and I both chose Mexican, then found the rest of the group trickling back to the spot Megan and Sam had staked out.

Van plopped down on a corner of a blanket, bending his knees outward, legs outstretched. He glanced up at me and winked as he gave a subtle nod to his lap.

As in, would I care to sit there? Right there—between his legs?

Yes. Yes, I would like to sit there, but I was pretty sure I'd drip queso all down my borrowed clothes if I did, from the sheer distraction of being that...intimately settled against Van.

Instead, willing my face to keep from bursting into flame for the hundredth time that night, I sat beside him as gracefully as possible, careful to cross my knees to the side in my dress. Though I did let my legs rest against Van's.

"What happens if I see cheese sauce at the corner of your mouth?" Van whispered as he cracked the tub of queso open and put it, steaming, on the ground in front of us so we could both reach it.

"Then you tell me?" I replied.

"I thought maybe I should lick it off. It seems like the gentlemanly thing to do," he quipped, still whispering in my ear.

I snorted. "Shut up and hand me the chips."

While I was quickly warming to the thought of kissing Van again—wanting to kiss Van again—I didn't want it to be so public. I was still inexperienced in these things, and wanted to practice in private before letting the whole world in.

The concert started, and I felt myself relax, surrounded by new friends, Van beside me, and the possibilities of what could be swirling happily inside me.

CHAPTER 47

DONOVAN

My ears buzzed with the bass that boomed through the speakers, even as my nerves buzzed with Katie leaning against me for most of the concert.

Wolf huffed happily. Progress. I could feel it. Katie was responding, and I desperately hoped she understood that I was serious in my pursuit of her.

About an hour and a half in, the band started a slow, slightly melancholy song. Katie stiffened beside me.

"I'm ready to go," Katie said softly as she stood and stretched.

"You guys heading out early?" Cade called from where he and Sarah sat cuddled on their plaid blanket next to us. I glanced up at Katie's faraway expression then nodded at Cade.

"We'll see you guys tomorrow. Thanks for the invite," I said, standing and bending to retrieve the borrowed blanket.

"That's okay. Just leave it. I'll take care of it," Raven said with a smile.

"Thanks." Katie smiled at the rest of the group before glancing at me shyly.

Twilight was falling, the sky a riot of orange, pink, and encroaching purples and blues. A few early stars dotted the blazing remnants as the sun set.

I grabbed Katie's fingers in mine, twining them before she could protest. She bit her lip but said nothing as we wove our way through the sprinkling of couples still on the grass as the music swelled.

"Did you have fun tonight?" I asked, hoping she had. Everything had been weighing on her. Her shoulders seemed to droop with the constant tension hanging over her. Tonight, they'd lifted. At least for a while.

"I did." She glanced up at me. "I really did. This was a good idea." Her fingers subtly squeezed mine. "Thanks, Van."

"You're welcome," I said, deciding to up the flirtation. I dropped her hand and looped my arm around her shoulders. She stiffened in surprise for a second before her muscles lost their rigidity. She curled into my side as we walked towards the crowded field where the vehicles were parked. She took a shuddering breath.

Wolf immediately went on alert. She'd been happy tonight. Why was she shutting down now?

"What's wrong, Katie?" I squeezed her shoulder lightly.

"I...that last song. It reminded me of my parents."

"Oh, Katie, I'm sorry." Regret curled in my chest. "I wanted tonight to be a fun outing—not something that made you sad."

"No. It's all right. I did have fun. I'm not...sad. Exactly. Just kind of suddenly got lost in memories."

I wasn't sure what to say to that. She leaned into me a little more as we exited the fairgrounds, their twinkling trees seeming to wave goodbye, and entered the lines of vehicles and headed towards Cade's borrowed truck.

"Van?"

"Yeah?"

"Do you know why I said my last name was Clay when you all found me?"

I halted beside Cade's truck and turned to look at her fully. "No, I don't." I let my arm slide from her shoulder but lightly kept her fingers in mine.

She took a shuddering breath. "When you and Angus found me on that mountain pass, bleeding, about dead, and terrified out of my mind, the first thing I remember smelling was clay and hazelnuts—I smelled you."

I didn't mean to, but I leaned in, my heart rate accelerating. Wolf swelled with pride.

"You were whispering to me. Telling me that you'd get me to safety, that you'd make sure I was all right." She blinked rapidly a few times. "I don't know why—especially after what I'd just gone through— but I immediately felt safe with you—believed you when you said you'd take care of me. And you have. The Hazelton pack took me in with no explanation, gave me a family when I had none. But because of that, I've always associated your scent with safety." She swallowed hard, and I brushed a strand of fiery black hair behind her ear, letting the pads of my fingers graze her cheek and the side of her neck. "So when it was time to tell you my name, Clay slipped out. It was so different from my own name, but it reminded me that I still had hope. That there were wolves out there who wanted to help me, who wouldn't hurt or betray me. All my girlish hopes were set on you that day on the mountain pass, though I don't know that I realized it at the time. It was unfair of me to put all that on you. I'm sorry if that has weighed unfairly on you and our friendship."

Emotion churned in my chest. Hot, fierce, and pulsing. So many different feelings, but one stood out the most. I loved Katie.

"What if I want you to? What if I want to be the wolf that holds your hopes?" I stepped closer, crowding her space until we were all but touching.

"Van," she murmured, her chest a hair's breadth from mine.

"What, Katie Clay?" I said, my voice rough, my insides on fire.

"This isn't Cade's truck."

I didn't move my eyes from her face, even as I registered what she was saying. Embarrassment threatened to crawl up my spine, but the red-hot desire to kiss her burned it away.

"I don't think its owner will mind if we borrow the door for a minute." I stepped closer, our chests touching, as my hands snaked around the waist of her dress, coming to rest on her sides.

Tension pinged between us as I stared at her lips, memorizing the bow of them. I could feel her heart beating like a hummingbird's wings.

"You know, it's getting really hard to keep my promise to you," I said, letting my eyes rove slowly over her face, lingering pointedly on her lips. Her fingers gripped my shirt. I leaned my head down, resting my forehead against hers.

"Maybe you could break it. Just once," Katie whispered.

I jerked back far enough to search her eyes. They were full and luminous, the sunset creating little fires that danced and whirled in the darkness of her enlarged pupils.

"Just once?" I whispered as my heart lurched into my throat.

She didn't speak, but a whimper escaped her throat as her hands released my shirt, one palm flat against my chest, the other sliding up my neck, tugging my face down to hers.

I didn't need any more encouragement. Wolf lunged, the ferocity of the movement taking me by surprise. I rocked with the momentum, my body pushing Katie's hard against the side of the truck that wasn't Cade's.

Blaring to life, the truck's alarm blasted my eardrums somewhere into sonic space.

"Oh, crap!"

Katie jerked even farther into my chest, my arms instinctively encircling her. A bubble of laughter escaped her throat. She tried to detangle herself from me, but she stepped on a rock, and twisted awkwardly, throwing me off balance, and sending me careening into the side of the car parked on the other side.

Another alarm shrieked through the stillness of the fairgrounds, competing with the music and the truck's pulsing noise that sent Wolf thrashing with every wail.

"Come on!" Katie yelped with a chuckle as she grabbed my hand and tugged me. Seeing the hilarity of the situation, even though I was mortified and desperate to taste her lips again, I laughed and ran after her—the two of us like kids caught with their hands in the proverbial cookie jar.

CHAPTER 48

KATIE

We were still laughing as we ran through the maze of vehicles, finally finding Cade's truck. Van popped the locks, and I didn't wait for him, suddenly shy, but opened the door and hopped in. Heat flooded my cheeks. I wanted him to kiss me. Had all but kissed him myself. I bit the inside of my cheek. Maybe it was time to tell Van I wanted to Claim him.

Van jumped in the other side and brought the truck to life. His eyes met mine playfully for a moment, long lashes giving his eyes a smoldery look that curled my toes.

Somehow, we managed to get back to the Rivers's house without too much awkward tension.

"Hang on," Van said as I reached for the door. "I didn't get to open it for you when we left. At least let me act like a gentleman once this evening." He winked and little skitters of anticipation winged over me. Goosebumps tingled up my legs at the memory of his fingers and his teasing.

It was only a few seconds before he was opening my door. I twisted in the seat, my legs sliding down to the ground, bare underneath my borrowed dress. I hesitated, wondering what he'd do. Suddenly, Van was there, in my space. His hands, wide and hot, slid around my waist. I gasped.

"You know, we were in a really good spot before we set off all the alarms," he said softly as he set me down but didn't let go. His eyes twinkled with a hint of mischief when I chanced a glance up at his face. I could make out his accelerated heartbeat as he nudged me with his fingers, his body grazing mine as he walked us a step backward. My shoulders touched the cool metal of the truck, his body moving with aching slowness, touching me—his chest to mine, my hips to his, legs tangled. Wolf panted and I swallowed hard.

"We were?" I squeaked as my hands snaked up to his biceps without my permission. *We're in a really good spot right now.*

"Mmhmm." The noise rumbled in his chest as he leaned down and let his nose skim my neck. Gooseflesh broke out on my arms to match my legs, and I audibly sucked in a breath. "In fact," he started slowly, "I'm fairly certain it was implied you might even like it if I kissed you."

"Once?" The word puffed from my lips, knowing full well that if I let him kiss me once, I'd want more.

"I'll take what I can get," he said, and I could hear the smirk in his voice, even as his hands tightened, and his breath brushed against my jaw. One hand slid lower to the curve of my hip as his other trailed white fire up my side, skimmed my upper arm and cupped the back of my neck. He pulled back far enough to look me in the eye. "Katie," his voice, suddenly serious, rasped, sending tingles shooting to my toes. My fingers tightened against the corded muscles of his arms. "I'm only kissing *you.*" Pain lurked in the depths of his eyes and my heart beat an extra measure. "I *only* want to kiss *you,*" he whispered. His thumb stroked along the edge of my jaw.

I believed him.

He must have seen what he wanted to because without hesitation his lips lowered, stopping just a hair's breadth from mine. Our breath mingled and longing speared me. Wolf nudged me forcefully.

Van's lips brushed against mine, like the barest hint of butterfly wings. My eyes shut and my body arched against him. I couldn't help it. I pulled his head down, and his mouth crushed against mine.

Sparks ignited inside me, and flames raged through my limbs. He groaned against my mouth, pressing against me, grasping me to his chest. Knees weak, heart soaring, my lips opened. Taking it as the invitation it was, Van's tongue slid into my mouth. His scent wrapped around me, making me dizzy.

The first time he'd kissed me, it'd been euphoric until I realized he wasn't kissing me. But there was none of that doubt this time.

"Katie," he whispered, his lips against my skin before his tongue found mine again. Heat danced over my limbs like embers. He whispered my name again, over, and over, letting me know he only wanted me. He only kissed me. Wolf surrendered, pushing us toward this boy we'd loved for so long.

Letting go of my insecurities, my fear that he couldn't want me the way I wanted him, I melted against his chest. His arms caught me around my back before his hands dragged to my shoulders, his lips searching, probing, dancing along the edge of my jaw, down where my pulse raged along my neck. His hands cradled my face as his mouth found mine again, parting my lips with his tongue.

"Katie, I love you." The whispered words shocked me to my core, erupting in molten rock and flooding my veins with magma. Wolf howled with abandon inside me. Van's lips didn't stop. He kissed me slowly, but with an intensity I hadn't realized one could be kissed with.

My fingers twisted into his hair, dragging myself closer to him so that not even air fit between us.

I wanted to say the words back to him, opened my mouth to, but he covered the words, our kiss affecting me so that the ground seemed to shake beneath me.

"I love you," he whispered roughly. "I love you," he said as his lips slowed even more. "I love you," he whispered as he pulled back. "I love you, Katie Clay." He said it looking me straight in the eye. My chest was heaving, my head spinning, Wolf barking with joy. My tongue, though it had been properly active moments before now seemed stuck to the roof of my mouth. "I love you," he said softly once more before he dipped his head and brushed his lips across mine once more.

We stood there, breathing heavy, staring at each other.

"I don't know that there's been a time I've known you that I didn't love you," I finally said. I still wasn't convinced I could have a future with this boy with my uncle still in play, but I knew I couldn't leave him in doubt of what I felt. Not after he'd laid himself bare before me. Not when Van was the future of my choice. A future I would fight for.

He dragged his thumb down the side of my jaw before leaning over and softly kissing my forehead. My eyes slid shut and I held onto him, unwilling to let the moment end. I needed to be held.

Van's arms stayed around me. He kissed my temple, rubbed my neck with one hand while his other stayed wrapped around me, cradling me against his chest. I took a shuddering breath.

"How about some hot tea and maybe an old movie?" Van suggested at length. "Or a bubble bath and a book if you'd rather be alone for a while," he added.

If my heart wasn't already utterly claimed, those words right there would have done it.

"Tea and a movie sounds perfect." I finally pulled back far enough to look at him.

"You'll always be safe with me, Katie Clay."

"I know," I whispered, heart soaring. I lifted on tip toe and pressed one more kiss to his mouth. He smiled down at me, eyes roving over my face. I'd never felt so *seen*. "Maybe we could interrupt the movie with a few more kisses?" I hedged with a smile.

He growled appreciatively. "Could we, please?"

I giggled, giddy and lighter than I'd felt in years.

Grasping my fingers in his, we slowly started up the sidewalk up to the front door.

Without warning, claws of agony ripped down my back. I cried out, crashing to the concrete as pain radiated through my bones. Without my permission, fur burst through my arms, my bones contorted, and fire raged through me, consuming me.

I screamed as my soul was torn from my body as my wolf expanded, grew, heaved. Muscles corded my forearms, my legs, twisted into hard knots over my abdomen.

"Katie!" Van yelled from somewhere far away. Agony lashed at me, yanking my wolf and I apart and smashing us back together. Chemicals flooded my system as bile rose in the back of my throat. Sweat slicked over my skin, matting my fur and the shredded remains of my borrowed dress and jacket.

At last, the torture stopped, and I gagged, spitting out the bile burning in the back of my mouth, slinging my wolf's head to rid myself of the taste. I shivered, shuddering as I took stock of myself. Cords emerged in my brain.

No. *No, no, no, NO.*

Hatred, agony, pain, snarling, gnashing, rage pulsated through my head, pounding with my heartbeat.

They were here. I was no longer the Beta.

I was the Alpha.

CHAPTER 49

DONOVAN

"Katie!" My heart pounded so hard in my chest, I feared it would explode against the back side of my ribs. She thrashed and grunted, her eyes rolling back in her head. Russet fur erupted through her skin, pushing out, receding, then shoving through again. Panic gripped me, indecision warring inside. I didn't know what to do—had no idea what was happening—just that Katie was in pain, and I was powerless to help her.

She screamed and Wolf thrashed, desperate to help her, to do something, but we were completely immobilized. Scents hurtled through me—sweat, fear, and something baser. Katie flailed on the hard concrete. I reached for her, but her claws caught my forearm, ripping my shirt and drawing a line of blood that welled and dripped to the ground.

Her scream turned into a howl, the mournful, terrified notes raising every hair on my body. Like a tidal wave, her scent crashed into me, shocking me as I realized what was happening to her.

She was becoming Alpha.

Her uncle was dead.

"Katie?" I asked tentatively. We sank together onto the ground, her wolf's form lurching from the concrete path then collapsing onto the grass, my arms reaching for her.

She whined, pawing at her face like she was trying to rid herself of a bad dream.

"Easy," I whispered, taking her paw, and gently moving it from her face. I stroked the sweaty fur back from around her eyes, letting my hands stoke soothingly over her ruff. "Do you know what's happened?"

She nodded miserably, a mournful whimper escaping her throat. Wolf paced inside, agitated, upset.

"Do you want to try to shift back—how can I help you? Katie, I...I don't know what to do." I was still at a loss—I'd never experienced this before, this changing from Beta to Alpha by force. "Come on, let's get into the house and we'll figure out what to do next." Because strategy was something active I could do. It gave me something to focus on besides the raw, cold terror trying to replace the blood in my veins.

Katie spent long agonizing minutes pacing, whining, sobbing, and growling in the kitchen. I'd retrieved her backpack and put it inside the doorway, but every time I tried to offer help or venture my head in, Katie snapped her jaws at me, effectively letting me know my presence wasn't wanted.

It about crushed my soul.

After an eternity had passed, I heard popping and the scratch of claws on the tile floor. Katie took a shuddering breath as her backpack unzipped.

Everything in me wanted to rush in and try to fix things. Instead, I clenched my fists and rocked on my heels, biting the inside of my cheek as I waited for her.

A few minutes later, her tear-streaked face appeared in the doorway of the kitchen. She swiped under her eyes, the skin pink and puffy. With a sniffle, she met my gaze and hesitated. Helpless, I lifted my arms in open invitation, unsure what she'd do, or what she needed. Her face crumpled before she swallowed hard and blew a hard breath, regaining some of her composure. She shook her head once then launched herself at me, jumping, and clamping her arms around my neck.

"Katie, I've got you. I've got you," I whispered as I held her tightly, letting one hand smooth over her tangled hair, wild down her back.

I walked us to the couch, Katie's feet barely touching the ground as she clung to me.

"Talk to me, Katie Clay. Please," I begged as I sat, pulling Katie onto my lap, unwilling to let her go any farther than the circle of my arms.

She pulled back far enough to look me in the eye. "They're here." She touched her temple. "I can't get rid of them. The mental block isn't working. The...the anger, the hate, the savageness. It's awful. Some of it is directed at me. Some of them feel abandoned, others hate that I'm now their Alpha. I don't know what's happened to my uncle, but if he's dead, and Ben is dead," she shrugged. "There can be no other alternative unless I die, too. I'm the Alpha of the remains of the Snowdon pack. My hand is forced."

We were quiet a minute, each of us processing.

"You could abdicate your position. It's extremely rare, but it could be done," I ventured.

"You can't hear them, Van. If I let them go now, they'd all go feral. The tether to the Alpha is the only thing keeping them sane. I'm the last biological heir of the Snowdon line. If I'm gone, there will be anarchy and chaos as the strongest fight it out and the rest flee to their own ends. I can feel it brewing. The whole link aches with sorrow and pent-up aggression." She shook her head as a solitary tear dripped from her lower lashes. "I don't think I'm strong enough to do this. I never wanted to be Alpha. I don't want it—don't want the pack that betrayed me, that stood by while my uncle killed my father, my mother, probably my brother. The pack that should have done everything in its power to protect me stripped away every single thing from me. They have betrayed me and broken my trust in a way that can never be mended. I want nothing to do with them." Her lip quivered. She bit down on it. "But if I let them go now, then I'm responsible for what happens afterward. What if they go and hurt someone? What if innocent people are killed because of my weakness? Because I cut their one tether loose. Enough people have died at the hands of that pack. No more." She leaned her forehead against mine and shut her eyes. "But that means I have no choice but to take my place as Alpha," she whispered raggedly.

"No," I insisted. They'd challenge her the second she stepped foot on Snowdon pack ground. "No. We'll find a way." I had no idea what we were going to do, but I did know that somehow, we'd find a way around this. Katie would not be trapped by her own pack. Not again. Not while I could do something about it.

"There's no use in hiding anymore." Katie raised her head, her hand lingering on my shoulder. "If Alan is dead, and I'm the Alpha, no one can force me to give up my inheritance. There is no reason for Kaylee Snowdon to stay dead."

"Unless you want her to." She'd told me that Kaylee was dead. Katie was who she was now.

She scrubbed her hands down her face. "I hate what my uncle has done. Hate that he's put me in this position at all. The whole thing just sucks."

"It does. I'm so sorry," I whispered in the dark, pushing a piece of hair behind her ear.

"Part of me wants to leave now. Just go, deal with it head on, even though the thought of Alan dead fills me with both elation and dread. Dread because...I don't know how he died. Did he fall off a cliff? Or, or did someone kill him? And are they just waiting for me to show up to finish the job?" She shivered. "The other part wants to stay hidden forever. But if I do, I'll never be able to silence the voices."

"So we sleep tonight. We start back tomorrow morning. We tell my Dad. We make a plan. You're not alone in this, Katie. You're not a scared little girl who hadn't even had her first shift. You are a strong, powerful woman, with strong, powerful allies who will rush to your side if you say the word." *I'd die for you.* Emotion churned in my gut.

She closed her eyes again, taking in measured breaths. Finally, she stared at me. "Link your dad. Tell him what has happened. See what he says. This has to end. One way or the other, it *will* end."

I called Dominic and let him know we'd be leaving the day after tomorrow.

"You all are welcome to stay longer. Is there anything else we can do?" Dominic graciously offered.

"The Wolfe pack has already done what was needed when you unquestioningly offered us shelter and a place to hide. We are in your debt. I believe we can handle things on our own from here." It was true. The Hazelton pack was sizeable, and Katie confirmed, the Snowdon pack was smaller. We outnumbered them easily. We only needed to out-strategize them, and we'd be okay.

Steve and Amalie came home about eleven o'clock. We were up, furiously planning, using game pieces as pawns and packs.

"You all making a new board game here?" Steve asked with a smile as he came into the room.

"Just preparing. We'll be heading out early Monday morning." I stood and shook Steve's hand. "Thank you for letting us stay here."

"Your hospitality has meant more than you'll ever know," Katie said, surprising me when she came forward and looped both Steve and Amalie into a hug.

"You're always welcome here," Amalie said, smiling as she patted Katie's back. "You, too, Donovan," she said.

I dipped my head, marveling at how much my life had changed in the past months, and how much of that change had happened because of the Rivers—both Steve and Amalie, but more importantly, Cade. If he had been less honorable, or if he hadn't already fallen in love with Sarah, it was likely I'd be mated to her by now. I shivered at the thought as Wolf snorted.

I would have no one but Katie.

That night we continued planning. Neither of us slept. We were too keyed up. Too much was at stake. I linked Dad and explained the situation, what had happened.

She's Alpha now? Dad asked again.

She is. Fully. The pack is there inside her head.

Who is her Beta?

Some beast named Brogan. Apparently, he was her uncle's best friend. No doubt they've been thick as thieves since Alan took over the pack.

That would confirm beyond doubt that her brother has been removed from the picture.

Right. Though we don't know how Alan died—that is a matter of concern.

Agreed. We will proceed with caution and make sure you go in with all senses on high alert. How is Katie handling things? Dad asked.

I glanced over to where Katie sat at the other end of the couch, pen moving manically over a notebook as she scribbled paragraph after paragraph. I wasn't exactly sure what she was doing, but I knew it was part of her planning and processing.

About as well as I supposed she can be? I offered.

She needs you, Son.

I know, Dad. We need you and the pack, too. On that note, here's what we're thinking. I explained our general plan to Dad.

We'll do it all on our side. Keep us looped.

I will, Dad.

And Donovan?

Yeah, Dad?

Be careful. I love you, Son.

Love you, too, Dad.

Dawn lit the sky with gray smudges by the time we solidified our plans.

"This is it," Katie said as she rubbed the heel of one hand against her eye.

"This is it," I repeated. We were as prepared strategy-wise as we could be. I glanced at the clock. It was nearly six in the morning. I scrubbed a tired hand down my face.

I tried to calculate how many hours it would take us to cover the miles between us and where we needed to go. We didn't have an easy mode of transportation, and I wasn't eager to hop another bus. My brain needed rest. I was aware enough to know I wasn't calculating well.

A quiet knock on the door sent Wolf racing to his feet, and my eyes dilated as fur prickled under my skin.

"Van?" Katie whispered, as on edge as I was.

"Stay in the kitchen," I told her. Quickly, I got up from the table in the dining room and went to the front door while Katie entered the kitchen.

I glanced out the window in the door and sighed in relief. "It's Dominic," I said softly, but loud enough I knew Katie would hear. Opening the door, a blast of pre-dawn air washed over me. Katie shivered in the chill.

"Dominic," I said, motioning with my arm that he should come in.

He shook his head. "Not staying. Just came to give you these. He held up something in his fist and dropped a key ring with a single key on it into my open palm.

I stared at it blankly, then glanced back to the leader of the Wolfe pack.

Dominic smirked at my lack of eloquence. "I tinker on old cars as a hobby. I keep one or two around that cannot be traced, just for times like this. Take this one. It's old, and has a lot of miles on it, but I've rebuilt the engine completely. It'll get you back home with no trouble. If anyone runs the plates, they'll come back all legal, but registered to a person in Florida. All things will check out, but will not lead back to us, or to you."

Gratitude swelled in my chest. This was the piece of the puzzle we'd been missing. We had nothing but our own paws in terms of transport, and this would let us enact our plan with speed and with rested bodies.

"Thank you," I said, emotion squeezing my throat.

"You're welcome." Dominic nodded once, clasped my extended forearm, turned, and walked into the mist.

Katie and I napped until early afternoon. Once we were functional, we packed up our few belongings. While we slept, Steve and Amalie had gone to the store and stocked the car with bags of non-perishables and water. It was exactly the kind of thoughtful, helpful behavior that sent appreciation rushing to my toes, never more grateful that we were allies with the Wolfe pack.

CHAPTER 50

KATIE

The goodbyes were harder than I expected. I'd grown to care for and deeply respect the wolves my own age in the packs at Rock Falls in the short week and a half I'd spent with them. I hadn't expected to make friends among them, especially with Sarah, but after a few rounds of profuse apologizing for shredding my borrowed clothes, I was convinced that they weren't angry with me, and I thought they might genuinely miss me the way I'd miss them.

Van and I stowed our scarce belongings in Dominic's gifted car, and after hugging the Rivers goodbye, we set off just before the crack of dawn Monday morning.

"Do we need a GPS location, Katie, or are you just going to give me general directions until we're closer?" Van asked as he pulled down the lane that would lead us to the highway and away from Rock Falls.

I sighed, sad to leave, terrified of what was coming and of what I didn't know, but resolved. The mantle of my responsibilities sat squarely on my shoulders. Wolf stood resolutely, ready to take on this burden. To deal with *them*. I wasn't sure how yet, but I would.

"Katie?" Van asked. He took his right hand off the steering wheel and rested it gently on my knee, giving me a little squeeze, though not hard enough to tickle.

"We've got to go to Washington."

"Any stops before then?"

I shook my head. "No. There will be two stops once we get inside the state, but until then, it's just you, me, and a lot of miles."

"I like the you and me part." He smiled.

I grinned back, strained, but appreciative of the effort. I twined my fingers with his still on top of my knee.

It was a lot of miles.

We drove until dark, stopping only when my bladder demanded it, or we needed gas.

"I think we might have made better time today than I did driving home with Angus," Van said as he grabbed his backpack and mine from the back seat of the car.

"You know he has to peruse the entire snack section anytime he stops," I said, smiling at memories of the few times I'd left the immediate Hazelton territory. Most of those times had been with Van and Angus.

I blinked against the neon of the lone sign as it flickered erratically. We were stopped at a cheap motel that took cash. There was no point in hiding in the brush. I was the Alpha. I was coming to the pack. We didn't want to draw unnecessary attention because I was still the *SnowSpace Tech* heiress, and with my face plastered on national news outlets, it was safer for me to remain in anonymity. So instead of the Ritz, here we were in the middle of nowhere.

Surprisingly, a whiff of freshness met us as Van unlocked the door.

"Wow. I have to say, for the rates we just paid, I'm seriously impressed." The room had been dirt cheap. I expected...not a lot. But even though the trappings on the bed and the carpet were worn, they appeared clean. Wolf sniffed, detecting laundry detergent and shampoo rather than old must.

My eyes zeroed in on the one bed as my heart kicked up.

One very small, twin-sized bed.

"And the couch even pulls out," Van said with a wink, probably hearing my accelerated pulse. My cheeks flushed.

I cleared my throat.

"Good," I squeaked. Wolf chuffed.

In the end, Van said the pull-out mattress was so thin, it was like sleeping on metal bars. He folded it back up and bunked on the couch. I offered him the bed, but he declined.

"It would be extremely ungentlemanly of me to take the bed. And I have Sasquatch butt points I need to make up. Give me two points and I'll happily take the couch."

I snorted. "Did you seriously just make up a random point system?"

"Yeah, I kinda did. But if it helps keep me in your good graces, I think I'll work on earning them anyway." He smiled and winked from across the room as he finished spreading the spare sheets over the once-stylish couch.

"And why would you want to stay in my good graces, Donovan Hazelton?" I teased, craving the light banter that took my mind from darker things that loomed.

"Because you're an excellent kisser. And I hear a man in a woman's good graces gets more kisses than one who isn't." His teeth twinkled as he smiled wide.

"That's probably true," I said as I handed him a folded blue fuzzy blanket down from the closet shelf. "I'd much rather kiss a man doing everything in his power to make me happy than kiss a Sasquatch butt. I'm not so much into that," I quipped.

Van chuckled. "I'll let you pick out a new book from Ms. Brisbane's shop once we're back in Arcadia Bay."

"Okay. I'm swooning now!" I flopped back dramatically onto the tiny bed, completing an exaggerated fainting spell.

"Mmm, let's make it a pile of books and see what that does." Van's throaty words drifted over my skin, raising gooseflesh. Suddenly he was hovering over me, the length of his body suspended over mine. Not touching but singeing me with electricity all the same. I stopped breathing.

Van smiled lazily. Leaning over, he placed a single sweet kiss on the end of my nose before he got off the bed. I was too immobilized by misfiring nerves to move. Van gently untied my shoes and took them off, putting them on the floor next to the end of the bed.

"Clearly the pile of books was the way to go." I could hear the smirk in his words. I gulped and sat up.

"Piles of books are good." It came out all breathy sounding. Van's eyes hooded, his expression turning all smoldery.

"I'll be sure to remember that." We stared at each other a heartbeat longer. It was as if an invisible hand reached inside my chest and, carefully cradling my heart, handed it to Van. I knew this time it wouldn't be misplaced.

Something whisked against the door and a shiver worked down my spine. Likely it was something the wind had knocked loose. Van was at the door in an instant, looking through the peephole. Wolf was on full alert, standing at the ready, waiting for the signal to burst through my skin to defend us.

"Just a can that blew across the parking lot and hit the door." He glanced around. "All the same. I'm glad this place has only a tiny window. I'm going to move the table in front of the door."

"Let me help."

We made quick work of moving the surprisingly heavy table in front of the door. It wasn't foolproof by any means, but it would certainly slow anyone down who tried to burst into our room.

"I don't expect anything odd to happen tonight, Katie, but would you feel safer if we took watches?"

I bit my lip. "Maybe?"

Van nodded. Reaching out, he tugged me to his chest where I gladly wrapped my arms around him as he held me against him. He plunked a kiss on the top of my hair.

"I'll take first watch. I napped in the car some today, and you drove the whole way," I said.

"You sure?"

"Yeah," I whispered before going up on tip toe and kissing him softly.

"Wake me in a few hours, okay?" he whispered against my lips, kissing me back once more.

"Will do."

The night passed uneventfully, and we were both able to get some solid hours in. It was still early when I crawled into the shower. As my hands lathered soap over my skin, my fingers halted at my belly. Swallowing, I looked down and let my fingers trace soapy lines down the wide, jagged scars that crisscrossed my abdomen. They weren't pretty. They were a painful reminder of what I'd endured the night my pack betrayed me. My scars had been a source of shame since I'd come to the Hazelton pack. Emma was the only other person in the world who had seen them. I'd kept them covered, something that took some doing in the wolf world where it wasn't uncommon to see flashes of skin in between shifts.

Werewolves got scars. But not often. We healed at an exponential rate. And of those wolves that did get scars, they weren't like these.

These were deep and told me I was weak. That I couldn't defend myself. My fingers reached the end of the longest scar, slicing through the white flesh of my belly and ending an inch below my belly button. My own pack had given me these. I wasn't even sure who. I'd been running for my life, grief and pain blocking out some of the details of that night.

Closing my eyes and swallowing hard, I shut off the water and got out of the shower. I dressed in t-shirt and jeans, wrapping my hair in a towel before exiting the bathroom in a cloud of steam.

"Okay if I shower?" Van asked, his gaze raking over me.

"Sure."

The shower turned back on, and I flipped my head over to towel dry my hair. Plugging in the complimentary hair dryer, I dried my hair for a few minutes but left it damp. The hot air felt good, but I didn't like not being able to hear my surroundings.

I shut it off and walked in front of the couch, where Van had already folded up the blankets, but paused in front of the tall mirror that hung on the wall. Biting the inside of my cheek, I slowly pulled up the bottom of my shirt. I forced myself to see my scars again. Tears pricked the back of my eyelids. I usually avoided them, but today, they seemed impossible to ignore.

"Katie?" Van's hushed voice catapulted my heart into my throat. So much for listening to my surroundings. He'd come out of the bathroom and stood staring at my reflection in the mirror. I yanked my shirt back down as blood rushed to my cheeks.

I couldn't move as Van tossed his towel to the corner and slowly walked to me. He stood behind me, electricity charging the sliver of air between us as we stared at each other in the mirror. With painstaking gentleness, he closed the distance between us, his chest meeting the back of my shoulders. His fingers touched the bottom of my shirt, hesitating, asking for permission.

I swallowed, tears stinging my eyes, anxious shame writhing in my middle. I nodded once before I could lose my nerve.

Van carefully raised the hem of my shirt. I sucked in an ugly breath as the remnants of the claws that had gouged open the soft flesh of my belly came into view. They seemed more hideous, redder, larger, more jagged with Van looking at them. Even though he only lifted my shirt over my stomach, I felt naked in front of him—totally exposed. A lone tear tracked down my cheek.

With aching tenderness, Van slid one of his big hands over the worst of my scars. A choked sob sounded in the back of my throat. His other arm wrapped around my shoulders over my chest, hugging me.

"They remind me that I wasn't strong enough," I finally choked into the silence. Van's fingers twitched against my skin.

"No, Katie. They don't show that you were weak." His breath brushed against my ear. "They tell you that you survived. That you were stronger than they were. That they couldn't take you down. That you healed. That you're now twice as strong." He paused, turning me so I faced him. He carefully put my shirt back down, letting his hands rest over the cotton at the waist of my jeans. "They tell your story. Painful though it has been, it's yours, and you should be so proud of who you have become. I love the woman you are. And as much as I hate what you went through—what we're going to finish—it's made you who you are and forged some of that fire inside you. And I love your fire." He brushed a damp strand of hair from my face, letting his hand trace down the outside of my ear to cup my jaw.

Sparkles raced through me, and Wolf puffed out her chest. Maybe Van was right. Maybe my scars didn't only say I'd been beaten. Maybe they did say I'd survived. Another thought ripped through me, and even though I felt stupid saying it out loud, I needed to know.

"They...they don't turn you off?"

Van barked out a surprised laugh. "Katie, I haven't seen all of you. Someday I really want to. Even so, I can assure you there isn't a single inch of your skin that *doesn't* turn me on. Because I love all of you."

My cheeks flushed again, but this time, a giddy tingling of acceptance burned pleasantly in my gut. I reached up on tiptoe and kissed him fully.

His lips were warm and soft, wanting against mine. I let my fingers bury themselves in the hair at the back of his head, my other hand skimming the defined planes of his chest, his soft t-shirt rumpling under my touch.

He gently nuzzled my neck and Wolf flopped onto her back, legs turning to jelly. I never wanted to stop kissing Van. I wanted *him*. This boy who saw my scars—both the inside ones and the outside ones. I needed him. Forever. A part of me had since the day I met him. But until recently, I hadn't let myself truly envision what a life with Van might look like. Because my past was always hanging over my head, there had been no room for a future beyond my eighteenth birthday. But it had passed, and things weren't perfect, far from it, but Van knew now. He knew *everything*. And he hadn't run. If anything, he'd planted himself more firmly in my life than ever before. I fell a little more in love with his stubbornness because of it.

A new appreciation of him stirred in my belly, and I kissed him harder, letting my lips express what I wasn't sure my words could. Van's hands slid down my sides, gripping my hips. Delicious heat spread from his grip to the rest of me. I tugged his head down and kissed his jaw, delighting in the way his breathing hitched and his fingers spasmed where they held me. My lips trailed his jaw and behind his ear. Kissing the sensitive spot, Van went rigid against me, a low groan escaping from deep in his chest.

"That's a good spot, Katie." He practically growled the words, and it sent a shot of passion through me. Pressing harder against him, I wanted to make him feel as good as he made me feel inside—show him how much I loved him. Intent on kissing him again in the same spot, I opened my mouth wider, my teeth lightly scraping his skin.

"Ah!" Every one of Van's muscles tightened into a hard, coiled line. "Katie," he gasped, crushing me against his chest, "Please don't use your teeth unless you're going to Claim me right now." A shiver worked over him.

My eyes dilated, wolf vision expanding momentarily as I pulled back far enough to look at his face. His eyes were wide, nostrils flared, desire pouring off him. I searched his face, wondering if I should Claim him then. Pheromones clogged my nose, and I wasn't sure if they were his, mine, or ours.

His breathing came in shallow, tight pants. He swallowed hard, shutting his eyes before opening them and staring into mine. Long moments passed as we searched each other, waiting, unsure. Van's breaths eased, though his heart still pounded beneath my hand. He tucked a strand of hair behind my ear, letting his finger graze down the side of my neck.

"I want to Claim you, Van." The whispered words escaped before I could censor them.

His expression softened. "I want to Claim you back, Katie Clay." His eyebrow arched and lips quirked mischievously. "And do all the Claimed things with you."

A laugh bubbled up my throat as heat rushed to my cheeks. He leaned in and kissed my lips softly, lingeringly.

"Do you want me to Claim you now?" I asked as he slowly pulled back. Nerves stuttered through me as Wolf thrummed with anxiety.

Van cocked his head to the side, a slight crease forming between his eyebrows. "I want you to Claim me, Katie. You and no one else. But I don't want you to do it until *you* feel ready. In every way. Your past is still hanging over you. If we need to finish with it first, then so be it. If you want to Claim me and get right to things this second, that's okay, too." He smiled, teasing me as his hands squeezed my hips. "Although this wouldn't have been my first choice of a honeymoon venue." The sincerity of his words cut something loose inside me. Reassurance was warm and comforting as I took in the face of this boy I loved. Who loved me back.

"I love you," I whispered the simple words out loud for the first time. I'd told him a part of me had loved him since he'd rescued me, but I'd never said those three most important words directly to him.

It was like the sun burst from behind the clouds. Van's whole face lit with joy.

"I love you," he said back.

"I want you to have my everything, Donovan Hazelton." I bit my lip. "But I don't think I can move forward until my pack and my past has been dealt with."

"I understand. It's okay. Let me help you. Let me do this with you—together." His eyes implored me. "So we can have a *long* time *together* after this."

I nodded. "Together?"

"Together."

CHAPTER 51

DONOVAN

It was hard to wrap my mind around everything that had happened in the past thirty-six hours. Katie had become an Alpha. We'd decided to take back her pack. We'd left Rock Falls with our alliance sealed even deeper. I'd kissed Katie. She'd kissed me back. Her lips had rocked the axis of my life—shifting my focus entirely. I'd nearly flipped her down onto the couch when her teeth had grazed my ear. Wolf went rigid again at the memory. There was something primal raised in a wolf anytime teeth were involved—either for war or for love.

Shaking my head, I tried to clear the hormone induced fog that had taken over my brain. I wasn't entirely successful. Katie's scent still clung to me. I blew a hot breath out as Katie sat tying her shoes at the edge of the bed.

She glanced up at me. "You okay, Van?"

"Yeah," I said tightly. She raised an eyebrow. I cleared my throat. "I'm looking forward to...things," I finished lamely, then wished I hadn't spoken at all.

Katie eyes widened, her whole face suddenly infused with red. "Oh," she said breathlessly.

"Come on. Looking at you on that bed is not helping."

She hesitated a moment as if debating if she wanted to get up or invite me onto the bed with her. The breath froze in my lungs. Wolf thrashed, thoughts of Claiming bursting across my mind.

Just when I thought I couldn't stand it any longer, she rose, coming to me and wrapping her arms around my neck.

"Soon, Van." She kissed me quickly then pulled back to look me in the eye. "Because I'm looking forward to *things*, too," she said with a cheeky smile. A growl of approval rumbled in my chest as Wolf pawed the ground, still wanting to get to things sooner rather than later.

"I'm glad to hear it."

She smiled. "Let's go get the unpleasantries over with so we can get back to planning a Claiming and...*things*."

"Not helpful. Already thinking about *things*."

She chuckled as we shouldered our packs and left the motel.

It was two more excruciatingly long days of driving. And two even longer nights. I dreamed about Katie both nights. In some of my dreams, Katie was chased by a feral wolf I took to be her uncle. In others he caught her and gave her those scars all over again. In some, I found her bleeding on the pass like I had all those years ago. With those dreams, I'd wake in a cold sweat, my need to make sure Katie was alive and well overwhelming.

When that happened, I'd take over keeping watch. But not before I kissed Katie. Once I dreamed we were already Claimed.

That was a fun dream.

By the rise of dawn on the third day we'd set out from Rock Falls, we knew we'd reach our first stop.

"Are you nervous?" I asked Katie around a mouthful of breakfast burrito.

"Yes, but not as much as I thought. I'm not looking forward to coming face to face with the pack again, but it's easier going forward, knowing that we're going in with a plan." She worried her lip in between bites of hash browns. "I think I'm almost as curious about the reactions today as I am nervous about all the things."

"That's probably fair. I imagine you'll cause some excitement and some stress for everyone involved," I said with a smile.

"Probably so," Katie agreed and took a slurp of coffee.

The building we needed came into view late afternoon.

"Here we go." Katie blew out a hard breath.

"Can I help you?" a receptionist with a perfectly coifed twist, muted red lipstick, and a disdaining eyebrow asked us as we approached her desk area.

Katie hesitated, and I let my hand drift to the small of her back for moral support. To let her know I was there and not leaving.

Katie swallowed. "I need to see Jeremy Lockhorn."

"I'm sorry, dear, but I don't think you're on Mr. Lockhorn's schedule. He's really a very busy man, and he can't move his schedule for unannounced appointments." The saccharine tone grated on my nerves, but not as much as the dismissive glance the receptionist gave us.

Katie's jaw locked. "He'll rearrange it for me. I'm Kaylee Snowdon."

The receptionist raised her other eyebrow.

"You are the fifth Kaylee Snowdon to enter this building this month. You'll excuse me if I'm a bit skeptical."

My teeth ground together.

Katie matched her glare for glare. "Well, in the event that I am the real Kaylee Snowdon, which I am, it would behoove you to call Mr. Lockhorn."

The receptionist sighed dramatically and pushed a button on her phone. "Mr. Lockhorn, there's another Kaylee Snowdon here to see you."

Ten minutes later we sat in plush chairs opposite Mr. Jeremy Lockhorn, Esquire, and executive of Michael Snowdon's estate. And Kaylee Snowdon's trust.

Mr. Lockhorn took off his spectacles, polishing them on a handkerchief. "I apologize for the delay, but as you've heard, you are not the first young woman to come claiming she's Kaylee Snowdon. After that story in the press, and having her sketched face flashed around, there's been quite a commotion. Some impressive impersonators as well," he said to himself with a grim smile as he replaced his glasses.

Katie sighed. "Give me the lock and I'll prove I'm who I say I am. I am the bio code."

Jeremy Lockhorn's eyes jerked to Katie's face. "The bio code?" he said, a disbelieving edge to his voice.

"I know my father changed his will days before his death, and I know he left everything to me. And he sealed it with a lock that requires a bio code. My blood is the only thing that will open it."

A more welcoming smile played at the corner of Mr. Lockhorn's lips. "We might have the real girl after all." He picked up his phone and pushed a few buttons. "Otto, bring me the Snowdon bio lock."

Two more minutes and Katie wrapped a tissue around her finger.

"Miss Snowdon, how may I be of service?" Mr. Lockhorn smiled graciously, all suspicion and pretense dropped now that Katie was proven Kaylee.

"Did any of the other Kaylee's come in with my father's brother, Alan Snowdon?" Katie asked, the slightest waver in her voice.

Mr. Lockhorn's eyebrows rose as recognition and then caution lit his eyes. "More than once. Your brother, too. Why do you ask?"

"I want to retain your services to continue to protect my trust. I came today to prove I'm still alive and well. I want to keep the money locked in the trust. But I want to change the access measures—both for the trust and for the allowance I can now draw."

"I'm listening," Mr. Lockhorn said. His eyes took on a new respect for Katie as he watched her keenly.

It was late by the time we left. Mr. Lockhorn ordered in Chinese for us while he and Katie finished solidifying the details of what she wanted.

I had never been more proud of Katie, and I told her so as we walked to the car. I looped an arm around her shoulders and kissed her temple.

"Thanks. I'm glad that part of things is over." She sniffed. "It makes me miss my parents more than usual."

I tightened my arm around her, no words for that. An ache rose in my own chest as a flash of my mom passed behind my eyes.

"Miss Snowdon! There's one last thing!" a voice rang out across the parking lot. My hackles rose as the snobby receptionist dashed across the black top in her heels. We stopped as she reached us. "I, I'm sorry. For," she glanced at the ground before looking back to us. "I'm sorry," she said. Her chin quivered before she turned and raced erratically back to the building in her too-tall heels.

A chill raked over my shoulders that had nothing to do with the cooling temperatures.

"Did that seem odd to you?" Katie asked.

"A little," I replied. Wolf pricked his ears forward. I let him up to the surface to scan our surroundings.

Nothing out of the ordinary.

I turned back to Katie. "Where to? You want to hit the pack tonight, or leave it one more day til morning?"

"No. Tonight. I feel like my mind is being tugged in two. I feel compelled. I need to go to them. I need to know what happened to Alan, find out if they're after me, too. Even though the human part of me still wants nothing to do with them." She sighed.

I opened her car door and waited until she was seated then closed it. I popped into my side, locked the doors just in case, and rolled the engine over.

"I know what you mean about the compulsion." I let my fingers reach out and feather along her jaw. "I want to link Dad before we go to make sure he's in position." My gaze dropped to her lips. "And I want to kiss you again, because it may be a while before we're able to be alone again like this." I smiled, already missing the close contact with Katie that I'd grown accustomed to.

Katie smiled back. "Then kiss me now and make me forget what I'm about to go do for at least a few minutes."

I did my best.

Based on Katie's response, I was successful.

CHAPTER 52

KATIE

Though I'd never done drugs, I was pretty sure kissing Van did a better job making me forget things I'd rather not remember than any illegal substance could.

With my heart drumming in my ears and my pulse racing, I didn't want to stop when Van slowly pulled back, his breath coming short and fast. He leaned his forehead against mine.

"Right. I've completely forgotten everything except what you taste like." His voice was throaty and sent tingles pinpricking down my arms.

"Same," I said, breathless too.

He swallowed. "Okay. Linking Dad now." With reluctance, he eased away from me, keeping his hand on my knee as he leaned back in his seat and closed his eyes.

Not for the first time, I wished I could hear what they said through the link. Soon enough. Soon enough I'd be bound to Van, and we'd share that intimacy as well as others. Wolf lolled her tongue out, eager to Claim Van.

"The Hazelton pack is in position. They're set up just outside where they can smell the boundary of the Snowdon pack lands. They're a little farther away than I'd like them to be, but if they cross territorial lines, that's only going to cause sparks and unnecessary tension. Unless you want them to cross over. You're the Alpha, so it's your pack and your lands. What do you want them to do?"

I tossed ideas in my head. "Better tell them to wait. I should be able to control them with Command if I have to, but I'm too new. Too inexperienced. Better not to rock the boat if I have another choice. Either to test my newfound status or to raise unnecessary hackles." I fervently hoped there wasn't an ambush waiting for me. I could use Command. I swallowed hard.

"Okay. I'll tell Dad to hold. Here we go. Are you ready?"

My eyeballs jiggled in their sockets with the thundering of my pulse. I gulped. "Nope. Let's go anyway."

I knew the second we crossed onto Snowden pack land. Every hair on my body stood at full attention and Wolf thrashed, shoving down old memories, and trying to reconcile this unwanted dominance, this responsibility that was ours, but that we didn't truly want. Not with this pack who had nearly destroyed us. My fingers grazed my belly, feeling the puckered scars beneath my shirt. Reminding myself that I survived. That these weren't marks of shame, they were marks of a fighter.

Van stopped the car. "Tell me what to do, Katie."

Inhale.

Exhale.

"Let's walk from here. I want to hear them coming." As the words left my mouth, the gleam of eyes poked through the darkness of the forest. A small measure of relief twisted over my shoulders. Maybe Alan stuck his finger in a light socket. Maybe no one was waiting to kill me outright.

"Too late. They're here." Van's hand clenched against the steering wheel.

I reached out with my mind, fighting not to recoil against the oiliness that seemed to coat the inside of my head as I did so. My brain obeyed like a rusty hinge. It had been so long since I had actively tried to use my own pack link. *Stand down. You will not harm the one with me.*

Before I could lose my courage, I cracked the door and got out, Van mirroring me. Low growls and a few yips sounded throughout the woods. We were surrounded.

You're the Alpha, I reminded myself. Wolf puffed her chest out, her neck bunching, jaw taut, ready to prove our Alpha status at a moment's notice.

I swallowed as fifteen pairs of eyes came into focus, tightening the circle around Van and me. I could smell Van's own dominance leaking into the night. He didn't like this.

Neither did I.

A few more growls sounded around the circle. "Enough," I barked audibly, letting Wolf lend weight to my words. "I am here. I am in charge." I glared, turning fully around the circle, letting my eyes meet every pair staring back at me from the gloom.

"Brogan." I sharply called the wolf I knew my uncle relied on. Who was now my Beta.

There was a snapping of tendons and cracking of bones. "Kaylee," he replied, a slight patronizing tone to his voice as he rose from his wolf's crouch to stand upright. Van's nostrils flared as he huffed a breath.

I suppressed a shiver at hearing my birth name drop from Brogan's lips. Anger clenched my jaw. He strode toward me nonchalantly, naked as the day he was born, at least a head taller, and twice as wide as me. Heavily muscled and flaunting his exposure, I instinctually knew he was trying to intimidate me. I refused to let it. Bracing myself for something I did *not* want to see, I purposefully let my eyes slide over him. All of him. With great disgust. Nasty. Meeting his gaze, I snorted disdainfully.

"If I were you, I wouldn't strut that proudly."

Van snorted appreciatively at my side, boldly meeting the death glare Brogan cast him.

"Tell me how Alan died." I didn't ask about Ben. I couldn't. Not yet. It was taking everything I had to keep it together right now.

Brogan smirked and held silent. Fury raged behind my eyes.

I was about to repeat my question when Wolf seized inside me.

Every cell in my body jerked to attention as horror clouded over all my senses.

"Katie!" Van said, a desperate edge to his voice, somewhere far in the distance.

Thunder boomed in my ears, my head ringing as Wolf thrashed and...shrank.

NO NO NO NO NO

My world reduced to a pinpoint before fire, light, and a blasting crescendo exploded in my brain. A whimper escaped my clamped teeth as pain lashed my body, muscles constricted, my bones sliced through my skin and retreated. Fur blazed along my arms and legs. My body completed a partial shift without my permission. I stumbled to the ground, sticks and small debris embedding into my palms. Bits of my clothes hung loose, still on me, but ripped where my Wolf form had pushed through.

I froze, gulping oxygen into my tattered lungs.

I was no longer the Alpha.

"Katie!" Van screamed.

"You idiot. Her name is Kaylee." A wet *thump* blistered through my awareness and Van's unconscious body slumped to the ground beside me.

Panic clawed at me.

"Van!" I struggled to shove the rasped word from my dry, cracking throat.

Heavy footsteps thudded near my head.

"Keep him down," a hard voice said. A voice that triggered memories. A voice that brought Wolf snarling to the fore. A voice that should be dead.

"No," I whispered. Wolf anchored herself against me, and with her help, I forced myself shaking to my feet and looked Alan Snowdon straight in the eye.

I was too horrified, traumatized, worried, and angry to flinch away from his steely gaze. His steely gaze that should have been rotting six feet under the ground along with the rest of him.

"Hello, niece," he said mockingly.

I bit the inside of my lip, tasting blood. I spat it at his feet.

His eyes narrowed. "I don't think that's any way to greet your long-lost uncle or *your Alpha*," he said, totally calm and in charge of the situation.

This was bad.

Unbelievably bad.

In all our strategizing, never once did we consider that Alan was anything other than dead. He was removed from the board entirely.

But now he was here, very much alive and in the flesh, and Van was slumped over in a heap at my feet. Unconscious and unable to contact the rest of the Hazelton pack.

Ice ran through my veins. I had no way to link with Hal.

I had never been more alone than I was in this moment.

Wolf heaved inside me, instantly calculating odds and running tactical scenarios I'd learned while with the Hazelton pack. They might not be here with me in fur, but that didn't mean I hadn't carried some of them with me.

My only chance to come out of this alive and intact was to challenge Alan.

And I had to win.

I needed time. Time to recover from my fluctuating wolf status hormones, for my head to clear enough to think rationally and logically.

Time for my heart to stop aching.

"How?" I asked, swallowing.

Alan's mouth tipped in a lazy grin. "There are some wonderful drugs out there on the black market these days. Some that will suppress a wolf. Those are not widely available but still more common. You've likely heard of those. Drugs that will keep a wolf bound inside its human skin."

I remembered hearing stories about Sam, Kyp and Bowen—how they'd had a similar drug used on them. I held in a shiver.

"What's less commonly known is that there is now a substance that immediately counteracts the effects of those drugs. So, dear niece, all I had to do was keep my wolf silent, unable to act as Alpha, let your genes draw your wolf out in my stead, then wait for you to show up. I got my call from Lockhorn's receptionist to let me know the real Kaylee Snowdon had been found, and I promptly gave myself a quick injection. Five minutes. I'm good as new. And here I am. And here you are." His slick smile turned menacing, showing his canines—too long to be completely human.

I thought I might hyperventilate.

"I want your money. Give it to me, and I'll let you live. You can even leave the pack if you want." He said it casually as if he were offering me a sandwich.

"No." I didn't want the money. But I would not give Alan that kind of power.

Alan smirked. "I'm shocked. Fine." He turned to Brogan and another hulking nudist who flanked Van, ready to knock him out again if he roused. "Kill him," Alan ordered, Alpha's Command chilling over me in a wave of icy power.

That brought my mind screeching to life, shredding the foggy haze of wolfish chemicals still dragging at my brain.

"Stop!" My Beta's voice wasn't enough to drown out an Alpha's Command, but it was enough to make the wolf hesitate. Quickly I turned to my uncle. "If you kill him, you'll never see a penny of my money. You know I've already visited the lawyer. I changed who can access my funds. If you kill him, even if you produce his body, you cannot access any of the millions my father left me." I swallowed. "Donovan has to be alive, breathing, and walk in of his own volition in order for you to get my money."

Alan growled, rage punctuating his narrow features. Grief struck me. Even though he was opposite my father in every possible way that mattered, he was still a thinner version of my dad.

I shoved those unhelpful revelations away, letting Wolf up to the fore again. I needed every advantage I could get. With Van out of commission, and no way to reach my allies, I was all on my own. I needed to go for the jugular.

Literally.

"You ruined my life once. You will not do it again. Consider yourself challenged." Even as I bit out the last word, my skin split, fur, teeth, and claws extended.

Lunging hard, back legs springs of coiled muscle, I collided with Alan in the middle of the forest floor. Pine needles and dirt cascaded up from our impact.

Alan snarled beneath me, his transformation swift. He bit at my neck, clawing at my ruff as my own incisors snapped millimeters from his jugular vein. Shoving for purchase, I snapped again, teeth nicking him. Not deep enough but drawing blood.

Alan roared in anger, flipping my much slighter wolf off and springing to his feet. Taking the moment, but leaving my eyes on Alan, I howled as loud as I could—if Hal was anywhere in the vicinity, he'd hear me, and know I needed help.

Alan circled. I licked my lips, my baser nature relishing the dark tang of my enemy's blood.

How does it feel to be blooded first by the girl you already failed to kill? I goaded, bravado leaking into our familial link.

Not as good as it will feel to break you. To feel your bones snap inside my mouth, to taste the same cowardice that ran through my brother's veins. Shall I tell you what I did to Ben? Would that be pleasant conversation for you?

His words were a spear to my shattered heart. Gritting my teeth, I shoved the mental link away the way Van had taught me. Using the link as a shield and praying it held better against Alan than it had against the whole pack, I focused on his sinewy body.

In the distance, a wolf howled.

The Hazeltons.

For one moment, Alan glanced away, distracted by the distant wolf. I took the opening.

The world stopped and seemed to spin in slow motion as I launched myself into the air. I came down hard on Alan's side. He wasn't quick enough to completely sidestep me, and I got a mouthful of the side of his neck.

Alan squeaked in surprise, a truly unmanly sound I registered with grim satisfaction as I sank my teeth into the flesh of his neck and shoulder. He barked and jerked, trying to sling me off. Knowing this might be the only chance I had to make purchase, I hung on—because my life—Van's life—literally depended on it.

Hal howled again, closer this time. I couldn't let go to howl back, and I prayed the scent of blood, and the musk of the wolf pack would be enough to lead them straight to us. Alan yipped and several of his—our—pack broke off to go meet the encroaching Hazeltons.

Alan shook wildly and pawed, gaining no new purchase. Adrenaline and desperation pulsed through me, careening like a stampede.

Unable to dislodge me, he flung himself back into the dirt, landing heavily on his side with me partially on the ground and partially on top of him.

I realized my mistake two seconds before the searing fire ripped into the soft flesh of my belly. His claws raked down my abdomen, shredding, ripping, destroying flesh, reopening my old scars and slicing new ones. Blood gushed from the deep wounds.

Powerless to stop myself from howling against the throbbing agony, my teeth lifted from Alan's neck. Triumphant, Alan shifted his weight to move. I had enough presence of mind to realize this was my last chance to end this.

Light flickered at the edges of my vision as I felt the blood rushing from my body.

Dread and determination settled on me as I bled out onto the forest floor. I wasn't going to survive. Sorrow and regret clashed with the determination driving my focus. I had to make my last moments count.

I needed to rid the world of Alan Snowdon.

Using a move I'd learned from the Hazeltons, I snatched Alan's front leg between my teeth and yanked my head sideways, effectively snapping his leg.

He fell hard with an anguished yelp.

"Katie, no!" Van's weak cry sounded. Relief that he was alive mingled with the soul-deep ache that I hadn't Claimed him when I had the chance. I'd never be able to show him the full extent of my love. I felt like I'd robbed him, robbed myself. Biting back a sob, with the last of my strength, I turned my head to Alan's hovering neck as he struggled to extricate himself from the mangled mess of my shredded flesh and his broken bones.

As the world started going fuzzy at the edges, I expended the last of my physical energy. I rallied Wolf, lunged weakly, bit down on the tender column of his exposed neck, and ripped out Alan's throat. Blood sprayed my face, instantly pooled beneath my fur as I lay panting, wheezing. Dying.

Alan twitched twice then went motionless. Tingling started in the base of my paws as Alphahood began to trickle back to me.

I wasn't strong enough. I couldn't be Alpha. I was dying. And I couldn't leave Brogan in control.

My last act as myself would be to right the wrong my uncle first committed when he stole the lawful power away from my father.

As my eyes shuttered and Wolf began to still, I willingly gave up my Alpha status, and transferred it and my allegiance to Van. I'd die a proper Hazelton. Van gasped, and I knew I'd successfully given my Alpha powers to him. Relief cocooned me as my vision failed, my last glimpse of this world the boy I loved as he struggled to reach my side.

I breathed once more, and let the darkness take me.

CHAPTER 53
DONOVAN

Alpha power rippled over me as despair threatened to crush the air from my lungs. Katie went still. Her chest stopped rising.

Some noise between a scream and a feral roar ripped through my throat as I finished crawling to Katie, her blood soaking into my jeans.

Her underside was in ribbons. I thought some of her organs might be mixed in with the mangled flesh lying on the pine needles. I choked as bile burned my throat. Tears blurred my vision as my heart cracked in two. I had no idea how to help her. As my anguish swallowed me whole, Wolf erupted through my skin, and I threw back my head and howled. My Hazelton pack immediately answered back, close by, and the sounds of battle intensified.

Dad thundered over the turf, dodging between trees as Alpha power leeched from Katie's motionless form and rippled over my fur. Looking down at Katie's nearly unrecognizable body, it was as if I could see mental cords of dominance coming off her, wrapping around me, then flowing into me. Dad crashed through the underbrush and immediately hovered over Katie and me, daring anyone to do so much as breathe in our direction.

Tears blurred my vision as Katie's power finished pouring into me where it swirled in confirmation, hesitating like the power was waiting for me to direct it. Division speared my brain. Tethers to the few remaining Snowdon wolves floated in my mind's periphery, tangling with the threads I already had with my own pack. The power waited, urging me to act, to step up and become my own Alpha of a separate pack. I didn't want to be Alpha. I just wanted Katie. Holding the power a beat longer, I breathed in once, twice, agony searing my lungs, then gave it up. I willingly let Katie's Alpha power course through me and to my father—my Alpha. The power slowly left, Dad's chest literally swelling as the full mantle of the combined pack Alpha fell on him. I flinched as three yelps and a bark sounded in the woods. Information from my pack sifted through my mental link. Not a single Snowdon remained alive.

Not a single one.

Katie.

Turning all my attention to Katie's silent wolf, I let the agony crush me. My body heaved as I gasped for air. I gulped a breath and forced myself to calm enough to lean over Katie's wolf, my own fur brushing over hers.

With reverence, I leaned down, letting my nose lightly touch hers. Opening my mouth, I gently closed my lips over her nose, biting down only enough she'd have felt the pressure if...

If she'd been alive for me to Claim her.

EPILOGUE
DONOVAN

I stared at the simple gray headstone. The wind sailed down from the mountains, brushing my cheeks, and drying my tears. I bent over and laid the flowers I'd brought—a bouquet of wildflowers—Katie's favorite kind—on the grass at the base of the stone. Brushing my hands on my pants, I sat down at the foot of the grave.

"Sorry I haven't visited in a while. Things have been happening. Things I want to tell you about. And because," I paused to wipe my eyes. My tears came quicker now. After the fight in Washington. "Because I think you'd be proud of me. Proud of who I've become, despite a few setbacks along the way." I smiled through my tears.

"I've tried hard this year. The Lacessere in Rock Falls wasn't at all what I'd planned, and neither was falling in love and making a hash of things, and neither was...what happened after." It was still hard for me to talk about. "I'll come back soon to tell you more, but I promised I'd be at the bookstore and bring lunch, so I need to go. It's been six months today.

"I just...wanted to drop by and tell you that I love you and I miss you." I stood, kissed my hand, and rested it on the tombstone. "Be back soon."

Books & Stuff came into view as I switched the bag of carry out from one hand to the other. Scents of cheesy quesadillas wafted up from the containers packed snuggly in the bag, but my mouth watered thinking about dessert, thick wedges of chocolate cake layered with ganache.

The bell over the door jingled as I opened it and the comforting scent of books wrapped around me like a hug. Books—especially their smell—always reminded me of her. The shop looked deserted.

"Ms. Brisbane? Are you back there?" I called.

"Nope. I sent her home early. Why don't you bring that food right here to the kitchenette? And bring your sexy Sasquatch butt with it." Katie popped her head out of the back hallway and gave me a saucy wink. Her toned arms braced on the sides of the hallway as her eyes lazily dragged over me, igniting my blood and propelling me forward. She tossed another suggestive smile over her shoulder and disappeared toward the break room. I happily followed. Wolves love to chase.

She met me at the doorway, dancing out of reach as I leaned in for a kiss. She took the bag of food from me and put it on the table, then leaned a hip against the countertop and crooked her finger at me.

A rumble sounded low in my chest as I closed the distance between us, lining my hips up with hers, and pushing her back against the counter.

She put a finger against my lips, halting their downward descent. "First, tell me how you're doing. Did you visit your mom's grave this morning?" Her eyes gentled in compassion as her hand brushed the hair back from my forehead. Nearly losing Katie had dragged up the trauma of losing my mom years before. I was still dealing with both, but we had support from our friends and families. And each other. We made it a point to talk each other through our feelings and our nightmares. It had brought us closer, having that raw, vulnerable honesty between us.

After Katie's Alpha power settled on me and I Claimed her as she lay dying on the forest floor in Washington, a curious thing happened. The power that had come from her had rested inside me. I didn't want it without her, so I let it funnel to Dad—essentially letting Alpha pass from Katie through me to my dad. But after I Claimed her, invisible cords wove themselves from me to her in a partial Claiming bond. As the cords to Katie solidified, power from Dad tore through me to the one-sided Claiming bond, then back into Katie. It wasn't the full mantle of her Alphahood; she'd given that up willingly. But somehow her wolf, my wolf, and Dad's wolf, had all worked together and infused her with just enough life left to hang on.

The road to recovery had been long and painful, but as soon as she was awake and lucid enough to do so, she Claimed me back. Right there in her hospital bed.

We'd had an enormous Claiming celebration once she was well enough, and consequently, we'd only been acting *fully* Claimed for a few weeks. Everything was new—in bright technicolor. I'd never been happier.

It wasn't long after Katie and I had our Claiming celebration that Ms. Brisbane declared she was too old to run the store full time and turned over the reins of management to Katie. They've got an unwritten agreement that Katie will buy the store from her once she's ready to fully retire.

Katie is thrilled.

I sighed, letting my thumbs brush over her lowest ribs as I brought myself back to the present. "I did. I still cried. But it feels good to talk to her again."

"Good. Was it okay going by yourself? Do you want me to come with you again next time?"

I smiled softly. "It was good. To go alone. I always like it when you come with me, but today definitely felt like a step toward healing."

Her eyes lit—both with happiness and a few regrets. "We've had our fair share of wounds, haven't we?"

"We have. But we're stronger for them," I whispered as I slipped my hands up her shirt, letting my fingers trace the mass of thick scar tissue that stretched across Katie's entire abdomen. My hands tracked to her sides, and she tipped her head back and closed her eyes, her hips pushing against mine and sending my pulse spiking.

"Happy six months, Van," she whispered, eyes opening to look at me, fire in their cinnamon depths.

"Happy six months," I replied as I leaned down and nibbled her neck. She arched into me, her hands snaking down my back toward my now lovingly termed Sasquatch butt.

It wasn't long before hands were wandering anywhere they pleased, and the kisses were deliciously heated. I was about to yank Katie's shirt over her head as her fingers coasted toward the button on my jeans.

"Oh! Gah! *My eyes!*"

Katie squeaked as Angus wheeled around in the hallway, dramatically and disgustedly covering his eyes with both hands. "Flaming fur balls, guys. Can't you lock the front door? Flip the closed sign? Wait till you get home? *Something* other than pawing each other in the middle of a public bookstore?" He scrubbed at his eyes. "Crap, guys, I want to go boil my eyeballs in bleach."

Katie giggled and blushed, hiding her face in my chest as regret that we wouldn't be finishing mixed with the embarrassment pinging through me.

"My fault," I called, swallowing. "I was supposed to flip the closed sign and lock the door." I leaned down next to Katie's ear and whispered,

"But I was too distracted by the vixen giving me *come hither* looks that lured me to back of the shop." Katie smiled against my chest

"Ugh," Angus groaned, still over dramatic. Though, in fairness, if I'd just walked in on my best friend and my adopted little sister in the break room...doing what we were doing in the break room...I might be overdramatic, too. "Seriously," he said again, "Emma just finished over at the bank. She'll come take the shop for the afternoon. Go. Eat. Be naked together somewhere I'll never see you." He shivered in revulsion.

"Angus, don't you go getting all self-righteous," I teased. "Do you have any idea how *not* insulated the walls of the barn are? All those times you and Emma sneaked away after you'd been Claimed? You were not so discreet."

I snorted as Angus's cheeks heated. He cleared his throat. "Is that right?"

I lifted an eyebrow and smirked.

"Well, if Emma has the shop this afternoon, and you're too disgusted to look at us right now, why don't you hold down the fort until Emma gets here, and we'll go eat lunch. And other things. Far away from you," Katie said sweetly, mercilessly teasing Angus.

"With my blessing!" No one missed the smile hiding at the corner of his lips.

I scooped up the bag of lunch and grabbed Katie's hand in my free one.

"Catch you later, Angus."

"Yup. Oh, and hey guys?"

"Yeah?" We turned in tandem.

"It's really good to have you both back. Happy six months."

I squeezed Katie's hand, and she squeezed back. "Thanks, Angus."

ABOUT THE AUTHOR

AJ Skelly is an author, reader, and lover of all things fantasy, medieval, and fairy-tale-romance. And werewolves. She has a serious soft spot for them. As an avid life-long reader and a former high school English teacher, she's always been fascinated with the written word. She lives with her husband, children, and many imaginary friends who often find their way into her stories. They all drink copious amounts of tea together and stay up reading far later than they should. You can read more of her short stories at www.ajs kelly.com.